AN [illegible]

and her [illegible]

THE SISTERHOOD OF THE QUEEN MAMAS

"Infused with humor and hometown charm, Jones's easygoing, chatty style will hook fans of chick lit and mom lit, as well as readers of Neta Jackson's Yada Yada Prayer Group series."

—*Library Journal*

MOM OVER MIAMI

"Hannah's struggles are down-to-earth and will touch hearts."

—*Romantic Times BOOKreviews*

SADIE-IN-WAITING

"Jones beautifully conveys a range of emotions, from the depth of despair to the pinnacle of joy.... Readers will nod their heads with empathy toward characters who seem like real people. Throughout the novel, compassion and family bonds bring hope, and God's love is shown to shine through even the darkest of circumstances."

—*Romantic Times BOOKreviews*

"Annie Jones writes about characters we all know and—despite their quirks—love. Sadie Pickett is an endearing character whose foibles and charms will leave you smiling as you think, *Yes, life is just like that.* Carry on, Sadie, and thanks for inviting us along for the ride!"

—Angela Hunt, author of *The Elevator*

Books by Annie Jones

Steeple Hill Single Title

Sadie-in-Waiting
Mom Over Miami
The Sisterhood of the Queen Mamas
The Barefoot Believers

Love Inspired

April in Bloom #343
Somebody's Baby #411

The Barefoot Believers

ANNIE JONES

Published by Steeple Hill Books™

STEEPLE HILL BOOKS

ISBN-13: 978-0-373-78603-9
ISBN-10: 0-373-78603-4

THE BAREFOOT BELIEVERS

This edition published by arrangement with Steeple Hill Books.

www.SteepleHill.com

Printed in U.S.A.

For Sarah

God holds you in the palm of his hand, and our family holds you always in the depths of our hearts.

Chapter One

Good ol' Kate.

Kate the bossy.

Kate the brave.

Kate the buttinsky.

Capable Kate. Commanding Kate. Clever Kate.

Even She's-So-Cranky-She-Needs-a-Date Kate.

Podiatrist Kate Cromwell would have gladly (*gladly* as in mustering up a genuine laugh, a less than enthusiastic smile and pleading, "Fun's over, knock it off now" between gritted teeth) answered to them all.

But the one name she would not respond to, the nickname she had worked long and hard to keep shoved down into the recesses of her long and vivid memory? The name she had vowed to keep off the tips of the tongues of anyone who knew her in the life she had so carefully crafted for herself over the last decade? The name given to her as a nervous, gangly child, always lurking about trying to listen in on grown-up conversations in hopes of finding out something, anything, that might answer some of her questions or help her learn how to heal her broken home? The name that reminded her of how she had, as a young woman, done a cold and hurtful thing that had cost her and two people she loved a chance for happiness as a family? That name she would not, *could* not, acknowledge, much less accept and respond to with a cheery smile.

"Well, let's get on with this, Scat-Kat-Katie!" Her two o'clock appointment checked the silver wristwatch that bit into the soft flesh of her age-spotted arm. She tapped the crystal above the yellowed face, with the hands clearly pointing to the two and a quarter hour past. She clucked her tongue. "You were born ten days past your due date and have been hurrying to catch up ever since, li'l Scat Kat."

"That's *Dr.* Scat…uh, that is *Kate,* if you don't mind." Control. That was what this situation called for. She had a job to do, an unpleasant one, and if she lost control now, Kate would never be able to follow through with her plans. She motioned toward the examining table with the chart in her hand.

"I *do* mind, I mind very much."

The woman hopped up with ease, plopped down and began to wriggle around, making the white paper beneath her crinkle. "Seeing as I was the one who carried you around those nine months and ten days. Add twenty-three hours of labor, thirty years of working as a single mom to provide a home for you and your sister, pay for your health care, your education, and put in thirty-eight years of pushing you *and* praying for you."

"That's all understood and appreciated." Soothing yet unyielding. That was the tone Kate had wanted to project.

Hard to do when wrestling with guilt that her mother had made an appointment, the only one Kate had scheduled for today, and Kate and her sister had concocted a plan to use that innocent action for their own purposes. On top of that, Kate was wrangling with her own inner child, who had grabbed a mental calculator and was doing some quick figuring.

Thirty years of work. Mom was sixty-six and had just retired. Dad had taken off when Kate was eight.... Close enough. But that other number bothered her. Thirty-eight years of pushing and praying.

Kate was thirty-nine. Did that mean her mother had started shaving years off out of shame over having a daughter unmarried and nearing forty? Or had Mom actually stopped praying for her sometime in the past year?

Maybe both...

Kate was a believer. She knew God's eye was on the sparrow and felt absolutely that He held her in the palm of His hand. But she also drew great strength from feeling her mother had her covered in prayers, as well. Now to wonder about that, and after the lousy year she had had trying to get her practice going, at the cost of a personal life and her life savings...

Her stomach clenched. She could hardly swallow.

She used every ounce of her professional decorum to excuse herself, then stepped quietly and confidently out of the examining room. From that point it took every bit of reserve she possessed not to simply run like crazy.

Scat-Kat indeed!

But the urge to run was only a symptom, not the real issue for Kate. In truth, of all the names people had given her, the real one they should have stuck her with was not Scat-Kat-Katie, but Scaredy-Kat-Kate.

Life frightened her. Not everything about it. Not the day-to-day tasks of just scraping by or of doing your duty, those she could handle just fine. Better than fine, if the respect and trust of others were any indication.

But the big things? The monumental decisions? The forks in the road that could forever alter the rest of her or someone else's days? *Yikes!*

How could anyone not be intimidated by those?

What if she made a mistake? What if she let people down? What if they gave up on her and left her high and dry? What if she made her choice then something better came along? With each thought, the knot in her stomach cinched tighter. How do you trust yourself with these issues when you know, deep down, you are basically clueless?

The urge to run rose like a wave ready to overwhelm her.

Thinking like that was one reason why she had gone from major to major in school, then from job to job, taking years to finally pursue her goal of going to med school. When she'd gotten there, she had specialized in emergency medicine, thinking the fast pace of it would prevent her from getting restless. One year in a real E.R. had dissuaded her of that and she'd been back furthering her education. One after another she had considered and rejected neurology, cardiology, pulmonology and every other *ology* available to her.

"I just worked my way down the body until there wasn't anything left but the feet!" she had joked.

But it really wasn't that far from the truth. She'd just kept thinking that as soon as she chose anything she'd find her real calling and not be able to follow it because of the previous commitment. It'd just seemed to her that something better just had to be waiting around the next corner.

At some point she'd had to choose. So she had. And then she'd found new ways to keep running. She'd become part of a practice, then had left. She'd worked for a chain of sports-medicine clinics. She'd even done a stint as an expert consultant for a small shoe company. And in between she'd filled in at emergency rooms to pick up a little extra cash. Nothing permanent. Nothing she liked well enough to want to make her stick around.

Finally, her search for something better had led her to the suburbs of Atlanta, where she'd thought living close to her mother's condo and at least sharing the same city with her also-ever-moving sister might finally help her to deal with all the old hurts.

She'd given it eleven months, two weeks and four days so far.

And had failed miserably.

Now whether she wanted to run or not, she would soon have to face the reality of having to leave her practice behind. The one time she hadn't run, she'd been driven out, through no fault of her own.

She couldn't help it if it was hard to find good office staff for what she could afford to pay. She couldn't help it if the fine print on the lease limited the size of the sign she could post, greatly hampering any chance she had of walk-in business. She couldn't help it if she'd opened an office in a place where everyone seemed to have good feet. Could she?

"People could analyze that kind of thinking to death," Kate told herself. "But I'm not one of them."

Her sister Jo, however, was. And when she got on her soapbox—er, psych-box?—Jo always brought Kate's restlessness back to the same source.

Vince Merchant.

"You are not able to make a life for yourself, Kate, because you left the life you really wanted back in Santa Sofia. Back with Vince," Jo had told her once in a fit of truthfulness, the likes of which the loving but guarded sisters rarely shared. "You will never find real peace until you let go of that time, of that man."

Let go. *Of Vince?*

Vince. Those four months after Kate had graduated college, they had shared the kind of intense but sweet romance that most people only dream of. Kate dreamed of it still. Sixteen years, a couple of almost-engagements and thousands of lousy dates later, this was the only man Kate still thought about and wondered, *What if?*

Marriage?

Kids?

A mortgage on a cozy house in a tidy little subdivision in...?

Kate forgot where Vince had actually lived when not spending his summers in Santa Sofia, Florida. But she knew he had wanted her to go there, help raise his son, Gentry, and grow old with him.

She had wanted that, too. In theory. Right up until the day four-year-old Gentry had said something that had sent Kate running—at first just away from the moment, then later from the engagement and, in doing that, away from the future they had hoped and planned to build together.

So, she'd grown older without Vince. She'd never owned a home or had kids. And she'd never gone back to Santa Sofia.

"If you're moving in the right direction, you have no reason to look back," her mom often said. "Go. Go. Go. Don't stop until you get what you want."

Apparently, Kate had never gotten what she wanted, because that urge to forge ahead, to keep moving, had never left her. Or her mother.

Come along and join this rally against fur or for this candidate. Sign this petition. Wear this button. Write this senator. Join our club. Visit our Web site. Tell your friends.

Dorothy—Dodie—Cromwell happily obliged. Then when her daughters tried to untangle the things she got herself tangled up in, she would sigh and chide them for not understanding her.

"Some people hang back and watch while the parade passes them by. But others hear the thump-thump-a-thump of the big bass drum and they've got to pick up their feet and march," she'd say. "I'm a marcher. I'm a thump-thump-a-thumper."

Kate had to admit she couldn't have come up with a better description of her mother herself. The problem was that this last parade her mother had decided to join—selling her condo to join with two elderly friends in a retirement co-op scheme they had concocted—left Kate's *head* feeling as if someone had used *it* as that big drum.

Now it fell to Kate to pick up the pieces and try to get her mother's life back on track. She couldn't get her own life on track, but her sister Jo had confidence that Kate could get their mom's life sorted out. And that she could do it quickly, without much fuss and no emotional or financial penalties attached.

Kate blinked and exhaled, as if either of those would clear her mind and prepare her for the task ahead. She gathered her senses and went back into the examining room.

"Sorry about that, Mom. I needed to find…" *My nerve.* Instead of saying that, of course, she bought time by patting her lab-coat pocket, then reaching in and producing a pair of pale blue half glasses, which she held aloft. Not a lie, she justified. Holding up eyeglasses was not a lie. It was just a…gesture.

Kate clenched her jaw at the rationalization.

"You need reading glasses to look at my feet, dear?"

It was time to call on Kate the bold. She'd promised she would do this thing. Her mother had presented her with this opportunity. She must act.

Even if the prospect of grabbing the baton, as it were, and commandeering her mother's thump-thump-thumping parade terrified her. What if…

"No." Kate tucked the glasses away. "No, Mom, I don't need glasses for this. I need…your cooperation."

Dodie squirmed.

"And full attention."

She scooted forward, gathering her purse in both hands.

"Obviously, I know everything you've done for me and I appreciate it. I do. But comes the time—"

"No."

"No? No what?"

"No buts." Dodie held up her right hand, eyes closed. For a moment, with her poise and pocketbook at the ready, she looked as though she were about to take an oath of citizenship. "I've reached an age where I cannot only say what I want but I can *hear* what I want as well. And I do not want to hear what you have in mind to say after that 'but.'"

Ah, not an oath of citizenship at all. An oath of independence.

"You can put your hand down, Mom. I'm just trying to tell you—"

"Oh, Katie, you should be sweet to me." Her mom moved back farther then farther still until the file folder

Kate had left on the exam table poked her backside. She quickly snapped it up as if to get it out of her way, but then before Kate could take it from her, flipped it open and began scanning her information. "Because, you know, I am so very…"

"Sneaky?" Kate snatched the file away.

"Frail," her mother boomed, snatching that file right back and with enough force to nearly drag Kate off her feet.

Kate sighed.

Mom finished her perusal and, obviously satisfied, handed the file back.

Kate set the file aside again. She didn't need it. She hadn't written in it the things she intended to tell her mother today, anyway. Dodie was not the only sneaky Cromwell in the bunch, after all.

"I know you are up to something." Dodie hunkered down on the table and the paper crackled. She gave her eldest girl what she and her sister had grown up calling the "confess and no one gets hurt" look.

Only it was too late for that. It had always been too late for that because the tight-knit—so tightly knit that they often poked one another with their metaphorical knitting needles—trio had lived most of their lives in their own particular world of hurt. It bound them together and yet kept them at arm's length—which was still close enough to get an emotional choke hold, if the need arose.

Despite the appearance of a cherub-faced Southern grandmother type—all warm hugs, high hair and a pocketbook full of hard candy—deep down inside Dodie Cromwell had a hole in her heart.

Not some kind of congenital defect that affected every aspect of her life, mind you, but something just as pervasive. Dodie Cromwell had lost a child.

And as long as she lived, Scat-Kat-Katie would always feel, because of her actions or lack of action, just a little bit responsible for that.

And on top of that, she'd lost the only photographs they had of the little chubby-cheeked girl named Christina.

"I know you're up to something." Dodie raised her chin, well, one of them. The second and third flaps of soft flesh that lay under her jawline sort of dangled lazily down along her neck as if they had been yanked up for no good reason a few times too many and had no intention of falling for that again. She crossed her ankles and arms, using body language that did not need an interpreter. "And I think it's only fair to warn you that you are wasting your time."

"*You* made the appointment, Mother. So if anyone is wasting anyone's time here..."

"It's not as if you couldn't use the—"

Practice? Money? Company? Nothing her mother ended that sentence with was going to make Kate feel good.

"—the situation to your advantage," Dodie finished then grinned. She had her daughter dead to rights. But then, she usually did.

"Would you sit still?" Kate used her most doctorly tone to both concede her mother's point and to try to keep things in hand. "All that wiggling makes it sound like you're trying to fish the last nut out of the popcorn bag."

Dodie Cromwell did her best to act shocked and wounded but her eyes glittered with pure impish pleasure as she demanded of her oldest daughter, "Who are you calling a nut?"

"If the shoe fits..." Kate bent down at last, easily uncrossed her mother's swollen ankles then worked her sensible but half-size-too-small pumps free. "Did these shoes *ever* fit?"

"They were on sale." Dodie wiggled her fat little piggies and let out a deep, satisfied sigh.

On sale. Waste not want not. One man's trash...is a resourceful woman's treasure. Kate had grown up with her mother's admonitions ringing in her ears. She respected them, understood where they came from but... "Treasure or not, you have got to stop trashing your feet, Mom."

"What?"

Kate met her mother's eyes, so like Kate's own, deep set and startling green. All the women in her mother's family had those green eyes. Kate and Jo had them and their baby sister... Well, no one could say for sure but they all believed she must. Her whole life, Kate had searched the face of every girl child the right age for another pair of green eyes like theirs.

"And don't get on your high horse with me, young lady." Her mother's voice drew her back instantly.

"You don't even know that popcorn doesn't have nuts, it has old maids."

Now it was Kate's turn to use the power of the green-eyed gaze and put on the indignant act. "Who are *you* calling an old maid?"

"Old maid?" Dodie went all gushy, her lips pushed out, her words not quite baby talk, not quite mindless mush, the way she might have spoken to an elderly pampered poodle if she had one. "You're not an old maid, sweetie pie. You're just…"

Kate held her breath. She hadn't intended to hold her breath. But her mother had that kind of effect on her—causing her to do all sorts of things she had never had any intentions of doing.

And with that thought, she exhaled in a whoosh that made her shoulders sag and blew her bangs upward. Before they could land in a brown fringe over her eyes again, her mother concluded her sentence.

"You're just *discerning.*"

"You mean too picky for my own good." Kate nodded.

"Both you girls are…"

Too picky for your own good. It hung in the air between them like another piece of the family's dirty laundry they tried so hard to ignore.

"…discerning," Dodie finished as she exhaled, looking adoring but glum. "I suppose I have only myself to blame."

Kate put her hand on her mother's leg. "No, Mom, I've never…"

Dodie reached out and placed her ruddy palm on

Kate's cheek. "Your father may have only loaded the baby into his brand-new overpriced pickup truck and driven off that awful night but he took a part of *all* of us with him."

Kate turned her back. It was the closest thing she could do to bolting for the door. She took her mother's foot in one hand as if she wanted to begin an exam. Actually, she just thought it was a good way to keep Dodie from kicking her aside and bolting as well when Kate said what she had planned to say. "But you took care of us then, Mom."

"I did."

Deep breath. She considered grabbing her mother's other foot, maybe throwing in a leg lock. Instead, she stood straight and turned. She'd promised Jo she'd do this and she *would* do it. This time she could not run. "And now it's our turn to take care of you."

"Oh, no." Dodie shook her feet free and slid off the table. She nabbed her shoes and headed for the door without even putting them on.

Kate couldn't run, but Dodie *could.*

Right out the examining-room door.

"No?" Kate stood in the doorway and called out, "You haven't even heard what I have to say."

"I don't have to hear." As Kate's lone assistant for the slow workday stared with her mouth open, Dodie's feet plopped softly over the stiff brown carpet of the outer office. She did not pause to put her shoes on, not even when she got to the main door. "I know what's coming. You think this same kind of thing hasn't happened to my friends? I should have recognized the signs. Getting me on your turf, taking away my shoes…"

"Mom, I'm a professional. I'm a podiatrist." *Not that anyone would know it from the pitiful lack of patients around here.* She glanced around the room, then called after her mother again, "You had an appointment."

"Yes, but *you* had another objective." She had jammed her hand down into her shoe so she could stab the pointed toe of the pump in her right hand. "And I want no part of it. I'm not some delicate old woman who needs looking after by her children."

"You just said you were frail."

She flung the door open, almost lost the shoe in her left hand, caught it and stuffed it, quite haphazardly, into her open purse. "You just said I was a nut."

And as if to disprove that notion to anyone within earshot, Dodie hustled out the door and into the hallway of the medical-arts building with her head high, one shoe poking out of her purse and the other firmly placed on her hand.

"No, Mom, I didn't." Kate followed as far as the door. "That was a joke. That was us just kidding around."

"Behind every joke is a kernel of…" She stopped, opened her mouth, then smiled. She yanked the shoe from her purse, fit it to her other hand and clapped both soles together like a pair of triumphant cymbals. "Kernels! That's what's in popcorn, isn't it?"

"See, Mom. You cannot focus. You go from one thing to another without thinking it through. One minute you're leaving in a huff, the next you're in this public hallway waving around those awful shoes that you will never be able to cram your feet back into."

Dodie frowned at the shoes.

When she did not try to prove Kate wrong by throwing the navy pumps down on the floor and beginning to shove her swollen tootsies back into them, Kate could tell her mother had taken the point to heart. She might not want to hear what needed to be said, but she *was* listening. So Kate pushed on. "Besides, you're going to slip in those stockings. Probably fall and break a hip. And then what?"

Dodie put her hand, uh, heel, on her hip, her penciled-on eyebrows furrowed over her worried gaze.

"You have no home of your own to go to and your lady friends are not capable of taking care of you when you're healthy much less when you need real care." Kate had not met these women, but she assumed they must be like her mother. And though she loved her with all her heart, the last person Kate would want hovering over her when she was seriously ill or in pain was her mother. "You haven't thought this through, just like you didn't think through selling your condo. Things like that are what have Jo and I…"

"Jo and you…?" Dodie mimicked the way Kate's voice trailed off then her face lit up. "Oh! That's right, I'm fleeing! I'm flying for my life."

"Fleeing? Really, Mom." Kate watched her mother now switch to careful baby steps.

"Remember when you and your sister used to put

on your father's old gym socks and skate on the hardwood floors?" she asked, making almost no progress at all heading for the large glass front doors.

Kate had insisted her office be on the ground floor, to better accommodate patients with aching feet. Little had she known she'd get the most benefit from that when trying to just do something sensible for her own mother. "Mom, this is hardly the time to—"

"Oh, that's right. That's right. Fleeing. Oh, and skating!" She put her weight into it and went gliding along the hallway. "Hey! The old girl has still got it! Try to catch me now Scat-Kat-Katie!"

"Mom, this isn't helping...."

And she hit the door.

Literally.

Went sailing right into it with a big thud. It knocked one of the pumps off her hands. That did not slow her down.

In fact, it just freed her up to open the door and rush headlong out into the bright afternoon sun, leaving a lone bargain pump lying on the floor à la Cinderella making her getaway.

If only Dodie's land yacht of a car would simply turn into a pumpkin. That would solve some of Kate's problems.

Oh, her mom would still try to drive it, of course, but people would be more apt to get out of her way.

Unfortunately for Kate, she didn't have sense enough to do just that.

"Mom, come back inside."

The driver's side door slammed. "Can't dear. I have someplace I have to go."

"Where?" Scat-Kat-Kate pushed aside her usual response to retreat and charged forward.

"Dream Away Bay Court!"

"Dream Away..." Kate knew that name. Wasn't it from a fairy tale or something? "What are you talking about, Mom?"

"Florida, darling. My friends and I are headed to our old vacation cottage in Santa Sofia." Dodie rammed the key into the ignition.

"Santa Sofia." The name tingled on Kate's lips. Or maybe that was the memory of the last kiss she'd shared with Vince in that very place.

The engine roared to a start.

"Mom, you can't be serious. We haven't used that place for like...sixteen years." They had a caretaker who, up until the last year or so, had kept it rented and they supposed in decent repair, but who knew? "Mom, stop. Think this over. Jo and I think you should come and live with one of us."

"Well, I think you should come and live with me. Nothing keeping you here. You want me as a roomie? You'll know where to find me." Dodie gave her a grin, a wave, and not one other bit of warning before she jerked the car into Reverse and hit the gas.

And her tire hit Kate's foot.

The wet snap of bones breaking got to Kate long before the actual pain.

Crunch.

Grind.

Squish.

Or maybe the squish came first.

On that, Kate could not be one-hundred-percent sure, what with her legs buckling, the agony overtaking her and her mind swerving randomly between a doctor's cool objectivity and a daughter's hot-headed frustration.

Neither lasted long.

Kate was down…but in a moment of realization that could only happen in her family, she knew she wasn't out.

Dodie had been stopped.

Kate had not run and for once she had succeeded, if only temporarily.

And as she faded into unconsciousness, she did so with a smile.

Chapter Two

Being perfect was not as satisfying as some people would have you believe. In fact, hotshot Realtor, Jo Cromwell, found it positively exhausting.

From the moment her sounds-of-nature alarm went off at 6:00 a.m. until she switched off her laptop and the satellite TV news mix—which allowed her to follow news, weather and financial reports on six channels simultaneously—at midnight, Jo's life was just one long list of putting out fires, putting plans into action and putting her best foot forward.

And every day she hated it more and more.

She hated the life she had created for herself.

She hated her unquenchable drive to push harder, climb higher.

She hated her desperate need to feel she had finally arrived by achieving more, by getting more, by *being* more. And she hated to admit that every day she failed.

Then every new morning she got up and tried to do

it all over again. She couldn't seem to help herself. Every day. Day after day. Year upon year.

Exhausting? To say the least.

And expensive.

The shoe aspect alone was a nightmare. Not only did it take a small fortune to keep shod in the latest trend, but the older she got the more she came to realize that the cuter the shoes, the more punishment they handed out to her feet. Her *fat* feet. Her *mother's* feet.

No designer names, expensive styles and accessories, not even an "awww" factor of "I'll skip lunch for a week to pay for these" times two in cuteness could change that.

"Thanks, Mom," she muttered.

"Hmm?" her passenger asked.

"Nothing." Jo gunned the engine and her car jumped forward a few feet, gaining her absolutely no real ground in the stifling Atlanta traffic.

Thanks, Mom, her mind echoed. Thanks for the fat feet, the weak ankles, the thin hair and the tendency to look like an hourglass with the sands of time drifting southward more and more each year.

"Green light! See it?"

And thanks, ever so much, for my sister Kate and for your latest means of allowing us to...be sweet...to each other. Jo gritted her teeth and eased her car forward.

Kate did not have to do anything to *appear* perfect.

Kate had traveled. Kate had sought and mastered a series of interesting and eclectic jobs. If that wasn't enough, at a time when other people might have been thinking of settling down, she up and went to medical school, became a doctor and now had opened her own practice.

Kate was the real deal. From her thick, gorgeous hair to her lean, athletic build, to her adorable little toes. Well, adorable up until a few days ago.

Jo shuddered. Her breath caught in her chest. She gripped the steering wheel and pulled into the parking lot of her apartment building with the chichi Atlanta address. She stole a peek at her sister in the seat next to her, now sitting serenely with her eyes closed.

"Perfect," she whispered before cutting the engine and plastering on a big smile. "We're here. Now sit tight and wait for me to come around and help you—"

Clunk. The passenger door of Jo's darling electric-blue PT Cruiser popped open.

"Kate!"

"I don't need any help. If I can just get myself upright, I can propel myself forward, get out and..."

"Fall on your face?" Jo clucked her tongue in good humor. How often did she get to play the rescuer role with Kate? She was going to savor every minute. She tugged on the hem of Kate's shirt to counterbalance the sudden forward pitch of her trying to climb out of the car on her own.

Ooomph. Kate came back down into the seat, her cheeks red and beads of sweat on her forehead.

"Stay put."

"You just stay out of my way," Kate joked, even though she looked as though she was about to be sick.

Jo shot out of the car, whomping her door shut with such force that it made the magnetic sign proclaiming Paul Powers Realty: The Powerhouse of Home Sellers slide down a full inch on one side. One day that sign would tout her name, represent her success. One day, Jo thought as she gritted her teeth and decided to leave the sign hanging lopsided, she would show Paul Powers she was not a girl to be toyed with. She would finally be somebody.

That was all she wanted. All she had ever wanted. *To be somebody.*

If Jo ever decided to have her own sign with a simple maxim to promote herself to the world it would be something eloquent yet energetic. Understated, yet it would speak volumes. It would evoke her style, her initiative, her…

Oh, who was she kidding? Jo didn't need a sign to proclaim to the world her fondest desire. It could be summed up in six words. *Pick me. Pick me. Pick me.*

An ideal sentiment for the kid who'd felt perpetually unwanted. Their father had chosen the youngest of the girls to take with him when he'd broken up the family. Mom had always leaned on Kate. But Jo?

Jo had gone into real estate and excelled at it because, in the end, she understood it. Every day all day she spent her time getting people to choose her. Then she took something that had been cast off and made someone want it, turned it into a complete must-have. Just like her.

In her line of work, Jo was the must-have agent. And she still felt unwanted, especially by her sister right now.

"This fierce independent act of yours may dazzle the corn-and-bunion set but I warn you it's about to trod on my very last nerve!" The springy curls of Jo's pale blond hair extensions bounced against the resolute stiffness of her shoulders in her eye-catching red suit jacket. "Just let me help you for once without it degenerating into a contest of wills."

In three long strides Jo had come around to her sister's side of the car and put her foot down.

In response, Kate put her cane down.

Jo narrowed her eyes on the spot just a hairbreadth away from her toe where the tip of Kate's cane rested on the blacktop of the parking lot. "These are three-hundred-dollar hand-crafted Italian sling backs!"

"Three hundred dollars for a pair of high-heeled toe crunchers? Where are your priorities?" Kate rolled her eyes.

"My priorities are just where they should be, thank you. If they weren't I'd have left you in that hospital at the mercy of every nurse and aide that you so enchanted with your constant demands to be released."

"I can't stand being confined. I have work waiting. A business to run…" Kate drew in her breath, but her face gave no hint if she was in physical pain or had just remembered that she had decided to close her office while she recovered from the accident. Maybe to never open it again.

"As do I. And yet here I am." Jo planted her foot on the edge of the open door, both to make her point and to block her sister from lurching up and out of the car and doing further damage to herself. "And I'm not going anywhere as long as you need me."

Kate glanced down. Her cane scraped softly along the ground in a gesture that suggested humility, like a shy child scuffing his toe in the dirt.

"Don't worry, you can thank me later," Jo murmured.

"*Thank* you? I was going to trip you so I could make my big break for it." Kate laughed without looking up, then bounced the tip of her cane on the ground a couple times. "Three hundred dollars! For three hundred dollars I would have carried you piggy-back through the streets of Atlanta, baby sister."

"Big talk from someone who can't even bear her own weight right now." Jo reached out to snatch away the barley twist mahogany walking stick with the brass cat's head handle. "And by the way, I scoured practically every thrift shop and antique store in Atlanta to find this cane for you. I'll thank you to be more ladylike with it."

"Ladylike?" Kate snorted. "Since when have either of us put any kind of a price on being considered ladylike?"

"Then just be a little less donkey-like with it, if you don't mind."

"But I do mind, Jo. I mind that my foot is in a cast and I am in a pickle when I was only trying to do a good deed. I mind that because of this, because of me, Mom now feels just awful and now neither of us can take care of her. Not to mention having to rely on you, my baby sister, who should be the one to count on me."

"If I needed to count on something I'd buy a calculator. Or an abacus. Or wear open-toed shoes. I certainly wouldn't turn to *you.*" She meant it as a challenge. The kind of joke meant to goad Kate back into acting like her old feisty self. But it didn't come off that way and Jo knew why. "That isn't to say people can't depend on you. In fact, you're the most dependable…"

"No. That's okay. You'd be wise not to depend on me. On ol' Scat-Kat-Katie."

Jo thought about putting her arms around her sister, leaning her head to Kate's and…

And what?

Telling her for the umpteenth time that there was nothing Kate could have done to keep their father from abducting their younger sister? Jo simply could not bear to bring that up, not in the first moments of the first evening of the first time she had ever had the chance to be the caregiver. The helper. The…Kate.

"It's sisterhood. It's not a competition," their mother often told them, usually on the heels of having heaped praise on Kate for some superhuman feat. Opening an olive jar, for example.

Competition or not, today, *Jo* was the good daughter. Jo was the hero. The star. Jo was on top.

It had taken Kate nearly being crippled for Jo to get on top but she wasn't going to nitpick about the process now. And she wasn't going to dredge up a lifetime of old hurts.

"Somebody had to step in and take charge of you." Jo lowered her foot and finally moved back enough so that Kate could swing her legs and her cane out the door. "You can't drive. You can't work. You can barely walk. Face it, Kate, you are totally dependent on me."

People liked to say they looked remarkably alike, always adding—for being complete opposites.

Jo didn't see it. The alike part. The opposites, that she understood to the depths of her being.

Yes, they both had the vivid green eyes of their mother's family. And they stood exactly the same height, barefoot. But Jo made it a point never to *go* barefoot, so that hardly counted. Where Jo had fair skin and natural blond hair—grown by naturally blond women in some distant Nordic country and naturally woven to the hair on Jo's scalp—Kate had their father's coloring. Dark blond hair with sun streaks, a dark tan from years of that outdoorsy life she loved so much, not to mention her dark sense of humor.

"Totally dependent on *you?* Where is Mom and her car when I need them? Maybe I can lie on the pavement and she can just finish me off." Kate gave a wry, throaty laugh. Just the thing to take the edge off her cutting remark. Of course.

Jo extended her hand to assist her sister up and out of the car. "Mom has hunkered down with one of her friends in her old condo building. I don't think we have to worry about her getting up to anything too ambitious until you're back on your feet."

"I *am* on my feet." She slapped Jo's hand away, tried to stand then staggered backward.

Jo caught her.

She winced.

This time she accepted the assistance with a heavy sigh, making it clear she did not like the situation, not one bit. "This is just temporary, you know. Three weeks, tops."

"Three weeks?"

Three weeks. The same amount of time Jo had until her own little house of cards would collapse around her. Instantly Jo saw that as one of those good news/bad news deals. The bad news was that she had three weeks to try to salvage her career and any scrap of self-worth she still possessed. The good news was that if she spent that time taking care of Kate, she probably wouldn't mind facing the end of her world quite so much.

She stepped in and anchored her feet to provide added support as Kate struggled to get stable on her feet. Foot. "Is that what the doctor told you? Three *weeks?*"

Kate mumbled something.

"What?" Jo cocked her head. "I don't believe I heard that."

"*Months.* The surgeon said three months before I could put my full weight on it for any length of time. *If* I have the other surgeries that he seems to think I am going to need…if I want to, you know, not walk with a limp and cane the rest of my life."

"*If* you have the surgery that will save your foot? There's some doubt?" Jo pulled her sister up until they stood shoulder to shoulder and yet still could not see eye to eye.

"Without the surgery I might be able to be back at work in a few weeks."

"And suffer so much damage that you might cut your career short by a few years? Not to mention the effect of not taking care of yourself and your general health and…" she paused to pointedly clear her throat "…well-being. Doesn't the Bible say something about physician heal thyself?"

"I refuse to take any guff from you on making choices that I should know better than to make." Kate raised her head and narrowed her eyes at the sleek white, impersonal building before them. "Realtors who live in rented apartments and all that."

Yes, the thirty-five-year-old fireball, noted as one of the city's "Realtors To Watch" in a sidebar for an article on the boom market in *Southern City Lifestyles,* did not actually own her own home. She had bought and flipped several houses and condos in the last four years but she had never lived in any of them. She'd find something she thought would make her happy, move in, paint, wallpaper, remodel, whatever it took, and the next thing she knew, she looked around her and realized she *wasn't* happy. So she'd go on the prowl again for a home, a haven, a…a…a…

It would help if she had any idea what it was she was really looking for. But to do that, she'd have to slow down long enough to examine her life and figure out what was missing.

"Are we going to hang out in your parking lot all day or are we going to actually make some use of this ritzy, three-hundred-dollar-shoe equivalent of an apartment of yours?"

Slow down? Examine her life? Like that was going to happen anytime soon!

"Don't pick on that apartment too much. It's going to be your headquarters for the next few weeks." She took a few steps backward, guiding her sister one hobble at a time. "Months if you know what's good for you."

"Again. Not taking guff from you on pushing myself too hard." Kate made it up the walk, using the cane and sheer willpower.

Before Jo could launch an argument, or even come up with one, her cell phone bleated out the opening notes of the old Crosby, Stills, Nash and Young song, "Our House." Luckily it did not blare out the lyrics that spoke of finding love and home. Apropos, Jo had thought, to her work. Yet so ironic to her personal life.

But irony was not what made Jo wince at her insistent ring tone.

"If you want to get that call, I can manage on my own." Kate took a step toward the sleek brass-and-glass door and winced.

"If it's important they can leave a message." Jo swept in and placed her hand on her sister's back more to provide a place to fall than to take control.

"You're a good sister."

Jo only felt a twinge of guilt that she let Kate think family love had motivated her refusing to answer the phone. While she had no idea, without checking, who might be on the other end of that call and what they would want from her, she did know it wouldn't be good. And unlike her sister, she would have no one to hold her up when the time came for her to take a fall.

Love. Fear. Guilt. At least she was acting out of some emotion and not just a blind sense of duty, right?

They made their way through the lobby and into the elevator. Then down the hallway… At least, Jo made it down the hallway.

Kate hung back, leaning on her cane and breathing hard.

"I should have rented a wheelchair," Jo said, even as she pulled her keys from her purse. "Let me unlock the door then I'll come back and get you."

"I am not helpless," Kate snapped, her usually friendly features lined with pain. She slumped against the wall for support.

Jo rushed to her. "Are you sure you're supposed to be out of the hospital?"

"So sayeth the insurance company," Kate joked.

"And your doctor?"

"I *am* a doctor." Kate grimaced.

"Truth, Kate."

Kate took a deep breath.

Her silence fueled Jo's suspicions.

"We don't have many traditions in our family, Kate. For that matter we don't even have much of a family. But when it mattered, you and I have always spoken the truth to each other. It's all we have."

Kate nodded then exhaled in a long, low breath.

"The truth is that my doctor thinks I've gone to the beach house."

"The beach…? You mean that ratty old cottage in Florida?"

"Hey, that ratty old cottage in Florida provided us with some of the wonderful experiences of our lives."

"You mean those vacations when we were kids?"

"No, I mean the rental money that paid for Mom to take a real vacation—away from us—once a year after we grew up."

"Be sweet," Jo warned with a laugh. They loved their mom with all their hearts, neither of them doubted that. She had done all she could to protect and nurture them—whether they needed it or not. She mothered them well with the underlying understanding—not unlike an electrical current that if exposed could wreak havoc—that Jo and Kate never needed to be mothered. They called this *good daughtering.*

Dodie *needed* them to need her. What an awesome responsibility to place on already emotionally shaky children. So Jo could forgive Kate for joking about the blessed break Dodie's vacation gave them. Because she understood it and because joking was the only way they dared broach the subject.

The thought of precarious subjects brought Jo instantly back to the real topic at hand. "Why would your doctor think you'd gone to the cottage in Florida?"

"Oh, the usual reasons."

"To moon over Vince Merchant?" If Kate insisted on giving nonanswers, Jo felt it completely within her rights as a little sister to respond with something Kate would have to react to.

"Vince Mer— Whatever made you think of him?" Kate, still leaning against the wall, twisted her upper body and gazed into the gold reflective elevator doors. "Of all the memories of that place, the cottage, the vacations, the sand in our shoes…our shorts…our hair…our ears—"

"I get it, sand."

"And, um, surf. And so many things connected to that place. Why, at the mention of Florida, would you go straight to Vince Merchant?"

"I'll answer that if you will." Jo smirked just a little. "But then, I guess, if you could answer it, then I wouldn't have to."

"Do not start, Jo. I have let go of that man. Of that time. It was a lifetime ago. It doesn't mean anything anymore."

"Uh-huh," Jo murmured at yet another evasive reply, the keys in her hand jangling as they went sliding along in her search for the right one.

"Besides, there is no way Vince Merchant ended up in Santa Sofia," Kate said so softly as she stared at the unblinking image of herself.

What was up with Kate? Jo paused to marvel. Refusing surgery. Misleading her doctor. After all these years to have that response to the mention of Vince. Was she about to run again? Why? And where could she go to escape the hurt she carried always in her heart?

"So tell me…" Jo drew a deep breath, considered the odds of getting a straight answer from her sister and asked instead, "Just why would your doctor think you would go to Florida?"

"Oh, you know." Kate looked down. Her shoulders rose and fell. "To rest. To relax. To rejuvenate."

"This doctor you're talking about?" She churned the key in the lock and pushed the door open with one shoulder before turning to face her sister and ask, "Has he ever actually *met* you?"

"Funny," Kate droned, limping past and into the nearly empty front room. "And yes, he did meet me. Even made rounds while I was in the hospital and formed some pretty strong opinions of me."

"I'll just bet." Jo moved inside, but not fully. She hung back by the open door, halfheartedly wishing she could slip into the hallway alone, take one fortifying deep breath before she and her sister became roomies for who knew how long.

Kate managed a rather pitiful-looking grin. "Why else do you think I told him I planned to go out of state for an extended recovery period?"

"You *lied?*" All right, that shocked her. Kate was more perfect than Mary Poppins, after all.

"I did not lie," Kate snapped in something that seemed like pain…or panic. She struggled to move forward with her cane and cast on the plush carpet.

"You lied to get out of having a doctor pester you to make follow-up visits." Jo took two hurried steps to lend support. "Visits that might save you from a lifetime of limping, I might add."

"Save your adding for that abacus you plan on

buying." Kate swatted away any attempt by Jo to aid her. "And don't be so…literal."

Jo stood back and folded her arms. "Literal?"

"*Lying?* It's such a harsh word."

"What would you call it?"

"I was thinking out loud." The comeback came quick and sure, as if Kate had maybe rehearsed it in her head a few times trying to convince herself. "Mom was standing there telling *my* caregiver that she intended to make sure I didn't spend any time at my practice, like she actually had that kind of influence with me, that kind of power over what I do with my time, that say-so about my work."

"And you couldn't stand the idea of it. You wanted to run so you invented a place you could run to and told yourself that was wishful thinking, not an outright fib."

"Mom started it," Kate protested. She attempted to put some of her weight on the foot in the large purple-and-white cast.

She looked so small. So vulnerable. Now, in the unkind artificial tract lighting, the circles under her eyes seemed so dark and the usually taut skin on her face and neck, drawn. It gave the impression of Kate being older than her years and much more intense, if that was possible, and anything but happy.

It made Kate look…

Jo drew in her breath and held it.

It made Kate look *like their father.*

Not that Jo remembered him so much as she remembered pictures of him. Pictures that had long ago disappeared from their home and faded from her memory. There was one in particular of him with his hand on her shoulder. Kate stood nearby. Dad had insisted it be taken to show off his new truck—the truck their father would drive away in forever a few days after the picture was taken. But being Mom, she'd only gotten the front fender and a part of their family. If other photos had been taken that day, Jo could not recall. Her parents had fought. They'd always fought. And their dad had left.

Now Jo looked at her sister and could see something familiar of him in her. It spooked her a little.

No, given Kate's suddenly uncharacteristic behavior and their father's bitter betrayal, it spooked Jo *a lot.*

Jo edged forward, her hands out.

Kate sucked air through her gritted teeth, her shoulders drew up but she still motioned to Jo to keep back. She took a step, gasped then shifted her weight back onto the antique cane and exhaled, her shoulders drooping. "Anyway, when my surgeon asked me what I might do with my time off, I looked at him and I looked at Mom and I couldn't help thinking about what she had said she planned to do and that I had promised I'd stop her from doing it, or doing *anything* so rash and—"

"Kate!"

The front door fell shut with a *wham.*

"And I said I *might* go to Florida." Kate didn't even pause in her rambling. *Step, gasp, shift.* Rambling *and* shuffling. "Just like that. *Might* go to Florida. Now is that lying, really?"

"Really? Yes, it is." Jo tossed her keys into the bowl on the table by the door. She didn't have to look to see if they landed. She heard the familiar clunk and the wobble caused by the one uneven table leg. Like everything else in her apartment, she had put it there for convenience on the day she'd moved in and had seen no reason to adjust or change anything about it since then.

She had enough decorating and dressing places in her side business flipping properties. She had expended a lot of energy learning how to do that to ensure a fast sale with maximum profits. She had gotten so good at it she could turn a house in a matter of six weeks, a month if pressed or maybe…

"Three weeks," she muttered. "Given the right market."

Fast sale. Maximum profits. Beach house in Florida.

Love. Fear. Guilt.

Rest. Relaxation. Rejuvenation.

Her goals and motivations as well as Kate's stated needs clicked through her mind just like that and one by one she placed a mental tick in the box beside each one.

Perfect. Perfect. Perfect.

"It most certainly *is* a lie. Unless…"

Kate put her hand on the back of the love seat in the center of the sparse space. "Unless what?"

Jo blinked. "Is it actually such a bad idea?"

"Lying?"

"Florida."

"Florida?"

"The cottage." Jo's heels clacked soft and swift over

the floor as she went to her sister's side. "We've been saying we need to get down there and go through things. Decide what to do with it all, with the place."

Sell. That was the solution to her situation. One big sale, one sudden influx of cash and she'd be on top again. "Perfect."

"It's worth some thought, I guess. It would get me away from..." Instead of finishing her thought, Kate looked around the room, her expression sour.

"Here." Jo caught her sister by the elbow. "Let's get you settled down and comfortable."

"Pick one." Kate dumped her cane onto the love seat and hopped around the side of it. "I can be settled down or I can be comfortable. I can't be both."

Jo knew what her always-restless sister meant but with this new idea burning through her thought process, she did not have time for empathy. "Sit. I'll get you some water so you can take your meds and the TV remote so you can stick your foot up on the coffee table and yell at the world."

In a matter of minutes Jo's French-manicured nails clattered over the keyboard of her laptop.

Florida real estate.

Property values.

Length of time on the market.

In a chair a few feet away, Kate flicked through the one-hundred-plus TV channels so fast that it created an almost strobe-light effect.

Crime show.

Crime show.

Crime show.

"If I have to spend the next three weeks watching this junk, I may go insane and do bodily harm to somebody." Another click, this time to a commercial…for a crime show. "Fortunately with all these forensic-science shows, I'll know how to do it without getting caught."

"Well, if you want to spare yourself the trouble of having to plan the perfect crime, there's always Florida," Jo said as she double clicked the mouse to scan yet another site on the hottest selling properties along the Gulf coast.

"What do you mean?"

Jo glanced up. "I, uh, it's just that it's been empty for two years now because no one rented it. Not sure what that means or what shape it's in but this opportunity *has* presented itself…."

"My losing the use of my foot is an opportunity?"

"The Lord works in mysterious ways." It was a pat answer, but not an altogether glib one. Kate and Jo were women of faith. Not particularly well-tended or studied faith but both of them had accepted Christ as their personal Savior while still teens. And hadn't Jo been praying and praying for some kind of resolution to the mess she had found herself in? Why couldn't this be the answer?

Of course to get to that answer, she just might have to go through her sister.

R-r-r-i-i-n-n-g. The phone cut through her scheming, um, musings and jarred her into reacting.

"I'm not here!" she shouted, even as Kate thrust out her own hand in the "get thee away from me" position and said the same.

"I'm not here."

Jo raised her head and met her sister's eyes. "If you're not here then where are you?"

R-r-r-i-i-n-n-g.

"Florida?" Kate ventured meekly.

Jo smiled and signed off the Internet with a decisive click. This was it. The answer to her prayer. And all she had to do to achieve it was convince her sister to dump the family home, the only thing besides the whole foot-recovery situation still holding their family together. "By this time tomorrow we'll be sitting on the veranda and sipping sweet tea, in Florida."

Chapter Three

"The porch is gone, Daddy." Moxie Weatherby, cell phone to her ear, climbed back into her almost-restored old red-and-white pickup truck sitting in the drive of the cute little rental cottage—correction, make that *once* cute little rental cottage—on Dream Away Bay Court.

"What do you mean the porch is gone, Moxie, honey?" The seventy-two-year-old man that everyone in town called Billy J rasped out a laugh. "Did it get up and move to greener pastures?"

"Well, it's green all right." She craned her neck to survey the scene she'd just left and in doing so caught a glimpse of her bloodshot, brown eyes and pink-tipped, turned-up nose in the rearview mirror. She wondered if she'd brought her allergy spray, because if she stayed, she was going to need it. "But I think the green part is mostly mold."

"Aw, a little mold never hurt nothing."

Moxie sniffled, swiped away a blob of runny

mascara then pulled back her thick hair, glad it had grown out enough to allow her to wad it into a knot at the nape of her neck again. That and/or a ball cap or simple round sunhat usually took care of hiding the drab mess of light brown, with copper and almost white-blond streaks she liked to call *beached blah-nd.* "Daddy, this is not a *little* mold. A little mold I could handle. We live in Florida, after all. This is a mold factory. The columns look like moss-covered trees from a primeval forest."

"You lived your whole life in Santa Sofia, girl. What do you know about forests?"

"I know those big, burly lumberjacks who work in them usually use chain saws to make any headway. I sure do wish I had one of those now."

"Chain saw?"

"Lumberjack." Moxie sighed.

"What would your fella say about that?"

"He'd probably tell me to put the lug to work and keep busy because he won't be able to see me again tonight."

"That Lionel Lloyd's just like his daddy, a hard worker."

"If he were just like his daddy, Daddy, he'd be a daddy himself," Moxie joked.

"Accept his proposal and he'd be halfway there." Her father snorted.

Moxie promptly sneezed. "Let's tackle one aversion at a time, please. The porch?"

"A little bleach, little elbow grease, you'll have the front of the old place shipshape in no time."

"Only if it's a *sunken* ship." She shook her head at the task before her.

"You trying to tell me that the house is taking on water?" Another raspy laugh, this one degenerating into a slight coughing fit.

Moxie waited it out. She always had, ever since Billy J and his wife—now ex-wife—had taken her in as a young child. She knew what brought it on and she knew what would follow.

A long, moaning kind of sigh. Another chuckle. A thump to the chest, one last sputtered cough and the promise that never quite came to fruition. "Got to see a doctor about that."

At that point she realized she had two choices. She could launch into her speech for the millionth time about the old man needing to stop smoking, start exercising and take care of his health. Or she could say a prayer that the Lord would keep the man she had called Daddy for most of her life alive and kicking a while longer. She opted for the second.

It was a reasonable choice. The Lord, after all, would at least listen to her petition whereas William Jay Weatherby would most certainly turn a deaf ear. And since he actually *had* a deaf ear, that made it all the easier for him to block her concerns out entirely.

"No, the house is high and dry as far as I can see. But the porch has seen better days." And she meant that.

A vacation spot, a home away from home, a refuge, even more than once a honeymoon haven. The little cottage had a happy history that stretched back to the days just after Pearl Harbor, when a soldier had built it for his beloved bride before going off to war. Years later they had built the smaller cottage across the way for their daughter and her husband so the families could always stay close.

Family and *close.* Two words that Moxie no longer had any reason to use together. Not with her mother off pursuing a new life and no siblings, and just the rumor of distant cousins living somewhere north of Florida. A picture of her aunt holding her as a baby hung behind the cash register in her father's business, but they had not made contact in the nearly thirty years since it had been taken. Families were hard, Moxie figured, and her father made them harder than they had to be. Which made it all the more important for her to show the old man she wasn't the kind to cut and run.

"Some of the floorboards are warped and split but serviceable. Maybe sometime next week, if the owners will spring for the paint, I can come by and spruce them up. The railings that are still standing are missing spindles but the railings that have fallen down look to be intact. No quick fix there but easy enough."

"How about the steps? Them fancy store-bought steps still there?"

"Yes." She smiled at his jab at her insistence four years back that they replace the old steps with the prefab kind people now used for decks and mobile homes. "The steps are in great shape."

"And the front door?"

"Still there." Thanks to Moxie's forethought in installing a glass-front storm door the year before she'd updated the steps, the original front door with the frosted oval window was still standing. "Though I shudder to think what's on the other side."

"Only one way to find out. Go up them steps and through that door and clap your eyes on the situation. Size 'er up. Make a plan. Dive right in. Do that and you can get a lot done and get gone before the owners turn up."

"Gone? After all these years working for them sight unseen, I kind of want to hang around and meet them."

"And have them think you'd just wait around long as it took for them to show? That they could have you at their beck and call the whole time they're here? Moxie, I raised you smarter than that."

"Daddy, that's a pretty dim view of these people."

"Well, in my experience, most folks *is* pretty dim." He chuckled, coughed, chuckled again. "Naw, girl, just a word of advice. These folks ain't like us. They been contented for first me then you to look after their property without so much as a call to ask how's it going or do we need anything. Then they decide to show back up, they don't give more than a day's notice?"

As far as anyone in Santa Sofia could remember, no one had seen the actual owners of the place for years. Since at least a year before Moxie had taken over the upkeep of the place. All their interchanges had happened through the mail, a business account and later e-mail.

"What does that say about them? You don't want nothing to do with folks like that." People often described Billy J as full of bluff and bluster, and that was exactly the tone he used now.

It seemed odd in this context. Odder still when her father's voice grew quiet, almost childlike in softness as he added, "Do you, Molly Christina?"

Molly Christina. Her daddy had called her that her whole childhood and his just saying it made her feel all of ten again as she answered, "I…I guess not."

"Good. Then you get to your work and get gone. The sooner begun, the sooner done."

"The sooner begun, the sooner done," she echoed, barely audibly.

"Then get gone. You done enough for these people."

"I have done a lot. For a lot of years I took care of the cottage and catered to the renters. These last two, of course, I've only had to keep an eye on it. Make sure we didn't have any unwelcome guests."

"Squatters," her father grumbled. Over forty years of dealing with the transient nature of things around here had not just made him ornery, but also a bit hardened toward people he didn't know well.

"I was thinking more of mice and snakes." Moxie shivered. "But I confess that was more for me than them. I kept thinking we'd get a renter and I'd have to go in and deal with who knew what if I didn't send someone in every now and then to give the place a going-over."

"There. Now see, you already know you don't have to deal with any vermin."

"Or squatters."

"I was talking about squatters," he groused.

"Well, I'm thankful for that. As for what all this place needs to make it livable?" Another look at the sagging structure. Then a quick check of the clock on her cell phone before pressing it to her overheated ear and saying, "I mean, it was one thing when we had rental money coming in and I could take it out of their profits as a business expense. But with it sitting empty for two years now?"

"Moxie, girl, you'd give a person the shirt off your back. When you work for someone, you give one hundred and ten percent. Time or two, I've known you to give certain folks a piece of your mind."

Certain folks? Moxie could only think of two, and she was talking to one of them.

"But when it comes to money?" The old man did that familiar laugh-cough thing again but managed to stave off another prolonged fit. "Well, you didn't get where you are today giving money away."

Where she was today? She exhaled and as the breath left her body, her shoulders slumped. "I hope they didn't expect me to reach into my own pocket to make repairs on *their* property."

"It's enough you giving them so much of your time and hard work. You should bill them for that."

"I am not going to bill them, Daddy." Her father would have. The man hadn't built up and maintained Billy's J's Bait Shack Seafood Buffet as a great spot to gather for both tourists and locals without being savvy about business. But sometimes business savvy was not good business. And it very often was not the way to get along with one's neighbors. "In case you've forgotten, I have new tenants moving in across the street this weekend and I don't want anyone to get off on the wrong foot."

"Tenants? I thought tenants paid rent."

"And I thought waitresses didn't get paid on days they didn't show up to work."

"That little girl is a single mom and it was just the one day. I'm sure things will turn around for her and I won't have to do that again."

That "little girl" was the same young woman Moxie had made special arrangements with to rent out the second cottage on Dream Away Bay Court. At about half of what she usually charged.

"Esperanza is not a single mom, Daddy. She has a husband and her baby has a father." And that baby's father had a father, a father who made it easy for the baby's father to act like a big baby and not live up to his fatherly responsibilities. Moxie clenched her jaw to keep from blurting all that out, not that she was sure she *could* blurt all that out. "Anyway, on my end of the deal, you know I'm not just giving her a cut rate on the rent. She's going to pay what she can in sweat equity."

"That don't sound proper for a young mother."

Moxie chuckled at her father's apprehension. "Just means doing yard work, upkeep, maybe help with my other properties."

"You know that girl is not going to do any of that.

Ain't that she's a bad girl, but, you know, with the baby and all."

She knew what her father was driving at, and all she could do was gaze at first one cottage and then the other, then sit back in the truck seat and shut her eyes. "It will get done."

"Well, not by me it won't, so I guess it's not my worry."

Translation: It's *your* worry, girl. I hope you know what you're getting into.

"I'll leave you to this, then," he finally said when she did not come back with a reply. "You know Billy J's famous words to live by—When the going gets tough, Billy J…"

"…goes fishing." She spoke the last line with him, with a practiced cadence and proper emphasis to match him syllable for syllable. "Thanks a lot, Daddy."

Not that she had expected to get any work out of the old fellow. It would have been nice for the company while she tackled the job, though.

"Been the Weatherby family motto for generations. Who am I to break with tradition at this late stage of life?"

"Who indeed?" she agreed with a puffy-eyed sniff and a soft laugh under her breath. Since she wasn't a Weatherby, at least not by birth, the motto didn't seem to apply to her. "So I guess I've run out of excuses. I'd better get after this mess and see what I can do before nightfall."

"See that you do." It came out sounding like an order.

Moxie did not like taking orders. "We'll see. It's a big job, after all."

"This job is only as big as you make it. Just do the basics and go," her father reminded her as he hung up.

She clicked the End button on her phone. "Do the basics and go?"

Certainly her father knew her better than that. Nothing in the makeup of her personality or her history spoke of a person would could do the basics then go.

Fifteen years ago, the year Moxie had turned sixteen, three momentous things had happened. That was not counting the getting her driver's license thing, which she *didn't* count because she'd been piloting boats and Jet Skis and zipping all over town via scooters long before she'd gotten a license to drive a car. And in Santa Sofia, who had anywhere to go, anyway, that having a car would mean so very much? So that wasn't the big deal for her that some other kids might have thought it.

No, when Moxie was sixteen her mom, the only mom she had ever known, ran off.

She'd gotten up one day, made Moxie and Billy J a big breakfast, washed up the dishes and when she was done, she'd written a note, packed her bags and left. All the note said was "Isn't there something better than this?"

A few days later they had learned that her notion of "something better" had come in the form of a thirty-something college professor who had been coming down to Santa Sofia for spring break for many years. She'd sent divorce papers and started her life over.

Billy J had gone fishing for the whole summer that

year and had come back with a two-pack-a-day cigarette habit and a chronic cough.

From that came the second momentous event. Moxie had changed her name.

Goodbye Molly Christina, a name that she had always felt made people think of a chubby-cheeked girl in a pleated plaid jumper that never fit right and with the personality of porridge.

Enter: Moxie. The girl who could take care of herself and rise to any challenge.

She only learned later that she, in fact, sort of liked porridge and that while *moxie* did mean spunky and bold, it was also the name of an old, mediciney-tasting soda pop. But by that time, the deed was done.

Lastly, she had asked, no *begged,* her father to allow her to take over the job of managing the cottage on Dream Away Bay Court for the absentee owners. She'd done it to ease her father's burden as much as she could but found quickly that she had a knack for property management.

Well, for people management, really, but she had discovered early on they were one and the same.

The work was easy enough. Clean, prep, mend, book the rooms, handle the accounting. But mostly she loved the chance to meet all those new and interesting people from all over. People who for a while—a long weekend or a whole season—pulled up roots, left their normal lives behind and came here. Some to get away from their problems. Some to seek out a whole new set of them—problems, that is. They didn't call it that of course; they called it "seeking adventure."

After that year, she'd started saving her money and by the time she was twenty-one and the only other cottage, the smaller of the two, on Dream Away Bay Court came up for sale, she'd bought it. Not long after that, a highway project had made it possible for people to go zipping along to more popular sites. Still, they had their regulars and every year a new crop of travelers "discovered" the peaceful serenity of Santa Sofia.

The town aged.

It lost favor with the younger tourist set. The older people no longer wanted to take care of houses they didn't live in year round.

More and more houses came up for grabs. Year after year, investment by investment she built her own little empire and looked after her dad. She never pulled up roots or took a vacation, not even for a little while. She never went in search of adventure or found the answer to her mother's question: *Isn't there something better than this?*

Not that Moxie wanted to leave Santa Sofia. She actually liked it here. She liked the way the town looked with its narrow streets, peculiar shops and mix of tacky beach culture and elegant old-world architecture. She liked the people, the quirky mix of native Floridians, Hispanic newcomers and people who'd come down to get away from it all.

Not too close to the Gulf but not too far away, Moxie had the best of town and oceanfront life.

Santa Sofia had the security and predictability of a small community peppered with the novelty and energy of a bona fide tourist trap. Moxie never felt bored here.

Snowbirds in the winter.

Family vacationers in the summer.

With a brief respite twice a year while most of the rest of the country enjoyed spring and fall. Santa Sofia had spring and fall, of course. They just didn't look or feel much different than the rest of the year.

Ever changing, never changed. That would have been a great motto for the town as it summed up the place's greatest charm…and its biggest drawback.

She sighed and opened the car door. "The sooner begun, the sooner done."

In a few steps she had the back down on the old truck and had pulled out her basic cleaning supplies. She wished she knew more about the owners. That would help her know where to focus. For some people the outside of their house—the part that other people saw—was the end all and be all. For others the outside could be a wreck as long as the beds were soft and the bathroom sparkling. Still others only wanted a fully stocked fridge to feel instantly right at home.

Not knowing what these people would want, Moxie decided to do a little bit of everything, concentrating heavily on the bathrooms, bedrooms and the kitchen.

The porch would have to wait.

"What are the odds that all they wanted to do was

drive here from Atlanta just to sit on the porch and drink tea, anyway?" she mused.

With that, she forged ahead, through the yard, up the steps and onto the porch. It groaned under her weight.

Moxie sneezed.

More groaning.

She held her breath, hoping it wouldn't fall in. Forget bleach and elbow grease, this thing needed major work. For the time being she decided she'd rope it off and stick up a sign saying to enter through the back door.

It took some wiggling of the key and a shove with her shoulder but she got the front door open.

"Not too bad," she muttered, moving into the front room. She put her cleaning supplies down by the stone fireplace with the polished driftwood mantel. From the bucket she withdrew a small notepad with a nub of a pencil tied to it by a short string.

She drew in a breath but didn't sneeze. "Musty but not moldy."

She ran her fingertips along the gnarled and knotted mantel. "Dusty but not disgusting."

She made notes.

She blew her nose.

She plumped a pillow on the overstuffed floral couch and eyeballed the ugly plaid monstrosity of a couch that hid what was probably a very uncomfortable pullout bed. "A little vacuuming, maybe throw something over them."

Her gaze went to an old cedar chest against the far wall where they used to store bed linens. She'd need to do a load of laundry now so she could have any blankets or quilts she found cleaned up before she left.

She wrote that down, sniffled then took a swipe under her eyes with the hem of her I'm Hooked on Billy J's Bait Shack Buffet T-shirt. Away from the mold on the porch, her scratchy throat, drippy nose and watery eyes had started to clear. Some.

Enough so that from the front room she could see all of the dining room and into the kitchen. It would need a scrubbing. As would the bathroom beyond.

Noted.

She pressed her lips together and adjusted the scrunchie holding her hair out of her way. As the list of things she had to do grew, she couldn't help focusing on the door hiding the enclosed stairway that led to the sleeping quarters.

The mattresses in the two tiny bedrooms should be turned at the very least. The rooms aired out. She'd have to check to see if she needed to haul any furniture up there—last time she'd looked, one of the dressers had gone missing and the lamp that had rested on it, broken. One dresser, one lamp. In all these years, she counted that a pretty good reflection on the town's people and the out-of-town people who found refuge here from time to time.

Still, she'd need to replace that dresser with something—maybe the chest of drawers from the dining room where they usually kept candlesticks and silverware? She winced at the thought of trying to wrestle that up the tight space and the steep wooden staircase.

"Where is that lumberjack when I need him?" Or her sweat-equity-promising renter-to-be, or—

"Resident handyman reporting for duty."

Moxie whipped around to see a tall man standing in the open doorway, his face in shadow. Of course, she didn't need to see that face to know exactly who she was dealing with. Her fingers tightened around the pad in her hand. Her whole body tensed. "Vince Merchant? What are you…? How did you…? Where did you ever dig up the courage to walk across my threshold again?"

He laughed. No surprise there—laughter was Vince's response to most anything. A jolly disposition, people liked to say of him.

Moxie didn't buy it. Nothing in life, particularly Vince Merchant's life, was a constant laughing matter. Sure, she could admire someone who found the bright side of every situation, but Vince never looked for the bright side. He used laughter to deflect that kind of effort, introspection, the scrutiny of others.

"Your dad called. I was already on my way over." He jerked his head in the direction of the cottage across the way. "So, I came over to help out."

"Help?" The man had come to offer the one thing she needed most. Help.

Didn't that just figure? Moxie had felt obliged to only give two people a piece of her mind in her lifetime. She'd just got off the phone with one of them and the other was standing before her now.

"Yeah. Help. Say the word. Point the direction. Slap

a hammer or a mop in my hand and turn me loose. What can I do?"

What couldn't he do? He was Vince Merchant.

Every small touristy town like this had its cast of characters. Some only played bit parts. Some came and went. Some, like her father and the man offering his help to her, rose to the level of icon.

Her father was the crusty old coot, for lack of a more complex description. And Vince?

Tall, with rugged good looks (which basically meant that women found him breathtaking and men couldn't see why), Vince Merchant filled the role of tragic heroic figure right down to the tousled golden hair, scar on his cheek and heart that he never shared with anyone. The young widower, raising a son on his own, had come to Santa Sofia to escape from the overwhelming weight of his loss and had found only more of the same.

And yet he had found the faith and the fortitude to carry on, to run his own handyman business and to still laugh. Often.

Too often, Moxie thought.

"Not even going to wait to see if Gentry or Esperanza are going to uphold their part of the bargain about helping me, huh?" It was what she would have done. What he *should* have done.

"I'm not doing it for them." He crossed into the room at last, and the light settled on his tanned face and showed the brilliant accents on his black Hawaiian shirt.

"Well, you're sure not doing it for me." Moxie and

Vince had known each other forever. He was like a big brother to her. Not the kind of big brother who taught you how to bait a hook, chased away the bullies and when you got old enough, bragged about you to his pals. But a big brother like the kind who thought he knew better than you how to run your life.

"What can I do?"

"I said you certainly aren't doing it for me. That's your cue to tell me why exactly you are doing this."

"Give me an assignment."

"You want an assignment? Write an essay in twenty-five words or less on why you have shown up out of the blue to pitch in with this project."

"The kitchen, you say?" He stretched his body so that he could peer in the general direction of the large, sunlit space beyond the dining room. "Yeah, I can handle cleaning the kitchen."

"Or you could make a phone call and get your son over here to get a head start on the work he's supposed to do as part of our rental agreement."

"Then after that, I'll go around front. Got a new power washer in the back of my truck, might was well see what that baby can do, see how much of the mold I can blast off the porch."

"Vince…"

"I don't want to talk about Gentry." Vince scratched the back of his neck with his blunt fingers, ruffling the shaggy waves of hair that fell just over his collar.

Vince never wanted to talk about Gentry. He would brag about Gentry. Make up excuses for Gentry. Even speak on behalf of Gentry. But talk about his son and the way Vince's overprotective parenting had left the kid unprepared for life, unavailable to those who counted on him and unmotivated to change?

No way.

"Just call him and—"

Vince started toward the kitchen, his eyes fixed forward to avoid Moxie's high-beam accusatory gaze.

Talk about his son? Or *to* him?

Clearly the man was not comfortable with the concept.

When Vince passed near her, Moxie couldn't hold her tongue any longer. "He's like twenty-four years old, Vince. A father. You can't keep fighting his battles for him."

"You don't understand how it is for him."

"To be a kid raised by a charming but sometimes maddening single father? Oh, I think I have some idea."

He conceded her point with a tight-lipped nod then added, "You had your mother until you were a teenager. Gentry never knew his. I always had to be both parents to him."

"I get that. But in time both parents have to let go. You have to let go, Vince."

"Yeah, I let go a couple years ago and the kid runs off and marries a girl he hardly knows."

"She's a good girl, Vince."

"Yeah, but she's a girl. And he's a boy. They had no idea what they were getting into."

"But they are in it. Together. If people would stand back and let them be together."

"I know you think I made it too easy for her to move out on him."

"No. I think you made it too easy for him to let her go."

"I thought letting go was good." He tried to laugh it off.

Moxie wasn't having any of it. In much the same way that Vince had never made Gentry be responsible for his own problems, nobody in town held Vince accountable for the way his son had turned out. Gentry wasn't a bad kid, far from it. He just never saw anything through. He never had to. Vince was always there to make excuses, fix things up, smooth things over.

Pretty handy having that kind of handyman cover your back your whole life. Moxie wondered if she would have turned out differently if her own father's shortcomings and quirks hadn't required she develop an independent streak.

No one in Santa Sofia had known Gentry's mother, but the story went that Vince and Toni had married young and started a family sooner than they had intended. Giving birth to Gentry had aggravated a congenital heart defect Toni hadn't even known she'd had. She had died when the child was only a week old.

"It's true. I had a mom, of sorts. A very unhappy mom, from the time I was a toddler until I was a teen. I have that over Gentry. But Gentry knows that his mother didn't abandon him. Not to mention that Gentry has you for a father and I have—" She cut herself off. Another sniffle, this time not entirely allergy related. She dabbed at the dampness under her eyes with her Bait Shop T-shirt once again. "I have to get back to work."

Vince nodded. He started for the kitchen then turned. "I appreciate what you're saying, Moxie. And that you care enough to say it to my face."

She nodded back.

"Oh, about me versus your dad?" He cleared his throat, ducked his head then peered toward the kitchen again. "Thanks."

"You're welcome." She dropped her gaze to the cleaning supplies and picked out a few things he'd need. She thrust them out toward him, compelled to add, "That doesn't mean I don't love my dad."

"I know."

"And appreciate all the things he's done for me."

"I know."

"Of course you know that but did you also know that I've even come to appreciate the things he didn't do for me?"

Vince held up his hand, the one with the spray glass cleaner in it. "I know where you're going with that and I am *not* going to go along with you."

"I'm just saying I still love my dad no matter what and Gentry will still love you even if you stop bailing him out of every fix and obligation he gets into." Moxie lifted her shoulders up.

"Okay," he said. "I'm going to hit the kitchen now."

At least she'd given him something to mull over, she thought, watching him go slowly. Perhaps, thoughtfully?

When he reached the beam of light, he paused.

Moxie held her breath, hoping he might share something deep, meaningful. That he might finally peel away that romantic, broody-hero image to reveal the real man beneath.

He turned.

She waited.

And in the stream of light, he met her gaze, shook his head and chuckled softly before heading off to do the job he should have demanded his son take on.

Chapter Four

"Are you sure this is the right place?" Jo had gotten out of the car and come around to help Kate.

The drive had taken longer than they had expected. First, they hadn't gotten away as early as they'd planned because they'd had to convince their mother that it would be a bad thing for her to tag along.

Despite getting Dodie to say she understood time and again why they wanted to go down first for a few weeks so Kate could heal and they could get a feel for the place, as soon as they started to get ready to go, their mom would hit a mental Reset button and hurry around trying to pack and come with them. The old girl wasn't loopy, she just thought that since Florida had been her idea, she ought to actually go there.

And if she went, it only seemed fair, came the next step in the reasoning process, that her girlfriends who wanted to share the property with her come along, too.

To which Kate promptly—and loudly—proclaimed that if they were all going, she wasn't.

And Jo would rush to point out that the primary purpose for the trip was to help Kate recuperate and having all these older ladies to chauffeur around and take care of would wreak havoc with Jo taking care of Kate.

The solution to it all came when Dodie offered to drive herself and her friends down. As soon as she heard *that,* Kate, making sad eyes and a truly pathetic whimpering sound, played her trump card.

"Drive, Mom?" She patted her cast. Winced and gripped the cane in a white-knuckled grasp. "I'd really feel safer if you didn't."

Dodie backed down.

Kate felt a wee bit bad about it.

Jo loaded up the car with Kate and all their cases, kissed her mom farewell, then headed down the nearest highway headed southeast.

They got away early but the drive itself dragged on forever. Atlanta traffic, Kate's need to keep fed and medicated, and to walk periodically to avoid problems from sitting too long in one position all played a part in the delay.

When they finally rolled into Santa Sofia, it was more than an hour past six o'clock, the time that they had told the caretaker to expect them. They called to let her know and learned that she was going to be unavailable to help them tonight. Something about a long steamy shower, a fistful of allergy medicine and a phone off the hook.

They didn't mind, they told her and hoped to see her the next day. Or the next. No big hurry. She hadn't seemed particularly anxious to encounter them, anyway.

They had some trouble finding the old place after that and, true to her word, when they called the caretaker, they got an answering machine. Nothing in town looked the way Kate remembered it. Here and there a landmark stood out. The pizzeria on the corner downtown, where she and Vince had taken Gentry every Friday night, had morphed into a mega-chain coffee shop.

"I can't believe what they did to that cute little pizza place. Remember how they used to actually toss the dough in the air and cook it in these big ovens?" Kate asked Jo. "And how upstairs was a... Oh, what was it?"

"A Junior League thrift shop?"

"You remember it?"

"No, I'm looking at it."

Kate followed her sister's line of vision. "Oh, great. Now I'm completely turned around."

A few right turns trying to get Kate set, well, *right* accidentally put them in position to see the orange glowing lights of Billy J's Bait Shack Seafood Buffet. Then it was as if the whole landscape fell into place and they were on their way.

Being early fall, it was not yet fully dark, but the best light of the day had begun to fade when they found the rusted and bent street sign proclaiming Dream Away Bay Co.

The rest had fallen off but they'd gotten the gist and gotten to the cottage.

Jo was relieved.

Kate was exhausted.

After helping Kate out of the car, Jo went around to open the trunk, then paused. She raised her head like a gazelle at a watering hole listening for lions. She frowned. “I thought this place was closer to the beach.”

“It was. Thirty years ago when you were a kid.” Kate walked, well, limped, really, up the drive. She leaned the hip bone that wasn’t connected to her nearly numb leg bone and soon-to-be-aching-again foot bone against the front fender, took a deep breath and let it out, slowly.

Seeing the old place again almost overwhelmed Kate. She hadn’t expected to feel such a…connection to it. To have the memories flood over her so fast and form so fully realized.

She and Jo as children.

Playing.

Laughing.

Mom, happy.

Well, relaxed, if not undeniably happy.

The sun.

The sand.

Vince.

The image of a young man, with Paul Newman eyes and just a hint of Alfred E. Neuman around the gap-toothed grin, broad shouldered and bronzed from the sun formed in her mind. No matter how much time had passed, this place would always remind her of him. There was no running away from that.

"We don't have to stay here if you don't want to," Jo called out.

"Oh, it's fine. It just needs a little TLC," Kate returned. "And a well-aimed hammer and nails."

The railings leaned decidedly to the left and inward. Their many missing spindles gave her the impression the cottage was greeting her with a toothy grin in need of a good dentist.

"Hammer and nails? Don't you mean a wrecking ball and an excavator?"

Kate laughed her sister off. "It's rustic."

"Okay, I'll give you that." Jo's lips twitched. "But can't you get tetanus from that much rust?"

"What did you expect?"

"Honestly, I don't know what I expected. But I sure hoped for something…" Her voice trailed off.

Kate didn't question her further. Instead she turned again to look at the facade of the old place.

The wicker flower box under the upstairs dormer window, which had always made the place look like something from a tropical watercolor painting, now hung higher on one side than the other. More dried twigs poked through the sides of it than shriveled, dead flowers swayed in the breeze on top. The dead petals scraped against the tarnished storm window screen with a sound that reminded Kate of a knife on burned toast.

The yard had bald patches. The bushes were overgrown. Bits of the scrollwork trim had broken off in the eaves. The trim around the porch was splintered. It all needed painting.

Over the sixteen years since she had last stood at this vantage point, the sidewalk had sunken down four inches in spots and jutted up in rocky slabs in others. Two big bins of trash, including a lot of brown and green bottles and crushed soda and beer cans, sat by the curb. A sign hung across the front door warning against stepping foot on the front porch and suggesting they go around back.

"It's a disaster," Jo muttered.

"I think it's wonderful," Kate murmured.

Try as she might to blame that response on her medication, she more honestly suspected she was seeing the sweet old cottage through the eyes of the five-year-old who had first come here full of anticipation. Not through the filter of the thirty-nine-year-old who had arrived today with a broken foot and a lifetime of broken expectations. Tears deluged her vision, and probably clouded her judgment as well, as she reached for her sister's hand and gave it a squeeze.

Jo didn't quite recoil but she did flinch slightly at Kate's unexpected touch. "Are you okay, Kate?"

She nodded, sniffled and seized the brass head of her cane with both hands. "Probably just a side effect of my pain medication."

"So, you going to explain to me how this place used to be closer to the beach thirty years ago or will that cause a total meltdown?" Jo had already turned her attention in the direction of the beautiful beach that lay somewhere out there, beyond her ability to see it, bordering the Gulf of Mexico.

"Back then, before the area got so developed, before they built the bypass and widened the highway, come nightfall we could sit in the backyard and hear the waves crashing on the beach. It was the lullaby that sang us to sleep at night and the thrilling charge that woke us in the morning."

She paused and listened.

No waves. No lullaby.

"It became a part of the way we thought of this place," she went on. "It set the rhythm of our days and became inextricably intertwined with our memories."

Kate took a deep breath but only smelled car exhaust, dust in the air and the slight hint of bleach. "So much so that being gone all these years we just sort of merged the ideal and the real. In my mind, when we first came to this place, it was on the ocean, and even though I can see that's not true, it still rings true for me today."

Jo crinkled her nose first at Kate then at the house. "Are you a podiatrist or a poet?"

"Can't I be both?" Kate raised her head. The sound of highway traffic greeted her, the buzz of cars and trucks trundling over the roads that had only been narrow streets years earlier. "At least Dream Away Bay Court is still isolated and undeveloped."

"You say that like it's a good thing." Jo squinted at the bumpy lane they had come down to reach the cul-de-sac with only two houses in it.

"If someone wants privacy. If they want a retreat from the world to be alone with his or her thoughts. If you want to make a spot that's yours alone. This is just the place." Kate tried to make it sound appealing even though Jo had to know that Kate, herself, found the very notion appalling.

"Privacy, sure. Except for having windows of the only other house around staring directly into yours." Jo turned to face the smaller cottage.

Designed in the same style as theirs, it only had one story. Though, as a child, Kate had attributed the old place with plenty of stories of her own making. "Ahh, the *mystery* house."

"The *what?*" Jo, who had popped up the tailgate of her Cruiser and had begun unloading suitcases, swung her head around so fast that even the hem of her blue-and-white sundress flounced in response. "This is the first I'm hearing of that. What mystery? Do not tell me something awful or untoward went on in that house and you never told me about it."

Kate smiled slyly, enjoying the ability to reclaim the right of the big sister to spin tales and enchant her younger sister, who had long ago become disenchanted with everything from men to these kinds of whimsical memories.

Jo went up on tiptoe, or as on tiptoe as she could in her stylish but ridiculously impractical shoes. She twisted her head over her shoulder to whisper. "It looks deserted."

"It always looked deserted." Kate made her way over to Jo, her head ducked down as though creeping along, trying to stay low and out of sight. Even though she stuck out like a sore…foot with her clunking cane and clumsy cast. Still, she grinned and whispered in her best late-night, under-the-covers, scary-story voice, "That's why I called it the mystery house."

"Nobody ever lived in it?"

"No one was ever home the weeks we were here." Kate shook her head trying to recall sharing the quiet cul-de-sac with any other vacationers or locals. "But look at it. So neat and well kept. Someone must live there or rent it out sometime or it would be in as bad a shape as…"

Jo followed Kate's line of vision, putting her facing their own cottage again. She let out a slow, muted sigh.

"Didn't you ever go over there and…"

"And what? Snoop?"

"Investigate." Jo raised her nose in the air, making her gorgeous blond curls shimmy over her squared, straight shoulders. "You never went over and rang the bell or knocked on the door to see if anyone was home?"

"Every year," Kate confessed. "But no one was ever there."

"Ever?"

"Nope. I mean, there was furniture from what I could see through the windows, you know, from standing on the porch."

"Uh-huh."

"It was as if whoever owned it packed up and left as soon as they heard our car come down the lane."

"Like those photos in documentaries about ships at sea that are found with the table still set for the evening meal?"

"Well, maybe not quite that dramatic but the place

looked like someone could come home at any minute and pick up their lives without much fuss or bother. The kitchen had all the appliances, fridge running and all."

"You looked in the fridge?"

"I could hear it humming."

"Standing outside?"

Kate ignored the loaded question. "And the place always had curtains and a window air-conditioning unit and a phone. Sometimes even a dish with hard candy in it on the coffee table and a new *TV Guide* by the armchair."

"But that was just what you could see from the porch, right?"

"Well, maybe when I was younger, I did press my nose to those windows."

"And?"

"And peeked through the old-fashioned keyhole in the back door."

Jo folded her arms to show she could hold her ground as long as Kate could stall. Longer, probably, given that Kate's foot had already begun to throb. "And?"

Kate exhaled and leaned on her cane. "And dragged a crate from the garage so I could climb partway through an open window with a torn screen around back."

"My word, Kate! You were guilty of breaking and entering."

"I was not. That screen was already broken when I got to it. And I only entered my head and most of my shoulders, just so I could get a good look around, you see."

"Well how do you do, Kate-the-cat-burglar." Jo snickered.

"I didn't burgle a thing! C'mon. I was a good kid, just…curious."

"Kate the curious," Jo echoed, somehow making it sound as if she were disappointed she couldn't use a more unflattering label.

"Didn't *you* ever do a little harmless pretend spying of your own when we came down here as kids?" Kate tried to remember the two of them engaging in the covert action but couldn't.

Jo went back to the task of unloading their things. She heaved a gym bag onto a plastic tote filled with sheets and towels and shook her head. "I was too busy spying on you."

"What?"

"Okay, not so much spying, since I didn't try to hide it. But the truth is most of my memories of this place center on you, not either of these cottages. From the time I can really remember coming here, all you cared about was going to the beach and hanging out with other teenagers and college kids. *You* didn't care about the house. So *I* didn't care about the house."

"You weren't even curious?"

"It had always been there." Jo shrugged. "I don't try to spy on my neighbors now, if that's any consolation to you."

"It is, in an odd way." Kate smiled, even though every second they stood there she could feel her medication waning. She took a deep breath and tipped her head toward the uneven walkway that led through the yard and around to the back. "Shall we?"

"Give me a sec." Jo pulled a tape measure out of her purse and extended the yellow metal strip from the chrome casing. She narrowed one eye, lifted her chin, lowered it, wagged her head side to side then let the metal slide back into place with a decisive whisk and clatter. "I remember it being bigger."

"What are you doing?" Kate scowled at her sister.

"Oh. This?" Jo blinked at the tool in her hand. "I, uh, force of habit, I guess."

"You guess?" If *Kate* were to hazard a guess, she'd *guess* her sister was up to something.

This whole adventure had her on edge. More than the usual edginess she applied to every situation of every minute of every day of her life. It had all come too easily, hadn't it? This trip. This sudden interest in a place neither of them had seen in sixteen years. Nothing with Jo, nothing between the two of them or anyone throughout the patchwork of relationships that made up their family had ever come that easily.

Complications. It was something the doctor had warned her to avoid. He'd meant with her bones knitting, range of motion in the joints and with the tissue healing, but Kate couldn't help thinking it applied here as well.

So she let the slightly strange action slide. If people ever decided to start calling *her* on every oddball thing she ever did, she'd…she'd feel as if her father had returned. Kate blinked and in that instant she remembered this cottage for the thing it had once been—a haven from her father's scorn, frustration and, sometimes, rage.

With that thought it was as if the whole scene before her transformed. The layers of chipped and peeling paint fell away. The small Victorian-*ish* style cottage stood in her mind fresh in buttery-yellow clapboard and brilliant white gingerbread scrollwork.

"Is it a fairy house?" she had clasped her hands together and asked her mother the first time they had driven up.

"It's a fairy-tale house," her father had muttered.

She had blinked, not understanding.

"Your father just means that there are no such things as fairies. But it certainly does look like a house straight out of a storybook."

"Don't put words in my mouth. I meant that it's a fairy tale to think us buying this house down here will change anything, will make anything better." He had laced his bitter grumblings with curses and name-calling. She wasn't sure, but the gist of it all was that she and her mother had come to this house with their hearts filled with hope and anticipation, and he wanted no part of it.

"You don't have to be here," her mother had said in reply, her green eyes scrunched down into slits and her always impeccably made-up lips pursed. She looked as if she had just sucked a lemon, Kate remembered thinking.

And her father had looked as if he was about to spit fire.

"Good." He had slammed the trunk of their car and dropped the suitcases on the drive. "I'll be back to pick you up in two weeks."

Two weeks out of every year without her father. Then it had seemed the best of all worlds. Later, after he had gone from their lives forever and taken her younger sister with him, Kate had wondered if things would have been different if it hadn't been so easy for him to leave that first time.

Her gut twisted knowing she had not run to him, wrapped her arms around his legs and begged him not to go. If only…

"It's awfully old-fashioned, isn't it?" Jo tilted her head one way and then the other.

Kate startled, then forced her attention to the place, which again looked like a poorly aging, once-grand lady. "I think it looks a bit like those Victorian conch cottages you find down in the Keys."

"And that would count for something if it were in the Keys. But here? It just looks…tired." Jo withdrew the tape measure and let it snap back in place again. Her mouth twitched to one side then the other. "Hardly an ideal spot for a home or a vacation getaway."

"Well, then it's the ideal spot for me, because I'm tired of standing out here. Make with the key so we can go inside and I can prop my foot up and start ordering you around."

"Key? I don't have the key."

"What do you mean you don't have the key? You were the one who packed up Mom's things after she sold the condo." And took a cut of the Realtor's fee for doing it. Kate had never faulted her sister for that, thinking that anyone who had held open houses and contract negotiations with their mom had earned every penny she got. But still, now, with sensation slowly returning to her foot and her patience waning, all she could think about was how Jo tended to look out for herself first and everyone else…never. "You should have gotten the key. Where do you think it is?"

Jo gathered the bags she had just unloaded, slinging them over her shoulders, her arms and filling both hands. "It's probably in a box in that storage unit I shoved everything in."

"Storage unit? Shoved? I thought you sifted through every knickknack and…paddy-whack, sorted it all out, bagged and boxed and organized…"

"Did I say I did all that?" She looked off at the cottage, her expression more inquisitive than evasive.

No, of course she hadn't said it. Kate had just assumed it. It was what *she* would have done on the occasion of her mother's latest big adventure, if Kate hadn't been so preoccupied with the disasters of her own life. In theory.

In reality, she'd probably have done anything to avoid dealing with it. Instead of the key being in a storage unit where their mother could retrieve it, under Scat-Kat Kate's care, it would probably have been moldering in a landfill.

Thunk.

Thunk.

Thump. Bump.

Thwack.

One by one, Jo divested herself of the luggage.

Kate exhaled and leaned on her cane. The tip sank into the rich damp soil beneath an island of thick, lush grass. "What now, then?"

"We call a locksmith." Jo already had her sleek cell phone in one hand, pressing numbers with her thumb even as she spoke.

"You have a number of a locksmith in Santa Sofia, Florida, in your cell-phone contact list?"

"No, but I have one in Atlanta and I presume they have connections down here."

"You are very good at your job," Kate noted when her sister finished up the series of calls that had someone winging their way to the rescue.

"Thank you." Jo tipped her head and her gorgeous blond hair—hair she hadn't had when she'd showed up at the E.R. five days earlier—went tumbling over her shoulder.

"How long?" Kate asked.

"How long have I been good at my job?" She seemed a bit more offended than a woman wearing someone else's hair should have been.

Kate chuckled. "No, how long until the locksmith shows up?"

"Oh. The locksmith." Jo nodded and looked down. She took a moment to shuffle her feet over some bits of crumbling concrete in the drive. While she didn't have on the three-hundred-dollar pair of pumps she'd worn two days earlier, the strappy beaded sandals with glitter and curved acrylic heels probably cost more than Kate had spent on her whole wardrobe of sensible, arch-supported doctor-approved—and she knew because she was that doctor—shoes.

Kate nudged the side of Jo's shoe near the strap lacing over her hot-pink pedicured toenails with her quickly getting grubby purple cast. She managed to wriggle her own ashen toes in a way that actually seemed to taunt her sister for her frivolousness, saying flatly, "Yes, the locksmith. When can we expect someone to show up and let us in?"

"Well, about that…"

"They aren't going to show up, are they?"

"Oh, yes, absolutely. They are going to show up."

"When?"

"Tomorrow afternoon."

"What are we supposed to do until then? Sleep under the stars?" Kate actually could do that. She'd brought a tent and some camping gear, just in case they came down and found the place roofless or without power. But being prepared to do something like that in a pinch and being forced to do it because your sister forgot to bring the key were two entirely different things.

"Some lack of imagination from someone already versed in the art of breaking and enter—"

"I told you it was already—"

"Broken. Yeah, I know. Well, looking at this place, it wouldn't surprise me if it were already a little bit 'broken,' too."

"What does that mean?"

"How hard could it be to get in?" Jo raised her hands out at her sides. "The locksmith said to try the back door or any windows in the back first, anyway. They're usually the ones most likely to have been left unlocked. If not…"

"You want us to break in to our own mother's cottage?"

"Why not? It's not like she's around to call the police."

"Jo!"

"I didn't mean it disrespectfully." She folded her arms and rotated her foot at the ankle to work the heel of her shoe free from the soft ground. She scowled at the clumps of earth and dried grass clinging to her expensive shoe. "Besides, it's not like she'd ever call the cops on *you.*"

"Can we save the woe-is-me chorus by the Mom-liked-you-best singers until we figure out what we are going to do here?"

"We already know what we are going to do."

"No, we do not."

"Well, I know what *I'm* going to do." And with that, she disappeared around the side of the house.

Kate would have followed but, from a practical point of view, by the time she got around to the back of the house Jo could well likely be inside already and have taken another route to the car to collect the luggage. Or she could have decided she couldn't *get* inside and come around to the front again. Kate was in no mood or in any shape to play a game of cat and mouse like that.

Besides, it had gotten darker as they'd stood out here talking and deciding what to do. The back of the house would be hard enough to navigate in daylight, what with the remnants of her mom's great rock-garden experiment. The whole back side of the house had been turned into a maze of hunks of lava rock, large chunks of petrified logs and a boulder shaped like the state of Kentucky. Kate couldn't imagine getting through that unscathed with two good feet much less…

"Jo! Jo! Wait!" She jerked her cane out of the ground with such force it sent her staggering backward. She did not let that impede her in her mission. Jo was literally walking into a disaster and only Kate could do anything about it.

She led with her cane only to find it plunging into the mud where there should have been dirt, as if someone had left the water hose running for the better part of the day and soaked the ground. She slowed her already snail's pace to an awkward lurch-and-lunge motion.

"This isn't going to work," she muttered. "Jo! Jo?"

Still no answer. What if she had run around back, tripped over a petrified log, pitched forward and been knocked unconscious by the western-most part of Kentucky? Kate chucked her cane to one side and did what she had to do—she hopped on her good foot faster and faster, calling out as she did, "Jo? Jo, I have to tell you something. Jo? Answer me. I have to tell you that—"

"What? What's so urgent? I almost had the back door jimmied open when I heard you—"

Wham!

The two of them collided.

Kate went careening into the side of the house. She whomped her head, her shoulder, her hip but somehow kept her foot protected from any impact.

Jo was not so fortunate.

"Why were you running toward me?" Kate demanded.

"Why were you *hopping* toward me?" Jo, sprawled out on the ground just inches away from having been impaled on a red metal birdhouse with See Rock City painted in white on the black roof, shouted back.

Kate swept her gaze over the "garden," which had "grown" over the years to include not just rocks but now also strange and tacky souvenir statues and knick-knacks from all over the southern states. She cringed, as much for her sister's pain as for the awfulness of the display. "I was trying to save you from getting hurt."

"I hope you'll understand if I don't give you a big gushy thanks for the heads-up." Jo pushed herself up on her scraped elbows. She didn't seem to even notice that her hair had suddenly become much longer on one side. It went positively lumpy along her scalp as she pushed the blond cascade back from her face and asked, "Are you okay?"

Kate slid her hand over her head, down her neck and then along her leg all the way to her cast. "Yeah. I think so."

"Good." Jo sat up and wound both of her delicate hands low on her calf. Her once-glittering shoe hung by one broken strap from her toes, battered, unbeaded and bedraggled. "Nothing hurt on me but my dignity. And my shoes."

"And I'm guessing you're the most upset about your shoes," Kate teased.

"Let's just say that with you as an older sister, I never got the chance to develop much of a false sense of pride, and leave it at that."

Kate didn't want to leave it at that but given the circumstances felt she had no choice.

"But taste in shoes?" Jo pressed on. "You were never an impediment to me developing great taste in shoes. Even though I am sure you would have advised me not to buy these. In fact, I can just bet you are thinking right now that I shouldn't even bother to get them repaired because I don't have any business wearing them around this place."

"Finally you've said something I can totally agree with."

"What?"

Hand on the side of the house, Kate leaned down. "You are not going to be wearing those shoes again for quite a while."

"Yes, but that's not because of your opinion of them, it's because they're broken."

"No, actually, baby sister, it's because you have sprained your ankle, and badly, too."

"What? No. It's just a little twisted."

"No, Jo, *you* are just a little twisted," Kate joked. "That ankle is sprained and my advice to you is to get inside, elevate it, ice it and don't try to put any weight on it for a couple days."

"You mean?"

"Welcome to the one-footed, rest-and-recuperation, you-ain't-going-nowhere and better-mind-your-doctor club."

Chapter Five

"This is serious, Jo."

"Oh, please. Maybe for an old lady like you this would be a serious setback but for your much younger sister?" Jo had pushed herself upward guarding her potentially injured ankle from bearing any weight.

"Much younger?" Kate challenged.

"You were born old, Kate." Deep breath. She could do this. The alternative? To not only acknowledge that Kate was right but to depend on her for who knew how long.

Jo shuddered.

"I was *not* born old." Kate extended her cane.

A peace offering? A way of taunting Jo to say "Here, you need this more than I do?" Or did she mean to prod her sister with it?

Kate honed her gaze on Jo, and concluded, "I grew old too fast."

Peace, prod *and* taunt, Jo decided. As ever, Kate

had found a way to do it all and do it with graceful efficiency. It made Jo want to go to great lengths to show her sister that she—Kate the correct—had gotten it all wrong.

So she did not hop her way around the old cottage. She did not hobble.

No, instead, she whisked off her battered shoes. She fluffed up her tattered weave. She straightened her dirt-covered dress. She held her head high, kept her mouth shut and she walked.

At least as long as Kate was watching.

The second she rounded the corner, Jo nearly collapsed against the side of the grungy old place. The paint was so old it turned to dust against her shoulder, leaving a grayish-white smudge. Ever the upbeat Realtor, she made a note to herself: *Original condition. Or maybe rustic charm.*

Buoyed by that reminder of just why she had come all this way and of all the work that awaited her, she grabbed a stick she found in the yard and used it as a makeshift crutch. On the return trip, she had the luxury of propping her injured ankle on the back of the small rolling luggage carrier. Probably a risky choice given that she had to navigate that crazy rock and hee-haw gewgaw garden again because the front porch was definitely off-limits.

But she managed to wrangle their things inside without showing too much of her discomfort to Kate, who was waiting inside with a hankie full of cloudy ice, chipped free from a plastic container she'd found in the freezer. Despite Jo's protests, Kate got her to prop her foot up and applied the pitiful ice pack.

Too late to actually help the swelling much, all it succeeded in doing was numbing the pain a bit.

"How do you feel?" Kate asked.

"Like I'm sporting a foot-sicle," Jo snapped back.

"I'll get you some aspirin. That should help."

"Only if you bring them to me in a pair of fuzzy slippers you warmed in the oven."

At that, Kate stopped. She did not face Jo. She simply looked around at their setting and her shoulders sank a little. "How did we get to be this way?"

"Mom ran over your foot and I tripped on Mom's rock garden." Jo knew Kate meant "How did we get to be so stubborn, so driven, so competitive with each other?" but she answered as if she meant "How did we both get banged up like this?"

The other question? Each member of their family had mulled that over for years and Jo found contemplating it yet again quite pointless. What did it matter how they got this way, after all, if they never asked themselves the real question that could make all the difference. What can we do about it?

Jo didn't have the answer.

Kate must not either since the smarty-pants hadn't offered it again and again over the years for everyone to ooh and aah over.

Easier to deflect any and all questions with a joke, even a joke tinged with an underlying and almost unthinkable sliver of truth.

"How did we end up with our tootsies in trauma?" Jo tried to wiggle her toes. Stiffly, slowly, she managed and somehow that gave her the boost of confidence to say, "Mom's car. Mom's creative endeavor. I guess with us, what those psychologists say is true—it always goes back to the mother."

Kate chuckled slightly and Jo knew her sister wasn't going to stick her toe any deeper into that quivering little pond of emotional quicksand.

Once they sold this old place, maybe it wouldn't matter, anyway.

Maybe this small deed, this tidying up and disposing of this last shard of their shattered past would finally grant them the one thing that could heal them at last. Closure.

That was the sweet fairy tale that Jo told herself to allow her mind to drift off to sleep that night. She wasn't here to merely solve her own problems, to make a desperate attempt to fix the looming financial mess she'd made with a couple of prideful business deals. By selling this house, she would finally get the real thing she had wanted for as long as she could remember. To finally be the hero.

Her.

"Not Kate."

"What did you say?"

Jo startled to find her sister crouched beside the big, sagging brown-and-gold plaid couch where Jo had spent the night, unable to navigate the narrow stairway to the two small bedrooms on the second floor. A quick glance over at the tangle of sheets, quilt and bunched-up pillow on the overstuffed yellow floral couch that sat on the other side of the coffee table told Jo that Kate had bunked there for the night.

"I said, um, never mind."

"Hmm." Kate's tone left Jo with the impression she'd at least caught her own name in Jo's mumblings.

"By the way, thank you."

"For what?"

"Watching over me last night."

"I thought you might get to hurting in the middle of the night and I wanted to be close at hand." Kate pushed back the covers from Jo's knee downward. "Or close at foot, as it were."

"Ha-ha." Jo intoned the universal notes for sarcastic humor. "Podiatrist humor. I'm sure it's funny. Somewhere."

"It is, trust me." Kate laid her chilly fingertips against the black-and-purple bulge that had once been Jo's slender—slender-*ish*—okay, less swollen and more attractive than a fat, overripe avocado—ankle bone and the top of her foot. "I'm a real knockout at our conventions."

"Sure, but can you really count boring people into a stupor as a knockout?" Jo sucked air through her teeth at the gentle probing.

"Count it? I depend on it," Kate countered just as smoothly as she rolled Jo's leg inward, then outward again to examine it from all angles. "Saves on anesthetic. Shall we give it a try now or are you ready to admit you've got a serious injury here?"

"Injury? Yes. Serious?" Jo glanced at her exposed ankle. It looked bad. Very bad. But it didn't hurt. *Much.* "What does that mean really? Do we have to go to the hospital?"

"No. I can take care of everything right here. *If* you promise to cooperate."

Jo couldn't afford to go to the hospital. She'd taken the risk and cut out her health insurance a few months back, hoping to apply the sizable sum she paid being self-employed to the never-ending sinkhole of a budget on her last real-estate flip. So she had no choice, really, even though it scalded her right down to her very last stretch of self-respect to say, "All right. If it means I don't have to go to the hospital, I'll cooperate."

"Good. I know I packed a first-aid kit in your trunk. Do you remember bringing it in last night?"

Jo shook her head. "I only brought the luggage that fit on the rack. Clothes, shoes, snacks, you know, the necessities."

"You couldn't have left the shoes?" Kate shook her head.

Jo gave a one-shouldered shrug. "Hope springs eternal."

"That's okay. I wouldn't mind getting outside for a few minutes. Stretching my good leg. Figuring out how to maneuver with this bum one."

"Checking to see if there is any activity at the mystery house."

Kate gave a sly smile but she did not deny Jo's accusation. "Do you need anything before I go?"

"A trip to the restroom." Jo pushed her fingers back through her hair, and they stuck. "And a professional hairdresser."

Kate winced.

Jo worked her hand free, making a mental note to get a comb, a mirror and maybe some scissors later, after she'd taken care of her other needs. "And breakfast."

"I can help you to the bathroom." Kate anchored her cane firmly on the old living-room carpet then crooked the elbow of her free arm to give Jo something substantial to grab on to. "Since I can't use the front door, I'm headed in that direction, anyway."

Jo nodded and scooted forward on the couch. Holding her injured ankle out at an awkward but presumably safe angle, she grabbed the coffee table with one hand and her sister with the other, allowing Kate to help her to her feet, uh, foot.

"Okay, let's coordinate." Kate wielded her cane then led with her intact foot. "Step."

Knee bent, Jo rested the top of her toes on the cushion behind her and made a half wobbling, half skipping movement forward with her strong leg. "Step."

"And…" Kate looked at her sister in horror. "Uh-oh."

"Uh-oh!" Jo repeated dutifully. A half a second later, the reality of their situation sank in.

Whump.

Back they fell, both of them landing in the relative comfort of the couch but with enough jarring force to rattle them for a moment. Then the laughter began.

"Uh-oh?" Jo gave her sister a playful elbow to the

ribs. "We're about to collapse into a pile and the only warning you can give me is 'uh-oh'?"

Kate tapped the tip of her cane lightly against her cast. "What has anyone in this family ever done to make you think we're good at issuing warnings?"

"Point taken." Jo exhaled. As her laughter subsided, the pain in her ankle intensified. She sat up, ready to try again. "Let's get this over with, right?"

"We can do this. No reason we shouldn't have learned from our mistake."

What has anyone in this family ever done to make you think we're good at learning from our mistakes? Jo considered paraphrasing and throwing Kate's own words back at her. Then Kate slipped her arm around Jo's shoulders and suddenly, she didn't feel like dredging up old hurts and grudges, at least not just then.

"Let's see, my cast is on my left foot." Kate dragged her cane over the floor as if she were doing complex math computations in the carpet. "Your sprain in on your right…"

"Wouldn't it figure that we'd even get hurt in exact opposition to each other?" Jo gritted her teeth and used humor, such as she could muster, to try to stave off the growing pain.

"No, now, don't fret. Maybe we can use this to our advantage. You know, like running a three-legged race."

"Yeah—without the *third* leg." Jo swept her hand out to remind her sister that their bad legs were side by side, making it pretty hard for them to bear weight much less move them forward.

"Maybe if I walk backward?"

"Oh, that can't possibly end up with me, um, *end up* by doing a nose plant right into this, uh, vintage-chic carpet." Jo laughed.

"Don't fight me on this." Kate positioned herself directly before Jo and met her gaze. "For once don't fight me and I think we can actually work this out."

Jo opened her mouth to make a joke. But a funny thing happened on her way to saying a funny thing. She looked into her sister's eyes, really looked. And suddenly she saw something in Kate she had never seen before and yet recognized as so familiar she could not refuse Kate's request.

Kate was afraid. And worried. And still, absolutely full of hope.

Jo took a deep breath and grabbed her sister's outstretched arms.

"Step." Kate inched her good foot backward.

"Step." They both moved their incapacitated limbs.

"Uh-oh!" they both exclaimed at the same time as Jo completed the first movement in their dance with a forward stride.

Using the "step, step, uh-oh" cadence, they made their way slowly through the front room where they had slept, through the wide arch that framed the open dining room and into the kitchen beyond. Thumping, bumping, bouncing off walls and giggling as they went.

"Don't make me laugh too hard, Kate, or I won't need to go back there anymore and you'll have to help me figure out how to change into some dry clothes."

"Hold on, we only have to get across the kitchen floor now and you're home free."

The bathroom, the real bathroom, the only full bath, complete with shower, sink, toilet and bathtub was ground-floor level…in the back of the house…through a heavy door just inches from the massive gas stove.

"Whose idea was it to put a bathroom right off the kitchen, do you suppose?" Jo stared into the large room with its sea-foam-green tile floors and walls and faded flamingo-pink fittings.

"Maybe it was an afterthought. Would they have included indoor plumbing when this thing was built in the forties?"

"Most houses did, but…these colors are definitely from the fifties."

"Probably the owner's idea of an ultramodern convenience."

"Or just the easiest place for an addition, with the kitchen already plumbed." Jo's mind was already trying to come up with ways to sell the odd placement.

She didn't have to think long. She had loved this huge, gaudy room as a kid, taking baths, being able to run in for a bathroom break and be out the back door again before Kate, who'd customarily played "it" in a game of hide-and-seek and could finish counting to one hundred.

Her mother had loved it as well, as it kept them from tracking sand all over the house.

But as a Realtor, it troubled Jo. It gave a first impression of being out of place, inconvenient and not very private. Coupled with the fact that the upstairs only had a half bath, and one that had been fit quite obviously into an old hall closet, she'd have her work cut out for her.

Ask anyone what people should consider when buying a house and you would most likely hear the old adage "location, location, location." They were instructed at Powers Realty to get sellers to clear away clutter and wash all the windows because "people are really buying light and space." But in her experience, Jo knew that most buyers could overlook a lot of things, but bathrooms and kitchens clinched the deal.

"I'm not going to close the door."

"Kate!"

"So I can leave a kitchen chair in the open doorway," she went on without missing a beat. "That way when you're done you can use the chair like a walker to get yourself over to the table. I set whatever is left of our travel snacks there and you can have at 'em."

"You sound like you're setting me up for a long wait. You're only going out to the car, not setting out to get help through the jungles of the Amazon."

"Oh, please. You're hungry and hurting. Fifteen minutes will seem like forever to you." Kate escorted Jo into the room and let her hold onto the sink for support.

"Fifteen minutes?"

"Or longer. It's going to take me a while to get to the car, find the first-aid kit and work my way around the house again."

"Not to mention the time you'll need to study the house across the street."

Kate threw back her shoulders and smoothed her hand down her thick, gorgeous hair. "That reminds me, did I see a pair of binoculars in your trunk?"

Jo puffed up a bit at not just nailing Kate on her covert intentions but on the fact that for once her sister hadn't tried to deny it, but had just gone with it. Could that mean they were getting a little more relaxed around each other? "Um, yeah. I have binoculars for work."

"To check out the…um, what?"

"Competition mostly. I use them to keep count of how many people come and go from open houses in a neighborhood where I have a property or to get info from yard signs."

"Maybe I should send you to do the investigation into the mystery house."

"Only if you want to put this one on the market." It was out before Jo had thought through the comment, but once it had slipped through her lips she determined to use it to her advantage. She narrowed her eyes on Kate's face, watching for even the slightest positive reaction to the idea.

"Sell the cottage?" Kate raised her head and made a sweeping survey of the place. "Hmm."

And just that fast, she turned away, leaving Jo with no more insight into her sister's thoughts than…well, than Jo *ever* had into her sister's thoughts.

Kate made her way out the door.

Jo took care of business in the bathroom. Real

business. Even as she saw to her own hygiene, she made mental measurements, eyeballing every inch for cracks, peeling paint, chipped tiles. She snapped on the faucets and the shower head, checking both the pressure and the water quality. All good.

"Ugh, but the colors," she muttered under her breath as she made one last scan. "If I were going to do this right, I'd have to gut this place just to make it border-line presentable."

Just then she caught a glimpse of herself in the mirror. "Talk about borderline presentable!"

She tugged and pushed and fluffed and smooshed her hair, trying to even it out. She did not succeed.

"Pick me, pick me, pick me," she muttered her would-be motto. "Yeah right."

Rumpled, slept-in clothes.

Positively gruesome-looking ankle.

Hair like a decades-old doll's, ratty and mashed into a mess on one side.

Pick her? For what?

Nobody would want her. Not like this. No one had ever wanted her, really. All the old fears ricocheted around her thoughts. Heading here, being here where she felt she might find some answers and where she had known mostly happiness, they had not plagued her for a whole day. Now, standing here in a bathroom that might well keep her from making that quick sale she needed, and looking, well, the way she looked?

"Don't do this," she told herself.

At least she could take some solace in the fact that

she didn't know a soul in town and wasn't going to run into anybody that she needed to impress.

"Hello?" A deep voice rang through the house from the back door.

Masculine. Decidedly so. And…strangely familiar.

Jo froze, her hands gripping the back of the chair until all the color drained from her fingers. "Who… Who is that?"

"You don't know me, ma'am. My name is Travis Brandt. I'm the—"

"Travis Brandt? *The* Travis Brandt?"

"The only Travis Brandt standing at your back door, yes." He still sounded every ounce as dreamy as he had seemed on TV.

"Of course I know who you are!" Travis Brandt. A bona fide blast from the past. A former college football hero turned pro, his name had been known throughout the South. With his great looks, powerful voice and a way of wrapping words in a Southern accent so rich it made your teeth ache, he'd gone into sportscasting, rising quickly through the larger markets on his way to taking a spot at whatever major network he chose.

Only he didn't chose. He'd just…dropped out of sight one day. People had speculated on the reasons for a time but then had forgotten about the man.

He'd had it all and now…

"Your sister said to call out first and make sure that you were decent."

She took a quick glance in the mirror again. *Decent?* That might be a bit too optimistic.

Jo had to do something and quick. She needed to make a good impression on this man, or at least not scare him off.

After all, Travis Brandt was just the kind of man she could sell a house to—fast. Or barring that, the kind of man who might know people who would want to invest in a business deal, giving her the funds to fix up the place for a slice of the profit when she flipped the cottage for top dollar.

Aren't you in deep enough trouble trying to do that in Atlanta? She clenched her jaw and pushed her anxiety over her situation aside. People fell in love with a house in the first thirty seconds. They did not give their fellow human beings that long.

Not that she wanted Travis Brandt to fall in love with her! How could he?

Her standing here looking as bedraggled as the house she wanted to unload?

"Um, ma'am? Did you hear me? Are you decent?"

Jo snapped to her senses. Or maybe something in her snapped and she took leave of them. Either way, she had to act. Grabbing a towel, she threw it over her head as if she had just come from the shower. It would mean she wouldn't get to feast her eyes on the man, but then he wouldn't have to jab his eyes out after seeing her, so that seemed a fair exchange.

She grabbed the back of the chair and began scooting it out into the kitchen as she announced in absolute truth, "I don't know about decent, but I can promise you, I'm covered up."

Chapter Six

"Stop whining." Kate settled down on the couch and adjusted the worn old quilt over her aching lower body. It wasn't quite noon and she was exhausted. She could blame it on not sleeping well last night. But she suspected it had more to do with the exertion of going out to the car to retrieve the first-aid kit.

Then going even farther, to the curb.

Then just a wee bit farther, out into the street. Using the binoculars, trying to see if there were any furnishings or landscaping or clues of any kind that might give away the secrets of the mystery house.

That it had begun to rain in the past hour did not do much to perk her up. She'd had plenty of patients who had claimed that changes in the weather played havoc with damaged joints, but Kate had always dismissed the notion as all in their heads.

"No, it's all in their toes," her mother had scolded.

"You are always in too big a hurry to really listen, Scat-Kat-Katie."

Now how had that dreaded nickname worked its way even into her daydreams? Kate's shoulders tensed for a moment before it occurred to her that the reminder of her own nervous habits probably came from the subject at hand. "It's your own fault that Travis Brandt couldn't wait to rocket out of here, Jo."

"Rock it?" Jo, moving with much more confidence, but still gingerly and plainly favoring her freshly wrapped ankle, joined Kate in the front room. Cautiously, she lowered herself onto the other couch then settled some things bundled in a towel beside her. She nestled down into the cushions as if the nubby fabric were as prickly as a cactus.

A pause.

Clunk. Followed by a more delicate clunk, but a clunk just the same as she blatantly used Mama's antique-*ish* colonial-style coffee table as a footstool.

"Rocket as in *ph-weeew.*" Kate slid her palms together in a quick upward motion that she hoped illustrated her admittedly weak imitation of a missile blasting off. In case that hadn't made her point, she offered a more direct description. "The way Mom would take off and explode if she saw you propping your feet up on her coffee table."

Jo flinched, slightly. A quick reflexive jerking action as if she couldn't get her feet down fast enough. But she didn't put them down. She paused instead, then planted them right back where they were.

Kate opened her mouth in shock at the sheer defiance of it.

Jo tipped up her nose. "Well, Mom isn't here, is she?"

"Neither is that cute preacher man." Kate made the sliding palm gesture again but decided to forgo the sound effects.

Jo's expression went positively glum.

Kate felt a twinge of guilt over her childish attempt to be the boss of her completely grown-up sister. A woman capable of doing whatever she wanted in a house that none of them had bothered to maintain, much less protect the furnishings in for way too many years.

Jo gazed at her reflection in the hand mirror she had drawn from the pale blue towel beside her. Using some solvent solution, she began to work to free a section of the long blond curls from where they had been attached to her scalp. "He did act like he had a fire lit under him."

"What did you expect? You carried on a whole conversation with him with that towel over your head."

"I couldn't let him see me with my hair, um, you know, not…uh, *done*." A long strand fell away like a wilted streamer an hour after the parade had passed. Half of her head looked like a yellow bath mat run through the dryer on high one time too many. The other half, a cascade of silky blond curls—that had also been run through the dryer on high, with poor Jo's head still attached to it. "Bad first impressions are very hard to overcome."

"And you somehow think that you made a *good* first impression?" Kate teased gently.

Jo dropped her hand into the swirls of blondness pooled in her lap. "Well, he *is* a minister. They're big on second chances, right?"

"And third chances and however many it takes, I guess." Kate rested one shoulder against the couch and watched her sister a moment.

"Some of us have a long learning curve," Jo whispered.

"When it comes to cute guys?" Kate was genuinely puzzled by her sister's comment.

Jo blinked a few times, as if processing the thought. She shifted her bandaged ankle, then shifted her eyes the way she used to do as a child about to fling out her arm and shout at Kate "Tag, you're it." "When it comes to cute guys some people, and I won't name names but I could say this someone is in this very room, wearing a purple cast and has an unnamed name that rhymes with Flatherine Flomwell…"

"Patherine Promwell? Zatherine Zomwell?" Kate suggested, tapping her cheek to show how very hard she had to think to unravel the riddle.

"…has a *very* long learning curve," Jo went on. "Sixteen years and holding, so far."

"I thought we were talking about *your* quest for second chances."

"We were talking about the kind of impression I wanted to make on Travis Brandt." Jo went back to work on her hair.

"We were, weren't we? Which means the real question is why does it matter to you?"

"It?"

"The kind of impression you make," Kate clarified. "You only just met the man."

"But his reputation preceded him."

Kate scrunched her mouth to one side. Even she had heard of the man, so she could not argue that point. "Still, you're not likely to see him again, unless we stay down here a while, and you're the one who has already been making sounds about not wanting to keep this place. So, why do you care what kind of impression you make on some local beach preacher?"

"I just thought…" She looked up and away. This positioned her face so that the last bits of gray morning light illuminated her expression. Her lips pursed. Her eyes gave the appearance of poignant wisdom.

"You just thought, what, Jo?"

After a few serene seconds, she lowered her gaze right into Kate's. "That's for me to know and you to find out!"

"Well!"

Jo stuck out her tongue at Kate.

Kate thought of doing likewise. Something about this house brought out the worst in them and did not help their already strained relationship. At least she could be grateful that Mom wasn't here to egg things on. She made a note to add that gratitude to her prayers, then pinched the bridge of her nose between her thumb and forefinger. "Fine. Clearly, you are up to something, baby sister. Something that you are not ready to discuss openly with me."

"Ya think?" She sounded like a churlish teenager,

which gave Kate some hope as it showed some maturity over the five-year-old her sister had acted like two minutes earlier.

Kate moved on to make her point before Jo regressed or shot straight on to acting like their mother. "I just don't see why this scheme of yours kept you from asking the man to run out and bring us back some groceries."

"Oh, really, how would that have looked? This was a man who had everything most people dream of. Wanted by every network, and who knows how many women?"

"I certainly don't want to know," Kate huffed.

"Yeah, me, either," Jo said softly. "Can you imagine it? Going from that to drumming up business for his church by going door to door."

"He was extending an invitation. It was nice. And the perfect opportunity for you to ask him to help us."

"Right. I can't talk to you directly or look you in the eye, pal, but I have no problem ordering you around like a cut-rate cabana boy?"

Kate cocked her head. "Why cut rate?"

Jo let out a long, heavy sigh. "Because if he were a high-priced cabana boy, I wouldn't need him to run errands, we'd be someplace where I could just use room service."

Kate took a second to soak that in before she gave her sister a short burst of soft applause. "You said that with such immediacy and conviction that I almost forgot…that it didn't make a lick of sense!"

"I know!" Jo massaged her scalp and groaned. "We've been cooped up in this house too long."

"Without a decent meal." Kate's stomach rumbled. All this talk of food only made the hunger worse.

"Don't start that again. I couldn't ask the man for that kind of dorky favor. The timing was all wrong."

"Because you plan to ask him for a bigger dorky favor later?"

Jo did not meet her eyes or even acknowledge Kate's wild guess. She just pulled free another piece of hair then shook it out as she said simply, "I just met him. It didn't seem right to impose. It's not like getting us a meal is part of his job."

"Really?" Kate adjusted her leg but that did not ease the quiet throbbing in her bones. She would never make it through this day if she had to both bicker with her sister *and* battle her body.

Jo worked free the last of her store-bought hair, gathered it up in the towel she had worn while talking to the preacher and set it aside. "Anyway, I noticed you didn't ask the man to run our errands for us, either."

"I was busy tending to your injury."

"And spying on the neighbors."

"And spying on the neighbors," Kate conceded. "Except there weren't any neighbors to spy on. I wonder if the place is going to sit empty the whole time we're here?"

"Maybe we should call the caretaker lady again."

"You think she'd know about the house across the street?"

"No, but if we explain our predicament, she might take pity on us and bring us by something to eat."

It was not an easy task to place the call. In the confusion of last night, neither of them had recharged their cell phones. That meant they had to find their chargers and plug them in and then get the caretaker's number and then when she answered…

"What?" Kate pressed the phone tight against her ear. "Ms. Weatherby? I…can't hear you."

"Swamped…" the woman shouted "…ing out…" Was all Kate heard next, then "Billy J's. Rain brings… in…sardines."

"We need food." Kate had matched the woman in volume but relied on small words in hopes that they would not be lost in the broken signal and the noise of the…*sardines?* "I have a broken foot. Can't drive. My sister fell coming in last night and now she can't drive, either."

"Oh, no! Not…front porch? Hey, put that fishing pole down and get back in that kitchen, mister!" That odd comment to someone on her end of the conversation came through loud and clear, of course, *especially* loud.

"Hearing you go on about fishing and sardines, not to mention the sounds of the buffet, are not helping." Kate had no clue how much of that got through.

"Don't start…closing this place up."

Kate sat up, even though it sent pain shooting through her leg to do so. "You're closing Billy J's?"

"Huh? Oh. No. No, my…always threatens…when people…eat all they can eat."

"We don't need all we can eat. We just need *some-*

thing to eat," she assured the woman. "We're really hungry here."

"Sit tight…know someone headed that way. He can…lunch…grocery list."

"Okay, we need milk and bread, and eggs, you know, the basics and…" That was when Kate realized she was talking to dead air. She considered calling back but decided to allow the caretaker to make that move, to allow her to get someplace where she could actually hear to take down the grocery list she had asked for. After a few minutes, when no call came back, Kate went back over the parts of the conversation and came to a conclusion. "I think she's going to send a man over with lunch from Billy J's."

Jo had spent the time while Kate had been on the phone fussing and fiddling with her hair and had it in a cute, if a bit finger-in-the-light-socket-esque hairdo that took years off her fresh, unmade-up face. "Did she take our order?"

"No."

"Then how will she know what to send?"

"It's batter-fried fish, batter-fried shrimp, batter-fried bread, batter-fried corn on the cob, for all I know they batter and fry the sodas right in the can. So, what does it matter what they bring? It will all taste the same."

"Delicious."

Kate nodded her agreement. She had always loved the food at Billy J's and it had done her heart good—in a way that only a place with the kind of food destined to give a body total cardiac failure can do—

to see it still open for business. "And it will all make us feel full."

"Did she give us a time frame?"

"No. But she mentioned lunch, so my guess is soon." And with that, Kate laid her head back, shut her eyes and…

"What shall we do while we wait?"

"I don't know." She glanced around the room and suddenly she knew exactly what they could do, and exactly how much Jo would hate the very suggestion. "Whenever we got restless around the cottage when we were younger, Mom would make us tidy up the closet."

"Oooh. Great idea."

"Really?" Kate considered demanding Jo tell her why the sudden interest in dealing with decades of old junk, then thought better of it. Jo wouldn't tell her a thing and if they started nitpicking again, what would that accomplish? "Okay, then let's see if we can—"

Before Kate could finish her sentence, Jo had jumped up to try to make her way to the closet a few feet across the room.

"Be careful. You can't go hopping around like that yet."

Jo's eyes practically glinted with bravado. "Is that a challenge?"

"That's sound medical advice!"

"Same thing to me." And off she went.

Kate pushed herself up and followed.

It was a small space under the narrow, enclosed stairway paneled with knotty pine that had aged into rich shades of honey-yellow and reddish-brown. Every personal effect their family had left behind at the cottage over the years seemed crammed into the tiny space. It smelled of mustiness and mothballs.

"Do they even make mothballs anymore?" Jo asked.

"If they do, they don't look like these." Kate frowned at the small white marble-sized balls strewn all over the floor. "Which only shows how long it has been since anyone has dealt with this storage problem."

"Or on the bright side, lets us know no one has messed with our belongings all these years."

"Jo! I never figured *you* for a bright-side kind of girl." Kate smiled at her sister.

Her sister returned that smile with a sly one of her own as she whipped something out from behind a three-foot-high tower of boxed board games and jigsaw puzzles. "You also never figured me for a world champion Wa Hoo player, but I proved you wrong about that a time or two."

"Wa Hoo," Kate whispered the name painted in squiggly letters over the old handmade game board. Their mother had bought the game and the bag of marbles for playing pieces from a roadside craftsman when they'd been quite young. They had spent hours playing it. So many hours that Dodie had often joked it was the only way she knew to get Kate to sit still.

"I'd forgotten all about that."

In turn, Kate had played it with Vince and his son, Gentry.

Jo handed her the board.

Kate trailed her fingers over the indentations, remembering the times spent laughing and chatting at the kitchen table. Of how full of himself Gentry had acted when he had beaten his father. He had always beaten his father.

Even as a young kid, he had told Kate he knew his dad was letting him win. Kate had tried to make that seem like a good thing, to point out how much Vince loved his son and wanted him to succeed.

Gentry had grudgingly agreed with her explanation then had rushed to add "I like it better when you and I play. Because then when I win, I know I did it because I'm go-oo-od."

"*When* you win? Don't you mean *if* you win?" she'd asked, waving the score pad in front of his adorable pug nose.

He'd gone quiet. "Even if I don't win, I like playing with you instead of Dad. He doesn't get this but I don't like winning all the time, not if it's not real."

"Being real is important," Kate had admitted.

"Yeah. But so is just being there, you know, like where a kid knows you're not going anywhere. That's important, too."

"Yes, it sure is."

"My dad is like that." Gentry had put the marbles in the leather pouch and set them in the center of the Wa Hoo board, looked up at her and asked, "And you, too, right? You're not going to go anywhere. We'll always be like this, like a family, right, Kate?"

"Kate?"

The sound of her sister's voice jarred Kate back to the present. She caressed the game board one last time then set it away from herself and fixed her attention on Jo. "What did you say?"

Jo began digging and pulling and scooting things around, seeming more intent on emptying the closet than on reviewing its contents. "I said that this is a great closet."

"Well, it's all right. As closets go, I suppose."

Jo yanked free then clunked a metal file box into Kate's lap without stopping to examine what she had just uncovered. "Are you kidding? People love deep, secure closets like this."

"People?" Kate looked up from the locked metal file box Jo had just discovered with the words Important Documents painted on it in what looked like nail polish. "What people?"

"Oh, just, you know, people. Hey, what's that?"

"This?" Kate smiled mostly to herself, her fingers running over the still-shiny chrome handle of the box. "Just a wee bit of buried treasure."

"Treasure? It says Documents on it, or rather Docu-*mints.*" Jo emphasized the pronunciation of a much younger Kate's mistake.

Kate hugged the box possessively. "Of course it does. Do you honestly think that if it said Kid's Treasure that any adult would have rescued it from a blazing fire or even bothered to preserve it all these years?"

"We had a fire here?"

"No, but I was planning ahead in case we did."

Jo pressed her lips together but to her credit she did not chide Kate about that whole "born old, grown old" debate. Nor did she point out that even as a child Kate had been prepared to pick up and run at a moment's notice.

Kate shrugged. "I had an overly dramatic imagination as a kid."

"Which you've completely gotten over, oh she of the obsession with the so-called mystery house?"

"I was just explaining my thinking when I wrote *documents* on the box where I kept my special keepsakes locked up."

"Ahh, keepsakes." For a split second Jo looked almost gooey with sentiment before she rubbed her hands together and demanded, gleefully, "Let's crack that baby open and see what's inside."

Kate hugged the box closer still. "I have a key."

"Of course. You *would.* Do you have it in a safety deposit box somewhere in abandoned salt mines that have been converted into an underground storage facility? Or have you kept it on your key chain all these years so you'd always be perfectly prepared?"

"It's hidden from a certain younger sister who used to spy on me and get into my things when she thought I wasn't looking."

"Hmm, I'll keep an eye out for that kid."

"And for the key. I forgot where I put it years ago. Good chance it's in here someplace." She gestured toward the games, puzzles, toys, piles of old clothes, mismatched sandals and secondhand musical instruments to indicate all the work that lay ahead of them.

"Great. You can look for it later, after I beat you a few dozen times at Wa Hoo."

"Jo, we can't play a game now. We still have a lot of work to do."

"Work? This?" Jo snatched up the leather sack filled with marbles. With the handmade board under her arm, she put her back to the chaos that had come out of the closet. "What's the rush? We can pack all that stuff up and get it out of here tomorrow."

"Pack? Get it out of here?" Kate struggled to stand without letting go of her treasure box in the process. "Who said anything about—"

"I call greensies!"

Greensies. Kate pursed her lips and blinked to keep at bay the tears that one silly word brought to her eyes. Their dad had always picked green in any game they'd played. Kate doubted that Jo even remembered that. "Okay, you can be greensies. For all the good it will do you, because I am in no mood to show you any mercy."

Jo offered just enough of a smile to show that she didn't believe her sister for one moment.

More than an hour later, after Kate and Jo had each won an equal amount of games and neither wanted to risk breaking the tie, Kate laid her head back on the couch and tried to make the most of their wait.

"Ka-aa-te?"

"Shhh."

"But, Kate, I'm bored."

"Be still."

"I don't really have much choice."

Kate put her finger to her lips.

"And I'm hungry."

"I thought you were bored."

"There's a difference?"

At that, Kate opened one eye to peer at her sister. Jo slumped against the side of the plaid couch with her legs covered by an old floral bedspread. With her short, choppy hair all awry and the bag of Wa Hoo marbles in her lap, she looked all of six years old.

That got to Kate.

"Okay. One minute." She shut her eyes and concluded softly, "Amen."

"You were praying?"

"Uh-huh."

"What were you praying for?"

Patience. Miraculous healing. Anything to get me through the rest of this rainy day, Kate could have said. But she kept those thoughts to herself. Jo was probably just as miserable as she was and, unlike Kate, Jo didn't have any prescription medication to take the edge off her physical discomfort.

And she was hungry.

And bored.

Kate exhaled. "You know, Jo, people don't only pray *for* things. Sometimes people just pray about things."

"I…I know that."

"But you don't put it into practice much?"

"I…uh…" She might as well have just thrown up

her hands and confessed, "You got me." The look on her face and tension in her formerly sprawled-out body spoke volumes. As did the surliness of her tone when she snarled, "When did you get to be so spiritually enlightened?"

"I don't know. I can't explain it but being here, with you, with all these memories…" She motioned toward the boxes of photos, papers and junk that they had hardly begun to look through, then to the old Wa Hoo board. "It just made me want to…"

"Pray for help?"

Kate smiled. "To say thank you."

"Thank you?" Jo tipped her head to one side then the other, as if she must physically turn the thought over and over in her mind. "Thank you. For…?"

"You."

"You're kidding!"

"No. You. And Mom. And this place."

Jo hung her head.

"You praying now?"

"Me? What? No. No, I…" She wove her fingers together, cleared her throat, looked toward the front door. "Maybe you should have prayed that the guy bringing our lunch would show up soon."

"We really are at his mercy, whoever it might be." Kate picked up her cell phone to check the time. "Which is why when I prayed I also asked for—"

"Aha!" Jo took a little too much joy in hearing her sister had, indeed, asked *for* something.

"—good neighbors," Kate finished her thought.

"You mean when you go back to Georgia and need help there?" Jo said it, more than asked it, seeming to want to lead Kate to confirm her take on things more than understand her sister's actual thinking.

"I mean here." Kate tapped one finger into her open palm. "In Santa Sofia. In the house across the street. *This* is where we need help, Jo."

"But this place is only temporary…I mean, for us."

"Everything *but* this place has been temporary for us, Jo." As Kate spoke the words, they took on a new and fuller meaning for her. She swallowed to push down the mix of sadness and regret welling up inside her. "We haven't even been here twenty-four hours and already I should be thinking about when I can get back to my practice. Or if I will even have a practice to go to when I've recovered, especially if I have the second surgery."

"I'm looking at some major upheavals of my own back home. Things that might mean I won't stay at my job. I may have to move out of my apartment."

"Again," Kate added softly.

"Again," Jo echoed in agreement.

"New jobs, new challenges, new living arrangements. Those only go to show that besides each other and Mom, Jo, this place—the cottage, the town—those have been the most consistent things in our lives."

"I…I hadn't thought of that."

"I hadn't much, either, until we got here, until we got stuck inside today." Kate looked around them. "I got to imagining how it would be if Mom really did move down here."

"Here?" Jo jabbed her finger toward the faded carpet. "In this very cottage?"

"Yes, of course here." Kate didn't know what else Jo had in mind and she didn't care. They were only talking "if" right now, anyway. "*If* she did stay here, then I'd want her to have good neighbors. Wouldn't you?"

"I guess, knowing how easy it would be to feel stranded out here, then yes. Yes, I would." Jo fluffed her hair then tucked the bedspread snugly around her legs. "And it wouldn't hurt if they were gorgeous, single guys on the high side of thirty."

Kate feigned shock then laughed. "I'm thinking of Mom here, Jo."

"Oh, me, too!" Her eyes grew wide and twinkled with fun. "Mom would definitely want us to have neighbors like that!"

"You're probably right." Her mother would love to see them both in love and married, and with kids of their own, Kate knew. A tall order for a woman who had raised her girls to feel as if nothing were permanent, no one stuck around for long. "But maybe we should think about the best kind of neighbors for Mom."

"And if they were not so great neighbors?"

Kate got up, grabbed her cane and headed toward the window that faced the mystery house. "That might go a long way toward influencing my vote on whether Mom moves down here or not."

"Really?" Jo nodded, her eyes narrowed.

Kate could practically see her sister filing away that little tidbit. Clearly, Jo did not see any advantage in keeping the old place and just wanted to find a way to get Kate to come around to her way of thinking.

"Really," Kate said softly as she pulled back the white lace curtain and stared in the direction of the only other house on Dream Away Bay Court. She flattened her palm to the glass where rain droplets exploded then trickled downward in dozens of wandering paths.

Neither of them spoke for a moment, then Jo groaned. "Why doesn't it stop raining? Did it rain this much here when we were kids?"

"Not that I recall. In my mind, I always picture this place as always sunny and warm."

"And closer to the ocean," Jo reminded her.

"Yeah." Kate raised her head, wishing she could hear the sound of the waves now. "Funny, huh?"

"Oh, yeah. Regular laugh riot. Apparently when we were kids this place had everything—location, looks, perpetual good weather. I wonder how it did it?"

"Did what?"

"Picked up its foundation and moved away from the beach and landed in some kind of urban rain forest."

"Without the forest."

"Or the urban, really. Have you noticed that now that we can't hear the highway because of the rain, we don't hear any traffic at all?"

"Not even the guy supposedly sent out here to bring us some lunch." Kate strained her neck to see as far down the bumpy road as possible. "I had my mouth all set for a big bite of… Truck!"

"Truck? I suppose if they put enough batter on it and deep fried it long enough—"

"Quit kidding around, Jo. There's a red truck turning in to the cul-de-sac." Kate spun around, nabbed her cane and took a few strides away from the window.

"Wait for me." But Jo couldn't seem to get herself up and steady without wincing in pain.

"You should have listened to doctor's orders." Kate limped by her sister, wondering if she should grab a blanket for the long trip around the back of the house to the front. "If you had iced and elevated that ankle today, you'd be able to get around at least a little by now."

"Don't pull rank on me now, the man has the wrong address."

"What?"

"You said he's pulling into the drive across the street. That means he's going to the wrong house."

"Maybe he lives there?"

"Maybe he's got our lunch. Do you really want to take that chance?"

Kate's stomach grumbled.

Dull pain coursed upward from her toes to her knee.

No. She did not want to take a chance of missing this guy. Even if he wasn't the man sent by the cottage caretaker, he was somebody with wheels who might help them out.

If she could attract his attention.

And fast.

She swiveled around. As much as a woman in her situation could swivel.

In a few faltering steps, she reached the front door.

"Kate, that's not safe."

"I'll just step out a tiny bit. Only enough so he can hear me when I holler. Don't worry."

"Scat-Kat-Kate is just a nickname. It doesn't mean you have nine lives."

Kate waved off Jo's warning and stepped out the door. The porch seemed safe enough. Solid, actually. She thumped it once with her cane.

The man across the street did not seem to notice her at all, just got out of the truck and headed for the other house.

She had to do something to get his attention. Between the rain and the hat he had pulled down low over his eyes and ears, she didn't think shouting from near the doorway would do it. She had to venture out farther onto the porch.

He rounded the truck and bounded up the stairs of the other house.

Kate had to act. She took a big step forward and stabbed her cane high into the air. She opened her mouth, filled her lungs and lost her footing.

Bump.

Crack.

Crash.

Kate's cane flew up, tumbling one end over the other like some fearsome fire baton flying skyward from a master twirler's hand. It caught on an overhead beam.

And Kate herself went down.

Down.

Down.

Right through a splintered plank of rotten wood went Kate's good leg, all the way up to her knee before she stopped with a jolt. Then she plummeted backward until the wild waving of her arms pitched her forward. She imagined if anyone was watching that she looked like one of those crash-test dummies caught on slow-motion film, back and forth, flailing helplessly until she came to a stop with her nose smashed against the spot where her foot should have been.

She took a deep breath and, ignoring the smell of bleach, enjoyed a brief moment of gratitude that she hadn't succeeded in attracting the man across the street after all.

"Clearly, you wanted to get my attention, but a simple yoo-hoo would have done the… Kate?"

At which point her cane came loose from the rafter and whopped Vince Merchant directly on the head.

Chapter Seven

"Vince?"

He rubbed the back of his head and looked at the cane lying at his feet.

Vince Merchant! It couldn't be! Her pulse raced. No, *raced* sounded too tame. Between the excitement of the fall and the shock of seeing Vince Merchant standing on her porch as big as day, her pulse *roared.* It made her head swim. She could hardly catch a breath.

She pushed at the edge of the hole in the porch with both hands trying to scoot herself out of it. The leg of her pajama pants snagged on the broken edge of the floorboards.

Pajama pants! Kate clutched her baggy T-shirt in both hands. Apparently falling through the porch waving a cane had not been quite spectacular enough. She had to add costuming. Unflattering and probably not the most sweet-smelling costuming. What must he think of her? She ventured a peek at him.

But he wasn't looking at her right now; he was looking up. Maybe trying to make sure nothing else could come raining down on him. Water from the leaky roof splashed on his cheek. "Where did that come from?"

She shook her head. "The real question is where did *you* come from?"

"Across the street." He crouched beside her as if it were the most natural thing in the world to find her here.

In town.

At the cottage.

In her pajamas.

Buried up to her knee in the splintered remains of the front porch.

"Why?" Suddenly Kate recalled her prayer for good neighbors. Though she found it nearly impossible to draw a deep breath, she did manage to ask "Is that your house?"

"Mine?" He glanced over his shoulder then stood. "No, I'm doing some handyman work there for…" He scowled.

Kate waited for him to finish his sentence but after a moment it became clear his thoughts had moved on.

"If I try to drag you out of there like this, I might end up going through the floor myself." He shifted his shoulders. His broad, muscular shoulders.

Not that Kate would notice such a thing, particularly from her disadvantaged vantage point. "Well, we both know the last thing I'd want is for you to be stuck here with me."

It was one of those things you don't realize how it

sounds until it's come out, bounced around the airwaves in a silence that lasts a little too long, and then falls like a dead weight between the two of you.

"I didn't—"

Vince held his hand up, graciously cutting her off before she did more damage. "There are some boards left over from trying to mend the railings. Let me just grab a couple and I can lay them down as a platform to bear more weight. Stay put, now."

"You thought I was going to go someplace?"

"Never can tell," he spoke to her over his shoulder as he gathered two long boards that had been leaning against the house. "You have a history of taking off without any warning."

"Oh, Vince," she murmured, unable to take her eyes from his face.

I'm sorry. The sentiment tugged at her heart. But she could not say it out loud. All these years her memories of her time with Vince had been edged with the pain and regret of her childish actions. At one moment she would think of the laughter they had shared, the warmth, and the next her heart would chill at the way she had ended things so poorly, the fact that she had let Vince say goodbye to Gentry for her instead of doing it herself.

How many times had she wished she had done things differently? How many times had she longed for a chance to go back and explain? How many times had she seen Vince's face and struggled to see forgiveness in those wonderful eyes?

She stared at him now. When he bent down to situate the first board in front of her, she could only murmur, "It *is* you."

"In the flesh." He smiled and gave her a wink before directing his attention to assessing her predicament further.

"Vince." This time she said it so softly he did not acknowledge it with even a blink of his eyes.

How may times had she imagined what it would be like to see him again after all these years? And now that he was here—in the flesh, as he had said—she couldn't imagine what to say or do or even think about it. She forced herself to breathe slowly as she took a moment to take it all in.

Older. He was older. But then, who wasn't?

But *his* older seemed so much more... What? Dignified? Powerful? Adorable?

She tried to squelch the urge to sigh at just the sight of him so near.

Yes, he was *still* adorable. Only in a more mature, more masculine way than his younger, more callow, scrawnier self. The lines accenting his eyes and mouth defined his character as much as they did his face. They marked him as a man who smiled easily and often. His hair had a golden sheen and the beginnings of silver streaks at the temples.

Kate tucked her own hair behind her ear, wondering if he had noticed the same kinds of things about her.

Wasn't he as amazed at finding her here as she was to see him?

"How can this be happening?" she whispered.

"Dry rot." He held the second board out as if trying to picture where to place it to do the most good.

"Dry..." She dragged her gaze from him to where her leg disappeared into a gaping hole. "No, not the porch."

She squirmed again to try to free herself, talking fast but firmly so as not to seem utterly awestruck to see him again. "No, I mean you don't live in Santa Sofia. Why are you here?"

"I *do* live in Santa Sofia." He squatted down beside her again and leaned his face close to hers as he slid the second board on the other side of the hole, directly under her backside. "And I'm *here* because you need me."

"Oh." *Awestruck* did not begin to cover how she felt when she heard that.

"Now, before we go on, tell me, are you okay?"

"I'm...awesome," she murmured.

"Yes." He gave a deep, soft chuckle. "I've always thought that about you."

Kate hadn't blushed in years. Maybe not since the first time she'd laid eyes on this very man, but she learned in that instant that she had not lost the ability.

"But let's face it, Kate, you don't look awesome." He tapped the board nearest her trapped knee. "You look like you could use some help."

She tensed. She could feel her blush deepen, brought on by total mortification. More wriggling without any success. The movement jarred her injured foot and she sucked air through her clenched teeth. "Actually, I *am* in quite a bit of pain."

He peered down past her leg into the hole. "Do you think anything is broken?"

"I'm sure of it." She tapped her cast. "But the rest of me is fine, maybe a little bruised." And that included her ego. "But fine."

"Maybe we should—"

"I *am* a doctor."

He stared at her for only a second before he broke into a short burst of benevolent laughter and finished his original thought. "Maybe we should get you out of this fix."

"Yes. Good idea. Just… Just stand back and I'll get myself out of here." She pushed and strained, using the stabilizing boards for leverage.

"Stop moving." He put a hand on her shoulder and fixed his gaze on hers. "I'll get you out."

"I can do it." She looked away and kicked the leg dangling in the hole to try to propel herself out of this mess. "I just need a little—"

"Put your arms around my neck." With no more warning than that, he pulled her against his upper body. One strong arm slid under her leg with the cast on it, the other lent support around her back.

"—help," she murmured softly to complete her sentence, even as she complied with his no-nonsense command.

He braced his legs and pushed upward. "Hang on."

As if she could do anything else.

Slowly, gently, with only a brief snag of her pajama pants, he lifted her clear of the broken floorboards.

He straightened and stood with what seemed like great ease.

"There," he said.

"Wow," she said in a barely audible whisper.

He stepped over the hole in the porch and up to the threshold of the cottage, still showing no strain.

At least no strain that she noticed. But then she could not take her gaze from his eyes.

Vince Merchant.

Here.

In Santa Sofia.

On her porch.

Holding her in his arms.

Suddenly everything felt right in the world. Or as if it could be *put* right again.

As if the past, her hurtful actions, his overprotectiveness of his son, it was at last behind them now.

He smelled of rain and aftershave.

Red colored the hollow of his cheeks and she wondered if he felt the same unspoken promise that she did or if…

"Kate?"

"What, Vince?" she asked, all breathless and hopeful.

"The door?"

"Oh!" She slipped her hand from beside the taut cords of his neck and reached for the doorknob, intent on using it to steady herself after she got her feet on the ground again.

"Still can't wait to get away from me, eh, Kate?"

"No. That is, yes, I don't need for you to carry me."

She tried to grip the door for support, only to feel it pull away. She startled and grabbed Vince's gaudy island-print shirt to keep from throwing them both off balance.

"Kate? Are you okay? I heard a…" Jo stood in the open doorway wearing a T-shirt, baggy sweatpants and an expression of total disbelief. "Wow!"

"You heard that 'wow' all the way in the house?" Vince grinned.

"Vince?" Jo looked to Kate for confirmation.

"Hey, squirt!" Before Kate could say a thing, Vince spoke up. "Last time I saw you, you had just graduated high school, worried incessantly about your hair, nails and clothes and could down more hot dogs at a single bonfire than any skinny teenaged boy or big-bellied fisherman I've ever met. How ya doin'?"

"Never mind that." Jo snapped her fingers then held out her hand. "What did you bring us to eat?"

Vince stepped over the threshold, compelling Jo to allow him inside the cottage with Kate still in his arms. "Well, at least you still have your appetite."

"No. I mean it." Even though Jo walked backward, albeit awkwardly, she did not back down an inch. "I'm starving here. Make with the groceries, lunch boy."

"Jo!" Kate would have swatted her sister away but that would have meant letting go of Vince. So she sort of swung her good leg out, toe pointed, to nudge her aside.

Jo did not budge.

"I'll see what I can do." Vince kept his tone light, even if he clearly felt his burden wasn't. "Can I put your sister down first before I throw my back out?"

"Yes! Put me down," Kate snapped. "I am capable of supporting my own weight even if I make the ground shake with every step."

"Yes, you are a true gargantuan," Vince joked as he bent at the knees and lowered Kate to sit on the plaid couch.

Kate slid from the ratty old hide-a-bed to Mom's antique coffee table. From there she easily transferred herself to the comfort of her nest of blankets and pillows on the floral couch. Then she tipped up her nose and met Vince's gaze. "You're the one who said I was breaking your back."

"No, years of, uh, well, basically back-breaking work have broken my back. Or, um, you know, messed it up pretty good." He frowned and looked from Kate to Jo. "Uh, pretty bad?"

"I see you're still the same old silver-tongued charmer you were in your twenties." Jo put her hands on her hips.

"Hey, I'm a man of action. Not words."

"Great." Jo batted her eyelashes at him and pointed to the front door. "Act like you're getting us some lunch."

Kate surveyed for injuries through the rip in her pajama pants and, satisfied there were none, threw the covers over both legs, more to conceal the reminder of the way Vince had found her than anything.

Vince sat on the edge of the plaid couch and turned to Kate. "So, you're okay?"

"Aside from a bloodless scrape on my knee and, I

think, my nose—" she touched the tip, unsure if contact with the wood or the bleach had left it stinging slightly "—I think my backside absorbed most of the impact."

"Knee? Nose? Backside? Impact?" Jo looked toward the still open door. "Did you fall out there or something?"

"Of course I fell." Kate pulled the covers up higher to protect against the chill of the damp fall air. "Why else would you think Vince would pick me up and carry me in here?"

"Oh, I could think of a few other reasons." Jo bit her lip and looked at Vince all moon-eyed and silly.

"Jo," Kate said flatly.

"What?" Jo's answer came back from a flirtatious fog.

"Go shut the door." Kate flung her arm out to point the way.

"Why?" Belligerence colored Jo's curt reply.

Kate didn't know if that came from not wanting to carry out the command or the mere fact that *Kate* had issued it. She didn't try to overanalyze it, just pointed more emphatically.

"Why should I shut the door? He's going right back out of it so he can get us something to eat, right?"

Vince looked from Kate to Jo then back to Kate again. "What's the deal here?"

"I could ask you the same thing," Kate said, still piecing together the reality of him here in the living room of their cottage once again. "In fact, I could ask you a million things."

"Yeah." He nodded. "Me, too. To you, that is."

"Dazzle us with your eloquence later." Jo prodded Vince's shoulder to get him up. "Fetch food for us, *now.* Please."

"How's Gentry?" Kate asked, knowing full well that after Vince had gone she would not recall a thing he had told her, only his eyes.

And his smile.

And her regrets.

"Good. Gentry's…good. He's like six-two now and—"

"And does he have a driver's license?"

Vince looked up at Jo as if he only now remembered she was still in the room. "Of course he does."

"Then give me his number and let me call him to do a grocery run." Jo plunked down on the arm of the couch and stretched out to retrieve her cell phone. "Unless he's at work and can't be bothered?"

"He's between opportunities right now. He stays pretty busy, though." The answer came too fast, too practiced and what did it mean, anyway?

Between opportunities?

Kate knew what it meant. The kid couldn't hold a job. And Vince wouldn't even make him responsible for a simple thing like running an errand for an old friend. "It's Wa Hoo all over again."

"Hmm?" Vince frowned at her.

Kate probably frowned back. She wasn't sure. She only knew she had not smiled or in any way shown that she accepted the flimsy excuse he made on his son's behalf.

"Wa Hoo? We don't have time for games, now, Kate. I'm hungry," Jo protested.

"What's the problem?" Vince asked Kate, not Jo.

Kate, always Kate. As though she were the only one in the room. In this house. In his world.

Her reservations about his relationship with his son fell to the side.

"Your cupboards bare? Your bank account empty? Your car broken down?"

"The cupboards are bare and so are our feet." Kate moved her cast as much as she dared. And she dared too much. She winced in pain.

"The lady who takes care of the cottage for us said she would send someone over with some food," Jo dove in, offering her own tightly wrapped ankle as evidence as she added, "Neither of us can drive."

"The lady?" Vince frowned.

"Ms. Weatherby?" Kate prompted.

"Oh, you mean Moxie!"

"Moxie?" Jo gave the same kind of look she usually saved for when Kate wore arch-supporting sneakers with a dress. "What kind of name is that?"

"Nick," ol' eloquent Vince supplied.

Jo's frown deepened. "Her name is Nick?"

"Pain has definitely affected your ability to think, Jo." Kate shook her head.

"Pain and hunger," Jo snapped.

"Actually all the information on the accounts says M. Weatherby so—"

"Yeah." Vince nodded. "It's the same person."

"I figured." Kate smiled. Probably a big, goofy, inappropriately dreamy smile given the mundane topic and yet, she didn't care. Vince Merchant was in Santa Sofia. Their paths had crossed again. And after she had prayed for the Lord to grant her good neighbors. She couldn't help grinning like an idiot. "And she, this M. Weatherby, said she'd send someone over. So when we saw your truck drive up across the street, we just thought—"

"Never fear! Your local beach preacher slash one-man welcoming committee slash amazin' aluminum crutch fairy is here!"

Vince looked from Travis Brandt standing in the doorway brandishing a pair of crepe-paper-wrapped metal crutches to Kate. "Friend of yours?"

"He's a friend of *mine,*" Jo claimed even as she propelled herself upward and began hopping straight at the poor unsuspecting man. "And I don't plan on letting him rocket out of here again unless he takes me along for the ride."

Chapter Eight

Travis Brandt stood in the doorway.

Her doorway. The family home's doorway, Jo corrected, though she had already come to think of the quaint cottage with great bones and good fixer-upper potential as "hers."

There he stood. Tall and…tall. Nothing else about him seemed to stand out now, not the way it had when he had been a sports-and-media darling. His once rich brown hair now looked muddied by too much sun, giving it reddish highlights that did not mix well with the coarse gray curls that licked at his ears and the collar of his simple button-down orange-sherbet-colored shirt. The shirt itself was rumpled. Not unkempt but as if he had ironed it a few days ago, worn it once briefly since then and hung it carefully on the doorknob of his closet. He'd thrown it on today, thinking, as men do, that since he could still see the lines of what had once been crisp creases, it was as good as putting on a shirt straight from the dry cleaners.

Jo tried not to find that probable sequence of events too endearing. Just as she tried not to notice that his white baggy pants were not so much pressed as flattened down the front of the legs. The backs of the knees, though? Crushed fabric in a half-dozen fan-like lines. A sure sign of a man realizing at the last minute he wanted to look more presentable and using an iron on just the parts he could see in the mirror—or that he could reach with the pants still on his body.

He came from a background of everyone hanging on your every word, so many women laughing at even your lamest jokes in hopes that you would notice and flirt with them, after all.

Flirt? Had Jo just flirted *with a minister?*

He shook his head and laughed, too.

Travis Brandt, *the minister,* was not allowed to flirt. Or invite anyone to flirt with him, even the harmless kind of flirting. Not the way that Travis Brandt the sports guy had, right? He had to think of his position in the community.

She laughed some more, knowing that *some* more was already way more than anyone in the room believed the moment called for.

Travis quirked his lips up on one side, still appearing amused. Or perhaps befuddled.

Had she befuddled him with her phony reaction? That only seemed fair since the very notion of what this man had done befuddled her.

To have gone from being *somebody* to serving just anybody. Jo wasn't sure how one made that kind of leap. Or why.

And she didn't plan on exploring the shift in the man's priorities today. She had her own priorities. First and foremost those included making the most of this guy showing up out of the blue by getting him alone and pressing him for information to help her sell the cottage.

"But I did stop by the church emergency supply closet and pick these up." Travis offered the decorated crutches to Jo. "For you."

"Me?" Travis Brandt had taken the time to do something kind for *her?* Not for Kate. Not in expectation of what he could get out of the good deed, but simply because he saw her, noticed what she needed and acted. "You did that for *me?*"

Jo didn't know what to make of that.

"You were the one with the towel over her head when I dropped by earlier, right?"

Jo thrust her fingers into her choppy, chin-length hair. It must look awful.

He pulled the crutches making a big, teasing pretense of glancing all around the cottage. "You don't have another sister hidden away, do you?"

"No." And her clothes, her ankle, her bare-faced face!

"No, that wasn't you?"

She thought for a moment of denying it. Bare-faced or not, she could not lie. "No, that was me."

"Shouldn't that be yes that was me?"

"Yes, that was me." She reached for the crutches. "No, I don't have another sister."

He withheld them. "Hey, I've read about this kind of thing. I'm not turning loose of these babies until I'm sure I'm giving them to the right girl."

Jo opened her mouth to say... Well, what *would* one say to that?

"Cinderella! Cinderella?" he called out, craning his neck to act as if he were searching and listening for the third sister to come rushing out from wherever Kate and Jo had imprisoned her.

"It's me." Jo held back the urge to laugh, which she knew would come off as too nervous and too much again.

"You're Cinderella?"

I wish. Cinderella whose prince has finally...

She blinked and dragged her thoughts back from that pointless little fantasy. "No, actually I'm the ugly towel-head sister."

She bent her head and ruffled her hands through her hair to demonstrate and to keep from looking too smug when his eyes went all dreamy and he said...

"Yeah, now I see it."

"You were supposed to say that I'm not ugly." She threw a pout in his direction.

"Why? You obviously already knew that. You aren't the shallow type who needs a man to lavish empty praise on you, are you?"

From across the room, Kate scoffed loud enough to make them both look her way.

Jo shot heat rays from her eyes at her sister. Or she

would have if she had been endowed with the power to shoot heat rays. Which, given the way people were treating her this afternoon, she suddenly wished she did.

"Let's start over." She pulled herself together and strove to keep her tone cordial, not pouty, not shallow, and definitely not superhero hot under the collar. "I'm the one with the sprained ankle you spoke to earlier."

He extended his arms, putting the crutches within her reach at last. "Then these must be for you."

"Thank you," she said. Or squeaked, actually. The kindness of the gesture and the cuteness of the gesture-*er* had the emotional effect of tightening her throat and raising the pitch of her voice. And that was only what the others could tell.

She stood on one foot and put her hands on the bars of the crutches.

"Not so fast. If I read my fairy tales right, you can't claim these until we make sure they fit."

"Fit?"

He moved around behind her. "Slide them under your arms and I'll make sure they're at the right height."

Jo fought to put on the outward appearance of calm and control. Despite that effort, she couldn't quell the sensation of an electrical current running just below the surface of her skin, raising her pulse, probably her blood pressure and elevating the whole scene to a big deal in her mind.

"Want some help?" Kate asked, pushing aside the mangled pile of covers to scoot to the edge of the couch she had all but laid claim to when they had first arrived.

"Thanks, but I've done this more than a time or two," Travis said.

"Silly me. Should have thought of that." Kate tapped her finger against her head. "Lots of football injuries?"

"More like Frisbee injuries," he muttered, his focus more on the position of the equipment than on Kate's interested questioning.

"What?" Kate turned her attention to Vince.

Jo made no pretense of not knowing that was exactly where Kate wanted her attention to fix.

"And volleyball injuries." Vince pointed to his knee.

"Oh?" Kate followed his movements.

"And stepping on everything from glass to hot coals injuries." He stuck out one foot. "Oh, and a surprising number of twisted ankles from getting tangled up in a leash while trying to walk a dog on the beach."

"That's right." Travis looked their way for a moment. "With Traveler's Wayside Chapel right on the beach, we have people wandering in asking for crutches once a week or so—you know, something just to get them to the urgent treatment center. I have the process down."

"Next to sunburn, tourists are most likely to suffer leg or foot injuries," Vince said, the way a kid throws in a piece of trivia to impress others.

"Cool." It certainly seemed to impress Kate.

"You think people hurting themselves is cool?" Vince folded his arms and leaned back.

"In a way, yes." Kate laughed. "It's my business to think it's cool."

Both Vince and Travis seemed intrigued by that statement.

That was why Jo had to act fast, to keep them from asking Kate about her work and having her go on and on about feet and toes and ankles and…

And leave Jo standing there watching yet again while everyone in her limited little world down here decided that Dr. Kate Cromwell hung the moon.

"Well, it's my business to make sure my sister has enough to eat so she can take her medicine and get better." So that they could sell this house, bail herself out and not have to worry about their mother living all the way down here in Florida with her daughters in Georgia.

Where did that last bit come from? Jo chose not to dwell on it. The first part had been enough to draw Travis's attention back to his task and that was all that mattered.

Jo only wanted to get on with the process so that she could get on with her plans to get Travis Brandt alone. To *talk.*

Just talk.

The mutual sharing of information.

Maybe planting a few seeds, shoveling on a little bit of…plant food, as it were…to help nurture those seeds to grow into fruitful ideas.

Fruit. Jo sighed.

Her stomach grumbled.

Talk *and* food, that was all she wanted from this man.

She wasn't being manipulative. Her business had a long history of dancing around the edge of a deal over a meal. And ministers were not slouches in that area, either. Luncheons, banquets, coffee and doughnuts in the fellowship hall.

Just a little pragmatic networking, that was all she was thinking about.

Travis knelt beside Jo and fiddled with the locking tab system, raising and lowering the pegs until he had the crutches just so. "How's that?"

She leaned forward, testing her weight on them. They wobbled slightly. Still, that offered an improvement over her current system of hopping from piece of furniture to piece of furniture for support. And she was in an awful hurry to get going. So, she wiggled them into a position she thought would give her the least discomfort and said, "Okay."

"'Okay' is not good enough." He went back to work, this time not just tinkering with the pegs but also standing up to make sure the pads didn't jab Jo under her arms.

He had to stand close to do this.

Not improperly close but close enough that she could smell the reassuring scents of beach and church on him. Beach smelling of the Gulf wind in his hair and sunscreen, even on a cloudy day, on his face and neck. That harder to describe church smell, she decided, reminded her of a hymnal opened for the first time after a week of sitting in a freshly lemon-oiled wooden pew rack. She liked them both.

"We don't want to settle for anything but the maximum comfort and security here."

Comfort and security. For a split second she thought of adding that to the list of things she wanted from Travis.

Her whole life she'd never felt those two things without reservation. Her mother offered comfort but, with her own hurts and issues to deal with, very little security. Jo's job also afforded her certain comforts but as her current situation proved, she could not rely on her work for a real sense of security. And Kate?

She looked at her sister quietly watching the goings-on, her fingers digging into the fat arm of the couch to keep herself from charging in and doing the job for Travis herself. Kate was all about security.

No matter what, Jo knew she could count on Kate.

It was one of the things that made her craziest about her sister. And one of the things that made it imperative that she get Travis alone. She needed to do her homework before she presented anything about selling the cottage to Kate. She owed her sister that much.

"There." Travis touched her lightly on the back and left his hand there. "How's that?"

"That's terrific." The heat from his warm palm sank into the tense muscles between her shoulder blades. She looked into his eyes and had to fight to keep her knees from going all weak and making him think she wasn't strong enough to go out. "Terrific."

Jo had come to Florida with a clearly defined objective in mind. She had to make use of every contact, every opportunity to advance that objective. Or else, in a little less than three weeks now, she would face certain disaster.

Unless, of course, something here changed all that for her.

Travis smiled.

The so-called electrical current that had been merely a low buzz under the surface of her skin throughout his working on the crutches suddenly surged. It took all of Jo's composure not to blow a fuse on the spot. Blow a fuse or overheat and melt into a puddle. So much for using this contact to advance her professional objectives.

"Great." He stood back and looked over his handiwork. And maybe a little bit more than his handiwork. "I have to say, even with your whole head covered by a towel and your swollen ankle propped up on a chair between us, I thought you were pretty cute. But this head-exposed, ankle-bandaged look really works, too."

"Yeah?"

"Yeah."

"She had a towel over her head?" Vince asked in a whisper meant to be overheard.

"Shh." Kate pressed her finger to her lips and leaned forward, clearly not wanting to miss a word.

Jo ignored them both, asking Travis, "You like this look better, huh?"

He pointed to the open space between where they stood and the couch. "Show me a runway walk so I can be sure."

Jo placed the tips of her crutches down, swung her body forward then stopped short. "Hey! I thought you were a minister! You're not supposed to ask a girl to go parading around in front of you like a swimsuit model!"

"So, I can be sure you know how to use those crutches?" He waggled his fingers to demonstrate walking. "Wouldn't be very nice, or neighborly, or much of a Christian act to saddle you with something without making sure you can use them properly."

"Oh. Yeah. Of course."

It was a delicate balance. Not the walking with crutches. But trying to strike the right chord with the former sports celebrity turned…minister…turned medical-equipment deliveryman.

Jo moved over the old carpet, trying not to make a million mental notes about her options—replacing it, shampooing it, tearing it up and hoping for hardwood underneath—for flooring as she did.

"Have you used crutches before?" Travis asked.

"No."

He crooked his smile up on one side "Well, you're a real natural at it. Very coordinated. Almost graceful."

If she were doing pretty much anything else—painting, cooking, even walking in a brand-new pair of super high heels—she'd have found that compliment charming—a bit awkward, given the source, yet still charming.

But said about walking on crutches? Just the idea of being a natural at that, graceful, even, made her pause. And pausing made her stumble.

In a single footfall, Travis stood beside her, one large hand spread across her back, the other helping to stabilize the crutch she had clunked down at an odd angle.

"Talk about awkward," she said, her head down,

trying to will her feet and the tips of her walking aids to all work together.

"Were we talking about awkward, Ms. Cromwell?" Travis asked.

"Jo," she said softly. "Call me Jo."

"Jo?" He said it as if the name didn't quite fit right in his mouth. Or maybe he thought it didn't fit right with her.

"As in the middle sister in *Little Women,*" Kate called out by way of explanation. Kate always rushed to tell people this insignificant tidbit because, like so many things in Jo's life, even her name came in Kate's shadow.

Little Women had been their mother's favorite old movie, so she had named her first daughter Katharine, after Katharine Hepburn, and when Jo had arrived—Jo was supposed to have been a boy to appease their father—Mom had hit upon the idea of naming her this boyish name, which was the character Hepburn had played in the movie. So, if one were the kind to analyze things too closely, and Jo was that kind, one could say that Kate was the real deal and Jo was merely an extension of her. And of her father's disappointment at not having a son.

"Jo." Travis tried the name again.

From his mouth, the name didn't sound like a synonym for a second-rate castoff. She responded immediately. "Yes?"

"I like it," he said.

"Thank you."

"And as for talking about awkward?" His hand

resting so lightly on her back it felt as fleeting as his breath, he nodded and finished up, "I thought we were talking about grace…Jo."

Jo looked up. Right into a pair of soft brown eyes focused on her. Not her sister's shadow. Not her father's disappointment.

Her.

Just her.

All her life she had wanted to see that look from someone who mattered. Who thought *she* actually mattered, if only as another person. She'd wanted it so badly that more than once she had made a pest of herself to her family and a fool of herself in questions of the heart. That yearning had dominated her actions for so long that she hardly knew how to do anything but seek that elusive affirmation.

And now it had come to her unbidden.

Without strings from him or manipulations on her part.

Travis Brandt had gone out of his way to do something kind—*for her.*

Her first impulse was to push him away. Then to make a joke, a caustic remark, an outright insult if she had to, to prove to him his lack of judgment for singling her out. If only he knew what had been going on in her mind, what had brought her to Florida.

Jo shivered and tore her gaze away from his, murmuring, "Grace. Yes. Grace. We were talking about that."

Suddenly the word took on a deeper meaning. Grace, not unlike the kindness and attention Travis had shown her, came undeserved, and often when one least expected it.

The mishmash of thoughts in Jo's mind troubled her. Yet they also reassured her.

"You steady now?" Travis released his hand on her crutch while his other hand still hovered close at her back. "Don't want you taking a tumble and twisting that other ankle."

"Steady?" She glanced into his eyes and wanted to shout at him *No! How could I be steady with you standing right there, looking at me like...like you actually care who I am and what I do?* "I, uh, yes. I don't think I'm in any danger of twisting my other ankle."

"Yet," Kate piped up clearly for Travis's benefit. Then she turned to Vince and smiled. "But given the crazy expensive stilts she wears for shoes, I'd say that other ankle is living on borrowed time at best."

"Spoken like a regular grumpy old woman who picks out her shoes for comfort," Jo retorted, knowing Kate would actually take the remark as something of a compliment.

"Hey, careful who you call *old,* baby sister. Don't make me have to prove you wrong by announcing both our ages. I'll do it. Right here. Right now."

Jo was not fussy about her age. In a few years, she might feel differently. But for now she could not count herself among the fluttering females who felt the subject of age too delicate to discuss in front of "gentlemen callers." But she was the kind of woman who did not want personal information broadcast by her snarky big sister in front of a potential business contact. That was her only reason for backing down, she told herself, business.

"I amend my comment. You are not a grumpy old woman. You are merely a grumpy woman. Who thinks she is so smart for her choice in footwear but hasn't stopped to consider that her clunky, ugly lace-up granny shoes didn't protect her from getting hurt any more than my adorable heels did me."

"Huh?" Vince looked from Kate to Jo to Kate again.

"I followed it." Travis stood back and stole a peek at Jo's lone pink fluffy house shoe. "The most sensible shoe in the world won't save the foot of a scatter-brained wearer."

"That's ri—hey!" Under normal circumstance Jo might have taken a playful swing at his arm, but out of fear of making one wrong move and falling on her face—thereby proving him right about the scatter-brained jab—she simply stamped her crutch and narrowed her eyes. "I thought you brought me these as an act of Christian charity, not because you thought I was too loopy to get around without help, Mr., um, Pastor? Rever—"

"Travis."

"Travis." She settled on the name quite easily. Too easily perhaps, which made her feel the need to ask, "But in a professional capacity, I should call you…?"

"Travis." His tucked his hands into his pockets, making his untucked shirttail crumple up. His shoulders shifted. "Everybody just calls me Travis."

Vince snorted his opinion of that. "I know some people who have called you a few other things, when they think about you just walking away from the life every guy dreams of having."

Travis shrugged but did not try to justify his choice or the opinions of other men.

How could he let that go so readily? Why did he not want to claim and enjoy the fame his hard work and accomplishments had brought him? Jo could not understand it. "But you do have the title, right? You didn't get ordained off the Internet or something?"

"No, I didn't get ordained off the Internet." Travis chuckled. "I have my doctorate and am a dually ordained and recognized member of the clergy."

"B-but people just call you Travis?"

"Why not? That's my name."

"But you earned that title. It says something about you."

"Yes, I'm sure it does. But, really, the kind of work I do, it's not *about* me. It's about who I serve."

"Don't you want the respect you're owed? Don't you want..." What was she doing? She'd gotten completely off track. She'd made this small thing personal, showing a little too much about her own feelings and not showing enough respect for his. She repositioned her hands on the handles, blew a blast of air through her lips and laughed, just the right amount this time, as she looked into those wonderful brown eyes. "Don't you want to take me to get those groceries?"

"Groceries?" Travis said it as if it were some kind of foreign word to him. Or at least a foreign concept.

Jo glanced at Kate. "Didn't that caretaker lady send you here to help us get groceries?"

"Caretaker lady?" Again a look from Travis that said, *No hablo nonsense.*

"Moxie," Vince explained.

Jo leaned on the crutches. "Yeah, that's the one."

"No, I came of my own volition. Just to bring you these." Travis tore off a loose piece of the decorative crepe paper.

He'd come *just* for her. She'd known he'd come to do this for her. That had touched her. But to know he had come *just* for her? That level of personal attention from a stranger? That…frightened her.

Not because she thought there was anything icky or out of line about the gesture from Travis but because… because she couldn't imagine why anyone would do that for her.

"I talked with this Moxie over an hour ago." Kate picked up her cell phone and looked at it briefly. "The connection was bad but I know she got the message that we needed help and she was going to send someone."

"So if she didn't send Vince and she didn't send Travis, who did she send?" Jo wondered aloud. "And how long do we have to wait for him or her to show up?"

"Him," Travis said quietly, and pointedly, to Vince. "As to how long you may have to wait for him—"

"It's not important. Travis and I are both here now."

"I think it is important." Jo hopped around until she

could see clearly out of the still-open door. "We trusted this woman with our home, with our mother's finances. And now we have a hole in our porch and someone she hand selected who hasn't shown up? Those are not signs of a responsible caretaker."

"None of this is Moxie's fault." Vince stepped forward, the way a man steps in front of a cowering dog to prevent the cruel owner from hurting it.

And odd reaction, Jo thought. Some might say an overreaction, unless Vince had something personal at stake with this…this Moxie.

"How can you be sure?" Kate demanded.

"We both know Moxie. Everyone in town knows her. She's a great kid. Hard worker. If she said she'd do something, rest assured, she upheld *her* end of the deal."

Now Travis sounded a bit too protective of the girl. Why that mattered to Jo, or why it even registered with her at all, she could not say. After all, the only thing she had in mind for this man was a possible business proposition.

She looked at Travis's face, then at the crutches he had given her, muttering under her breath, "Just for me," then the firm reminder, "just business."

Kate looked at Jo. The unspoken agreement that passed between them pretty much said, *I won't force the issue if you won't.*

"I guess it could all be a simple misunderstanding," Kate conceded.

"You two did have a hard time hearing each other," Jo said.

"Bad signal," Kate explained to Vince.

He nodded, though the wariness had not left his expression.

"And didn't you say there was a lot of background noise?"

"Yeah. She was at—"

"Billy J's," both Travis and Vince said in almost the same breath.

"Yeah. Billy J's." Kate fell back against the cushions and sighed. "I was sort of hoping that whoever she sent over would come bearing a plate piled high with steaming, delicious seafood and sides hot off the buffet."

"Stop." Jo couldn't reach through the crutches to clutch her complaining stomach so she just leaned forward even more to show her suffering as she moaned, "You're killing me."

"Then let's go." Travis tugged a set of car keys from his pants pocket.

"Give me a chance to change my clothes," Jo said before the keys could so much as jangle. "Kate, tell Travis what you want us to bring you."

"Bring? Why can't I go with?" Kate asked.

Travis gave his keys a shake. "No reason we can't all go down there and fill up now."

Jo could think of a reason. She didn't *want* them all to go. She wanted this chance to talk to Travis about selling the house, about whom he knew and—-

"And then on the way back we can stop by the grocery store. You wouldn't mind that, would you, Vince?"

"That might put too much strain on Kate's foot," Jo

spoke up before Vince could. "She had surgery only ten days ago."

"And you sprained your ankle just yesterday." Kate scooted to the edge of the couch, ready to push herself up. "If you can do this, I can do this."

"Maybe I can't do it," Jo offered, grasping at anything to try to get her plan back on track.

"Don't worry." Travis moved to her side. "I'll catch you if you fall."

"You promise?" she whispered without meaning to.

"I promise," he whispered right back, sounding very sure.

Jo wanted to be alone with Travis now more than ever.

Which was why she knew she could not let that happen. Business and romance simply did not mix. That was how she had gotten herself into this awful mess to begin with.

She could not risk adding insult to…irrationality, again. She had to stick with her original plan, even if it meant changing those plans at a moment's notice.

"Let's do it, then," she said as she hurried to the back of the house so she could change into something a little less…slept in. "Let's all go to Billy J's together!"

Chapter Nine

A steady stream of people had flowed in to the Bait Shack Seafood Buffet since the doors had opened at eleven.

In.

But not out again.

Every available space along the two rows of highly varnished picnic-style tables that filled the center of the huge dining room was full. Every booth by every plate-glass, fogged-over window that lined the walls, too. Every stool sitting haphazardly around what had once been a bar and now was officially called the "drink station," where waitstaff grabbed sodas and specialty juice concoctions, was occupied.

There was a line at the buffet. A cluster of people waited for tables to come open—or to spot someone they knew well enough to squeeze in beside. A few folks who didn't have the patience for that had simply taken the chairs from the waiting-to-be-seated area and set themselves down wherever they could find a spot.

"Hey, put that chair back where you got it!" The infamous Billy J stabbed his finger, or what was left of it after an unfortunate fishing accident, at two of the buffet interlopers. "You tryin' to get them to come out here and close this place down?"

"If your bad cooking ain't made them do that yet, I doubt my sitting in this chair eating the stuff will," one of the robust fellows called back before popping a hush puppy into his mouth then puffing out his already round cheeks.

"'Sides, you ol' coot, you the one al'ays sayin' you gonna close this place down anyways. Why you care if we hurries things along a bit?" the scruffy fellow next to him threw in.

"Now, I ain't foolin', folks. Listen up, here." Billy J lifted both of his fleshy arms, which, coupled with the soft flab flapping under his chin, made him look a little like an old, proprietary pelican trying to scare scavenger crabs and gulls away from his catch.

He did it to draw attention to himself, of course. As if he needed to do anything to accomplish that.

Wherever he went, Billy J *commanded* attention. Bearded, wearing shirts roughly the size of and with the same subtle array of colors as a circus tent, and never without his white captain's hat with a parrot feather in the brim, he sort of naturally drew people's eyes. Children often mistook him for Santa Claus off on a tropical vacation. Adults often thought of him as some kind of mythical creature as well, they just never agreed on which one.

"I will close this place down," he barked. "You just watch me."

That was about the time everyone looked away.

See, they had heard this promise before.

"One more group of folks comes through that door before some of you overstuffed freeloaders leave, I won't have no choice." He gave them all what people called the not-so-evil eye. Nothing about Billy J. Weatherby could be construed as anything but benevolent. And everyone knew it.

Moxie most of all. She sighed and laughed at his antics.

He caught her gaze and smiled back. Not the big, goofy grin he bestowed on strangers and old friends alike. No, this smile was for Moxie alone and came with a twinkle in his blue eyes and a twist of his lips that said without a sound, *There's my girl.*

He often spoke about how the Lord had "rained down a double fistful of blessings" on him by bringing his Molly Christina into his undeserving life. And he never let her forget how much she meant to him.

Moxie smiled back at her dad, smiled then shook her head as if to let him know she didn't buy his claim about closing down any more than his customers did.

"Bam!" He slapped his meaty hands together as he made his way back toward the kitchen muttering—loudly. "Shut them doors and head off fishin' and leave y'all locked in here till Christmas."

"It's a fire-code violation," Moxie called to chair-sneaks. She jerked her thumb toward the place in the waiting area where they had taken the chairs, and the men grudgingly got up and relocated.

Someone called out to her, asking for more sweet tea.

A drawn-out creaking, rising then falling in pitch and loudness, made Moxie turn.

Yet another couple crowded in through the front doors.

In. But not out again.

Rain did that in Santa Sofia. Made people restless. Bored. Hungry.

"Hungry!" Moxie remembered her promise to get someone to go by the house to pick up a grocery list for the Cromwells and realized she hadn't followed up with Gentry to make sure he'd done it.

Surely he'd done it.

Moxie had explained that it was important. The women needed Gentry's help. And he was going to be in the area, anyway, helping Esperanza and the baby move in, right?

"Right?" The hardness she interjected into the single-syllable word struck her nerves like a hammer on a piano string. Gentry Merchant was a twenty-three-year-old man. Despite his father's insistence on treating him like a kid, he was a *man.* A man with a child to look after. Moxie had done the right thing in asking that man, okay, that *young* man, to do this small favor.

"Right?" she whispered.

He'd said he would.

No.

He'd listened to her lecture and then had said, "All right. All right."

Did that actually constitute a bargain struck between them? Knowing him, he would find a way to argue that he hadn't committed to helping the Cromwells at all, but had merely conceded that he should be helping his wife and child move into the rental cottage on Dream Away Bay Court.

She thought about calling the Cromwells back but she couldn't hear a thing in here, even on a good day when the reception was strong. Besides, they had her number. If Gentry hadn't shown up yet to collect a grocery list for them and run their errands, surely they would have called her back.

She thought of all the years they had not bothered to call or inquire in any significant way about the cottage. Clearly, follow-up was not their forte. Moxie chewed at her lower lip.

She tried to get a glimpse of the clock on the shelf behind the cashier's stand. She had to squint to fully concentrate on the kitschy Kit Kat clock ticking happily away amid the confusion of seashells, strings of paper lanterns and pink-flamingo lights, rubber fish, crabs, lobsters and starfish tacked to the wall.

"After two," she murmured as her gaze drifted downward to fix on the framed photo of herself as a baby.

A photo faded into shades of green, ruddy brown, violet and a sky bereft of blue, left stark white by the passage of time, it was the only memento of her life before Billy J and his wife had taken her in. She paused for a moment, as she always did when she became suddenly aware of the photo, to stare into the eyes of the woman holding her. Her aunt, or something like that. Her birth father hadn't given Billy J more details before he'd abandoned her.

"A relative." Billy J had told her to settle for that, then had added, "A person who knows where you was and who you was and still hadn't come a-lookin' for you. Why get all-fired fired up about that kind of connection anyways?"

Usually after a bluster like that, he'd begin to cough. And cough. And say he needed to see a doctor.

The man loved her. He needed her. He could not tolerate the idea that anything would ever interfere with that.

So Moxie let it drop.

Okay, she stopped asking or talking about it.

But every now and then it caught her unawares and she had to stare. Were the woman's eyes really that green or was that a trick of the aging ink colors? Had she really once loved Moxie as much as it looked like in the photo? Then why hadn't the woman tried to find her?

Moxie had certainly tried to find her birth family, but to no avail. She had so little information, after all. No paperwork from before the Weatherbys had adopted her. No memories to help guide her. Her birth father, who had died in an accident as a long-haul trucker when Moxie was three or four, had left nothing for them to go on—except this picture, which they had found in the glove compartment of his old pickup truck.

She had often studied the background of the photo for some hint as to where it might have been taken. But it just looked like an ordinary driveway in Anytown, America.

She could thank the old picture for one thing, though—it had inspired her to buy and restore her vintage truck. Somehow, she felt it gave her some connection to her past.

"Here's a full pitcher, boss." A young waiter pressed a plastic handle into her palm, ignoring the amber liquid the hasty action sent slopping everywhere.

Moxie shook the sweet tea from her hands and called after the kid as he retreated, "I am not the boss around here."

A statement that was greeted with a lot of jeers and laughter.

"I'm not!" she insisted.

And she wasn't. She had no interest in running the Bait Shack Seafood Buffet, even if she had the skills to do it…blindfolded, or at least with a patch over one eye…and a wooden peg leg that made her spill as much tea when she hopped from table to table as she poured when she got there. Her skills didn't matter. This was her father's domain. Her father's dream.

Not hers.

Not that Moxie had a dream. She looked again toward the cash register and the picture.

"I don't want to run this place," she said firmly again for anyone listening to hear.

She only worked here to help him out on days like today, when the rain brought people in like driftwood on the tide but didn't wash them out again.

Moxie pushed her way through the crowd, holding the pitcher of sweet tea almost above her head as she went.

"I hate the rain. Just hate it." Billy J met her in the middle of the main dining room, pushing along an empty high chair as he strode toward her.

"Rain can't be that bad, Mr. Weatherby. It sure is good for your business," the fresh-faced father who slid his baby into the seat joked as the old man abandoned the chair and pushed on past.

"Good for…?" A short cough cut him off. The old man's already ruddy cheeks puffed out and grew an even deeper shade of red.

"You've done it now." Moxie tried to get to her father before he exploded. It wasn't the customers Moxie feared for, but her father and the effects his getting all worked up would have on his precarious health.

"You'd think that, wouldn't you? And at first it does seem that way when so many folks stop by meaning just to dry off and grab a quick feed." Redder and redder. His eyes became dark and beady above his ballooning cheeks. He wasn't angry so much as on a roll—a roll that wasn't going to stop until it had flattened somebody! Another short cough, a deep breath, then he launched in again. "Then you look around and realize folks is hunkered down and settled in for the long haul."

"Daddy, calm down," she said, knowing she might as well tell it to the plastic hammerhead shark hanging just above them as to the hardheaded man in front of her.

"The lunch crowd becomes the dinner crowd." Cough. "The dinner crowd stays through the night, gabbing and grabbing fourth and fifth helpings of food for which they's only paid once." A flurry of coughs that quickly subsided.

"Daddy, it's an all-you-can-eat buffet, you have to expect this to happen from time to time."

"Look at 'em." He scowled. He coughed into his powerful fist, then raised his head and scolded, "Look at yourselves! All of you who tell yourselves you just come in outta the rain for a bite. Only bite that gets taken on days like these, gets taken is outta…" Cough, cough. "Outta…" More coughing before he rallied and said at last in one indignant huff, "…outta *my* profits."

He paused and took a good long look around. He closed one eye and put his fist on his hip, his lip snarled up on one side like some grizzled old sea dog. "I think some of you are taking advantage of my sweet and gentle nature."

The room greeted him with silence. For one second. Two.

Then all at once people began to whistle, to stomp their feet, to laugh, clap and cheer. Yes, the whole lot of them had seen Billy J's rabid fit of temper for exactly what it was. The greatest performance they were likely to see this evening.

He snorted. Held back a cough, then waved the

response away with one hand, part aw-shucks humility, part dismissive bravado.

"Why don't you go spread some of your sunny disposition around?" Moxie pressed the pitcher into his hand, tugged free the dish towel she had been wearing as an apron and threw it over his shoulder.

"The only sunny thing I want to spread around is the real thing. I hate the rain, I tell you." He started to stalk off, then paused to stop and refill a few glasses at the nearest table.

Old habits, Moxie thought. He could complain all he wanted but deep down, the man loved what he did. He knew everyone in town. He probably even knew the Cromwell sisters.

"Daddy?"

"Give me a warm afternoon and a room full of people so rarin' to get out into the open air that they fill their plates once, good and full, but they don't go back because they want to get fed and…"

A young boy lifted his glass.

Billy J refilled it with a smile and a wink then turned to face Moxie, all thunder and grump, concluding, "…and get out."

Moxie shook her head, laughing. "I'll believe you when you do as I've suggested over and over again. Fix up the place into a nice, quiet sit-down restaurant where patrons are not so inclined to gather and linger."

"The days of Santa Sofia supportin' a fancy eatin' spot are long over."

"Not fancy." She pointed toward a booth across the

room stuffed with mom, dad and two teenage boys. The table was piled high with plates and every glass among them empty. "Family."

"Family? You mean one of them places where they tack posters and neon signs on the walls?" He gestured toward his beloved rough-hewn paneled walls covered in fishing nets and cheap, tacky souvenirs. "Fill the menu with stuff that's more trend than taste and make the whole staff line up and sing a made-up song to customers on their birthdays over some stale brownie and topping concoction?"

"Something like that."

"Can't picture it."

Moxie couldn't, either. Oh, she could conjure up the image, thanks in part to her father's detailed description, but as for putting her father as the owner of such a place? Nope. He'd run Billy J's pretty much as it looked today since before she was born. The Bait Shack was part of this town, just like the weary Traveler's Wayside Chapel and the historied cottages on Dream Away Bay Court.

That thought snapped her back to her earlier concerns. "What do you know about the Cromwell sisters?"

"Who?" Suddenly the man who had ignored her silent direction to tend to the distant booth couldn't make his way across the room, and away from Moxie, fast enough.

So she just followed him. "The ones who own the cottage on Dream Away Bay Court?"

"Sisters?" He put his huge back to her and began

pouring tea into the glasses, even the ones that clearly should have had juice in them. "I thought there was only the one lady. Single mother. Dottie? Dorie?"

Moxie frowned. Her father never forgot names. "Dorothy."

"Dorothy Cromwell? Sounds right. Haven't spoken to her since you took over handling the cottage upkeep."

"Ten years? You haven't spoken to her for fifteen years?"

"That how long it's been? Hmm."

"Time flies when you're going fishing."

He chuckled, looked pensive then chuckled again. "But to answer your question, no, I don't know a thing about them sisters and ain't particularly interested in making a study of them."

The front door creaked again. Moxie turned just to see where the newest customers would find to wedge themselves in. And she couldn't help but smile. "So I guess it wouldn't interest you at all that the Cromwell sisters just walked in the door?"

"That's it! I've reached my limit!" Billy J spun around, his huge arms spread wide. "If you ain't paid yet, settle up now. If you ain't ate, fill a plate and take it home with ya. This is not a drill, people. I repeat, this is not a drill."

"Daddy? What are you doing?"

"I'm... I'm... I'm going fishing, sweetheart," he said softly. Then he gave her cheek a pat and began moving through the dining room, directing people to pay up and skedaddle. "Everybody out!" Billy J called again. "I'm closing this place down!"

Chapter Ten

"That felt like the longest day of my life." Jo slumped into a wooden kitchen chair with leatherette padding on the back and seat.

Travis stacked the leftovers from their meal in the refrigerator, moving the newly stocked milk, eggs, lunch meat, fruit and vegetables around to accommodate the large white to-go box from the Bait Shack Seafood Buffet.

Jo let out a sigh that was more like a moan, or a moan that was almost a sigh. Anyway, she made a sound that she thought summed up her weariness and frustration then went to work trying to elevate her throbbing ankle.

Before she could maneuver her leg more than a foot off the kitchen floor, Travis had slid his hand under her knee, gently bending and raising her leg as he scooted the other chair up to provide a resting place for her foot.

"Thanks." She nodded.

He nodded right back, saying nothing as he let his hand linger, lending support a moment longer than the situation really warranted.

"I'm okay," she said, finally able to straighten her leg, in a crooked, tense, ready-to-yank-it-out-of-harm's-way sort of way.

He stepped back.

She missed the warmth of his touch immediately. So she asked a totally pointless question, hoping to keep him from making some excuse and heading out the door. "Coffee?"

"Don't mind if I do. I didn't get any work done today for the chapel. I'll be up late playing catch-up."

Jo should have felt bad about that but she didn't. Whatever he had done, he had done because he wanted to. He was a grown man, after all.

After all, before all, and all in all!

A real live, grown-up, wonderful man, who was, at this moment, making coffee in the kitchen of the house she had heretofore only associated with childhood and childlike hopes, dreams and memories.

There had never been a man in this kitchen that she knew of. Oh, wait, Vince Merchant.

Jo glanced toward the front room where Kate had sacked out on the couch already. Poor Vince. They had barely gotten back from the buffet, after a side trip to the grocery, and eaten their considerably cooled-off meal when Kate couldn't endure it any longer. She'd had to have one of her pills.

Kate had fought off the pain as long as she could,

but with her tummy full for the first time today, the doctor in her had taken over and she'd taken her meds. And conked out within a half hour. Not that she'd made a lot of sense during the last fifteen minutes of that half hour. So that had given her less than fifteen minutes to talk to Vince after more than fifteen years apart.

Kate was going to kick herself in the morning.

A fate that Jo determined would not befall *her.* Travis was here. They were alone at last. She was going to make the most of it. By pumping him for information, of course.

She put one elbow on the table and watched Travis move about the kitchen gathering the goods he had just helped stash away. Filter, coffee, creamer, cups. His fingers barely fit into the drawer handles as he went looking for a spoon. When he found one, the size of his hand dwarfed the slender silver utensil.

Jo could have watched him all day. Um, night, she corrected, looking out at the crescent moon framed in the tiny cottage window. The day that had seemed almost endless was winding down.

She rested her chin in her hand, with her cool fingertips along her cheek. "Is every day this long down here?"

"Same as everywhere else. Twenty-four hours." He raised his head, not quite looking over his shoulder, then switched on the coffeemaker as he said, "Though Santa Sofia does move at a slower pace, if that's what you mean."

"Slower pace." Jo mulled the notion over. "Guess

that's why tourists and snowbirds have sought it out for so many years."

"Actually, I think that's probably why in recent years tourists especially have begun to avoid it."

"Avoid it?" Jo sat up. That news did not bode well for what she hoped to do here.

The coffeemaker gurgled and the dark, rich-smelling liquid began to drip, drip, drip into the carafe.

Despite her conviction that bathrooms and kitchens sold houses, she knew that locations set market values. They determined how much people would pay, brand spanking newly renovated kitchens and baths notwithstanding. A town fallen from favor with tourists meant a town with a depressed market.

Drip.

A depressed market meant desperate sellers.

Drip.

Desperate sellers meant…

Drip.

Desperate and depressed Realtors.

Jo thought of all the things she had seen over the years. Prices reduced below real value. Unrealistic demands from buyers. Gimmicks. Giveaways. Kissing her potential windfall goodbye.

Drip. Drip. Drip.

"But the snowbirds, they still come back to Santa Sofia, don't they?" That was the real market, she told herself.

Travis gripped the handle of the carafe for a moment and paused to make sure the process had finished up before he yanked it free and began pouring. "Every winter there are fewer and fewer of them."

One lone last drop fell from the filter bin. It hissed on the hot plate, followed by the odor of burned coffee.

"The bulk of them used to descend on the town right around Thanksgiving. Blue-haired ladies and baggy-pants men in big old cars loaded down with trunks and suitcases with just enough room to see out the back window, if a yappy little dog hadn't taken up residence there."

He held up the creamer to offer Jo some in her cup.

She shook her head.

He sloshed a slug of it into his own cup, not bothering to measure it out, and began to stir as he went on. "They flocked to the beach, swarmed the farmers' market and relied on locals to shepherd them around. It wouldn't be uncommon for great gaggles of them to cross paths all over town."

"You sound as if you're describing an actual migration of wild creatures instead of the yearly convergence of mostly elderly folks fleeing the cold climates of the Northern states."

"You ever seen these wild snowbirds?" he asked, waggling his dark eyebrows at her as he set a cup before her with a clunk.

"No," she confessed.

"Then stick around a while, why don't you? It's more fun than watching Animal Planet."

Stick around? Not in her plans. Jo gazed down into the coffee cup to keep from letting her expression give away too much as she asked, "But you said there still are people who have winter homes here, right?"

"Sure. Some pass properties down through families, well, like your family obviously has."

She took a sip. It was hot but that was easier to deal with that than the intensity of Travis's curious gaze when she failed to affirm his statement.

"And some come back year after year because they have made friends here. They don't see any reason to try to find a new place somewhere else."

"Doesn't anybody ever see a reason to find a new place here in Santa Sofia?"

"Oh, sure."

That got her to look up.

"We've seen quite a few people come back because they remember how it was here when they were kids. Again like—"

"Like me and Kate," she supplied the rest. Only she hadn't come back here to recapture a happier time. And almost told him so.

"That's a funny thing about this town, people can't get it out of their heads. They have some good times here and they want to come back. They spend enough time here and they never want to leave."

She pressed her lips together.

The room went quiet.

The quiet grew around them.

Then it seemed to press down on them, making them each squirm a little.

Say something, Jo's mind screamed. But she didn't

dare. The only things she could think to say were too personal. *Is that what happened to you? You came here and you never wanted to leave? Or are you talking about what you hope will happen with me? Do you really want me to stick around? What would you think of me if you knew I have no intention of doing that—and why I can't?*

Jo shifted in her chair.

The floorboards squeaked.

She should say something about needing her rest and calling it a night, she thought.

She took another sip of coffee then stared into the black liquid splashing against the inside of her cup.

Finally, Travis leaned back against the kitchen counter and folded his arms, not tightly, just laid them across his chest, his cup all but swallowed in one of his hands. "You had regular winter renters here for a long time, didn't you?"

"The McGreggors."

"The McGreggors," he echoed as if the name had been right on the tip of his tongue. As if he had known them almost as long as her family had.

Only he couldn't have.

"Mr. McGreggor died almost a decade ago and his wife, Ora, went to a nursing home a few years ago." Jo folded her arms to mirror him in a not-so-subtle way of letting him know she had seen right through his so-called natural charm right down to the oldest of sales tricks. "You were still in broadcasting around that time. So you couldn't possibly have known them."

"Ora and her only daughter stopped coming to Santa Sofia four years ago. But her last winter, she was an avid supporter of the Traveler's Wayside Chapel." He rested the heel of his empty hand next to the deep old soapstone sink. He crossed his long legs at the ankle and looked up then all around the room, leaving the impression he had stood in that very spot before, probably with Ora McGreggor. "Only knew her the one year and hadn't thought of her in a long, long while. Did you know her well?"

"No, not well." She tried to picture the couple and their child, or had they had a dog they'd treated like a child? Jo couldn't say for sure. "The McGreggors were some kind of distant relation on my mother's side. That's how they came to rent the cottage for the winter. They called her to ask about it or she called them to offer.... Something like that. It worked out because with them here every year, neither Kate nor Mom nor I felt anxious about the condition of the cottage, even after we stopped coming to it in the summers."

"Why did you stop coming here?"

Because Kate wanted to. And whatever Kate wanted, the whole family did.

That was the simple answer. But as is the way of most simple answers, it was, in fact, really very much more complex than that.

"We stopped coming because..." It wasn't any of his business, this business of how she felt unwanted even in her own family. Of how her wishes hadn't mattered when Kate the Great spoke. It wasn't his business and it wouldn't matter in the long run and…and the last thing she wanted to reveal to this man was how unimportant she felt to the most important people in her life.

Still, she had to say something, so she told a shorthand version of the story, one that cut her out of the mix entirely. Which struck her as painfully appropriate. "We stopped coming because Vince Merchant broke Kate's heart."

"Really?" He set his cup aside and straightened out of his casual slouch by the sink.

"Or she broke his. Honestly, I can't tell you which. Like I said, I was practically a kid."

"So they have a history?" He looked through the open doorway, past the dining room and into the front room where all that showed of Kate was her cast propped up on Mom's good table and one hand dangling out from a snarl of covers. "Definitely an undercurrent there this afternoon but I thought it had more to do with Vince trying to cover for his son not showing up with your groceries."

"Gentry? I can't believe he's old enough to drive."

"Oh, he's old enough to do a lot more than driving." Travis chose that moment to rub his eyes, effectively concealing any further clues to what he meant by that. "Anyway, very interesting about your sister and Vince. Curious to see how that plays out."

"Plays out?" It just now hit Jo. Vince and Kate. After all these years, they had crossed paths again. That totally changed everything. For the good or for the bad, they were not in the situation now that Jo had expected them to be in when she'd proposed this trip.

"Yeah, plays out. Who knows? They may rekindle the old flame."

He was right. Kate might want to stay here now more than ever.

"Or Kate might want to run out of here faster than a…a Scat-Kat-Katie."

"A what?"

"Nothing." Jo shook her head then frowned. "Weren't we talking about something interesting before we got onto why we stopped coming to the cottage?"

"Interesting? Not much. Just the McGreggors." He looked into his cup and chuckled. "Of course, that Ora was pretty interesting. A real pistol."

"Do you happen to know, was she the one responsible for all those tacky souvenirs in the rock garden?"

"She gave me the impression those had some connection to your family."

Jo frowned.

"Or I could have heard her wrong. I don't recall any details, just that even in that last winter down here that Ora was a force to be reckoned with. I'm glad you reminded me of her."

"I remind you of Ora?" There were worse things he could have said. Ora McGreggor had always gladly given reports on the old place's upkeep, from new cracks in the foundation to missing shingles on the roof—which she would have personally climbed out on to check on. Travis was right. Ora was a pistol, to say the very least.

"Talking to you reminded me about her," he corrected, then paused, stroked his chin and cocked his head. "But now that I see you in this light…"

"Hey!"

He chuckled. "Seriously. I liked that ol' gal. Liked her from the moment I saw her. She had a fire in her, you know? A fire to serve the Lord as well as her fellow man."

Jo wanted to ask why that would possibly remind him of her but she couldn't bring herself to tarnish Travis's memory of Ora, or his kind opinion of Jo.

So it wasn't a trick. The man was, indeed, naturally charming. He remembered people's names and things about them, even ones he hadn't known long or well. People mattered to him. But did some people matter to him more than others?

Jo gazed up at him for the first time in several minutes.

He met her gaze. "So, did you know any of your other renters?"

She unwound her rigid arms and pressed her shoulders back, lacing her fingers together in her lap.

Cute. Kind. No tricks. If the man were a house, she could sell time shares in him for every week of the year, even in a market like Santa Sofia.

"Jo?"

"Hmm?"

"I asked you a question."

"Did I answer?" Her head cocked to one side. She could sell time shares in him, but why would she want to share a guy like that with anyone?

"No, you *didn't* answer."

"What?"

"My question." He set his coffee cup down.

Jo startled. She blinked. She replayed the conversation, or lack of one, in her mind. She probably blushed. She certainly stammered.

She had let this get completely beyond her control and she had to rein it in, get it back on track, focus on her goal. And to do it now while she still had Travis all to herself.

"Did you know any of your other renters?" he asked, for at least the second time.

"Um, no. Maybe. I don't know. Mom might have. Or Kate. Like I said, I stopped coming here the summer after I graduated from high school, so I was a kid, mostly." She tried to prevent her imagination from dwelling on the possibilities—*Travis all to herself.* Just to stare at the guy. Listen to his voice.

Ply him for information. An edict from an earlier ambition wedged its way in through her flustered confusion.

"But my mother probably got to know them. Or made a point of *not* knowing them. You never know when *who* you know and *what* you *don't* know will come in handy, after all. You know what I mean?"

He gave her a patently fake scowl and shook his head. "No, I don't."

She laughed, yes a bit more than she should have. But then, it came easily now, here, with him. And before she could overthink that, she seized control of the situation again. "So, you say there is a younger element looking to buy homes in the Santa Sofia area?"

"Did I say that?" He appeared genuinely puzzled.

"You said people who had come here as kids were returning now. Wanting to give their own children the same kind of happy memories, I suppose?" Suppose nothing. She was hoping like mad this was the case. Nostalgia sold like crazy. And if ever there was a house packed to the rafters with nostalgia—and maybe a little crazy—this was it.

"Yeah. I guess. Some. We had a few families like that attending services at the chapel this past summer."

"Title holders or lessees?"

"Methodists, I believe."

Jo huffed. "What I was driving at—"

"I know what you were driving at." He held his hand up. "Jo, don't kid yourself. I know what you're up to here."

In other words, while she had sat there quietly sizing him up and fighting the urge to sit, stare and perhaps drool over him, he'd done the same with her. Only he didn't sound as enthralled with the conclusions he had reached. She adjusted her ankle, clenching her jaw against the renewed rush of pain that caused and asked, "Up to? You make me sound so sneaky."

"Aren't you?" He held his finger and thumb close together, adding, "Little bit?"

How do you answer a question with the truth when the truth is the last thing you want somebody to learn about you? Jo sat there, sulking and silent.

He leaned forward just enough to chuck her under the chin then spell it all out for her. "You're obviously trying to weasel information out of me. And I suspect, given the opportunity, you'd take it a step further and ask me who I know who might want to buy a place like, oh, say *this* very house."

Jo pursed her lips. She wanted to say something. But she was unable to deny his keen observation, and given his tone, unwilling to concede his implication. *Sneaky? Weasel?*

"Admit it, Jo. If I hadn't stopped you just now, you'd have followed the line of questioning just as I said."

She tipped her head to, sort of, acquiesce without actually owning up to anything.

"And when I told you the truth, that I'm just a nobody servant of God who has an efficiency apartment over the lone Sunday-school classroom in a church-owned sliver of Santa Sofia beachfront property, you'd have taken another tack. Probably asked me if the chapel had ever considered shelling out for a parsonage for me. Or if they had a program to buy homes for widows and orphans."

He didn't sound angry as he said it, just earnest.

And maybe a little bit hurt.

"So?" he asked.

"So?" She wondered what, exactly, he expected of her. "You want me to stop you right there and deny it all?"

"Quite the contrary." He pulled the chair out across from her, hesitated, then sank into it. Not formal like a minister about to enter into a counseling session but kind of lazy-like lounging, legs sprawled and hands behind his head, like a friend open and ready to listen. "I want you to spill it all. If *you* want to."

"Spill?"

"Tell me what's going on. What you're really up to and why. And most of all, how can I help?"

"Help? A minute ago you sounded as if you wanted to do anything but help me sell this house."

"Not help you sell it. Help you do the right thing, even if that includes selling it."

"Fair enough." Not that she had asked him for that kind of help or that measure of fairness. But here they sat. They had sized one another up and were still here, able to meet one another's gaze.

Finally it was his eyes that made her do it. Spill it all. Confess. Say simply, "I'm in a fix."

"A fix?"

"A pickle." She tried again.

"A pickle?"

"Is there an echo in here?" It was a cornball old gag but it worked to break the tension in the room.

Travis dropped his constant, caring gaze long enough for Jo to catch her breath and regroup.

She looked out into the front room.

Kate moaned, moved slightly, then fell back into her soft, buzzing snore-breath-snore pattern.

Jo swallowed to clear her throat, then raised her eyes to Travis and began again. "I made a mistake."

"And?"

She took a deep breath, allowing her shoulders to rise and fall before she summed it up succinctly. "And now I have to fix it."

With his brow lined in concern, he studied her a moment then asked, "Selling your family's summer cottage will fix it?"

"Fix the financial part of it."

"Ahh. Debt." His expression relaxed.

"Not just debt. Not buying too many expensive shoes or unpaid student loans, Travis. This is business debt."

"Business debt is worse?"

"Business debt comes with strings." In her case, yards and yards of string. Knotted up and tangled with years of rock-bottom self-esteem and dreams of a girl who'd never felt wanted. "And there are other people involved. There are consequences that go beyond whatever problems it raises for me."

"Jo, whatever it is, you can just say it outright to me."

She believed his words, so she told him. "There's a man involved."

"A man?" He tipped the chair up on two legs, tilting his head back to stare at the ceiling. "A...lover?"

"No! I mean, a... We're not... I don't... Not that he hasn't made overtures...but I couldn't. Not until..."

"Until?"

She liked this man too much to sit here and blurt out the *M* word—*marriage*—in front of him. Sure, he was a minister and he would understand, laud her even. But forever after he also would not be able to look at her without thinking, *That's the girl who just wants to get married.* That kind of message sent men running in the opposite direction.

Still, she couldn't lie to him. So she decided, in one blinding, rash moment, to tell him the greater truth behind her choice. "I led him on, just a little, because I knew I wasn't going to just fall into bed with him and…and I wanted him to like me."

The chair legs came down hard on the old floor.

Jo braced herself for the ridicule she felt was due her.

"Jo. I'd tell you that you should know better but…"

"But you don't know me, Travis. I'm the girl that nobody ever wanted. Me. Just for myself."

"I find that very hard to believe."

She did not respond to his comment, just forged on with her story. "So when Paul Powers singled me out at work and made a big deal about grooming me for partnership, I felt special for the first time in my life."

"Because he put the moves on you?"

"Because he saw something in me that nobody else ever bothered to notice—that I was there!"

"Trust me on this, Jo. He was not the first person, nor will he be the last, to notice you are here."

"Was that a compliment? I honestly can't tell."

He just shook his head. "And then?"

"Then ninety days ago—"

"Ninety days?" He seemed amused at the exactness of her recollection.

"Roughly ninety days. In just under three weeks it

will be ninety days. I know that because it was part of a contract negotiation."

"You two had a contract?"

Jo nodded. "For a flip."

"A what?"

"A flip. You know when you buy a broken-down house cheap, go in and fix it up and resell it before the first payment is due and make a bundle."

"Ahh."

"Well, I'd done it a few times and had some really good outcomes." Jo paused to relive the waves of fear she had felt when she'd signed those contracts, the thrill of the chase to get the work done in time, the pride she felt at seeing her bank account rise with each sale. And how, when Paul Powers had noticed her success and picked her as his protégé, she had finally felt as if she mattered to someone. "So Paul came to me with this opportunity. High risk, but potential for a major payoff."

"Or a major loss."

She conceded as much with a single nod. "The deal is, I sank everything I had into this project, and it hasn't been enough."

"Why didn't you go to your boss to help you out?"

"I did. He said I'd made my bed and I could just lie in it. He wanted no part of it, or me." Tears filled Jo's eyes. She tipped her head back to keep them from falling onto her cheeks. The humiliation of Paul Powers's reaction still stung all these weeks and all these miles away.

Though she could not see him, she heard Travis

shifting his weight. She imagined him gritting his teeth at her girlish insecurity. She felt so ashamed.

"Jo?"

"What?" She still could not look at him.

"If the house you're flipping and your financial problems are both in Atlanta—" he spoke with a quiet intensity that showed kindness if not sympathy as he finished his question "—why are *you* in Santa Sofia?"

She dropped her hands onto the table, thought for a moment, then admitted, freely, "Because this is where I believe my answers lie."

"Oh, really?" He slipped his hands from behind his head and rested them on the table, near hers.

"When she retired, Mom put Kate and me on the deed. At first she did it for inheritance and estate reasons then later—when the house stopped being rented—"

"After they built the highway project," Travis interjected.

"Yes, that makes sense. That's what precipitated it, only we no longer had Ora down here to tell us that. Anyway, when the rental money wasn't paying for her vacations anymore, Mom came to think of this house as our family nest egg and told us it was here for all of us to use as we saw fit."

"And you see fit to cash in on it and hope to find a way to make them see things your way?"

"Don't make it sound so ugly. This is how the real world operates."

"Don't lecture me on how the real world operates. I know it all too well. I get what it means to live from deal to deal, to make more money than you deserve then spend it as if it were your birthright to live like Solomon. I know how scary it can be to be the one everyone is looking at, some waiting for you to do greater things. And just as many or more expecting you to fail."

"Not fail so much as not try," she told him. "To flounder and keep floundering until everyone gives up on you. That's my fear. That I will always live down to everyone's lowest expectations of me."

He touched her fingertips, not quite taking her hand in his. "I know the fear and angst the 'real world' can deliver. I also know there is a love that changes all that, a perfect love that casts out fear."

"You're quoting scripture?"

"First John 4:18."

"You have the whole Bible memorized?"

"Nope." He shook his head. "But I *like* First John, chapter four."

"Hmm." She thought about asking him to quote more but knew it wouldn't throw him off track. He'd only find a way to use the Word to bring it all back to doing the right thing. She moved her hands away from his and dropped her gaze. "This isn't my spiritual life, Travis. This is business."

"You honestly think you can separate the two?"

"It's not that easy. I don't have a lot of options."

"You always have options. You always have choices."

The only other option Jo had, besides getting a

windfall from selling the cottage, was to go back to Georgia and sell the flip house as is, under value. For that, she would be rewarded with a mountain of debt and her reputation as a go-getter Realtor thrown down a dark hole.

But she would be free. Free of the bitterness. Free of the neediness. Free of Paul Powers. Free to start over.

"I'll think about that," she finally said.

"And if you ever need anyone to talk to about it—"

She knew he meant that. "Saying thank you doesn't seem like enough."

"It's enough." He pushed his chair back, a signal he was preparing to leave.

He would leave and what then? Jo didn't know. She did know that they only had this moment and she did not want to waste it. "I wish I could kiss you."

He froze, his eyes searching hers for a moment before he said, "You can."

If she'd known it would be that easy, she'd have asked it earlier. "Yeah?"

"On the cheek." He grinned.

"That's all?"

"For now, yes."

For now? Meaning at some point in the future...? Jo didn't voice that question, and Travis went on to explain.

"We have to set boundaries, Jo. I am not going to court temptation."

She'd already told him her greatest fear and he hadn't laughed. She'd asked for a kiss and he'd said *yes* and *for now* not *no way, never.* So she decided to take one more risk. "What about me?"

"I don't want to put you in the path of temptation, either."

"No, you said you wouldn't court temptation…"

He didn't catch on.

"So I said, what about me?"

"You mean?"

"Would you ever consider courting me?"

"We just met."

Jo couldn't believe her boldness. But she'd never met a man like Travis and deep down, she wondered if maybe she was just looking for a reason to stay in Santa Sofia. "So?"

He bent down, putting his face before hers, and touched her cheek.

She brushed the lightest of kisses over the tanned, whisker-stubbled skin.

He smiled and turned to face her, nose to nose.

His gaze sank into hers.

Jo caught her breath.

"Gnn-aaaa-rrr-pp." Kate let out a big ol' pig-snuffling-through-a-trash-trough kind of snore.

Both of them startled, then broke into laughter.

"So much for the path of temptation," she whispered.

"I think you have enough to deal with without adding in stolen kisses and starting a relationship with someone you plan to leave behind in a matter of weeks."

Jo knew he was right. But as she watched him walk out the back door, she couldn't help but wonder, if she stayed off the path of temptation, what path would the Lord lead her to instead?

Back to Georgia? Or maybe just off to the hardware store to get the goods to start fixing this place up to sell?

Chapter Eleven

Kate tossed the pencil and the pad with her notes on it onto the coffee table. "Done and done."

She leaned on her cane. Though exhausted, she just couldn't face another minute sitting on that lumpy floral couch.

Then don't sit there on your face, she could just hear Jo teasing.

Jo could afford to tease because her ankle had gotten strong enough that she felt up to getting out and able to drive her car. Except for the fairly physically and socially uncomfortable trip to Billy J's and a quick stop off at the grocery store, Kate had stayed right here in this house.

From her vantage point in the front room, she took a moment to do a 360-degree look-see around her.

Jo had asked her, after she saw to a few housekeeping duties, to look around the place and write down her first impressions. In one column Jo had instructed her to note what looked outdated, what seemed dingy, what appeared downright disastrous. In the next column, a list of the high points, paying particular attention to things with strong emotional appeal.

"Strong points," she'd said. Kate suspected her sister had wanted to say *selling points.* "Tell me what you find compelling about the place. What makes it inviting or cozy."

It all looked that way to Kate. Inviting. Outdated. Compelling. Emotional. Cozy. Disastrous.

"You know…" she whispered. She looked toward the window that framed their view of the mystery house and echoed the last word she had written on the strong point side of the list. "Home."

But it was *not* her home. Not likely it ever would be, especially not if Jo carried out her plan. The plan she thought she had so cleverly concealed from everyone. In reality she might as well have hammered a For Sale sign in the yard the minute they'd driven up. She wanted, very, very much, to get rid of the old place.

And Kate might have gladly gone along with that plan earlier. A few days ago, all the way back to ten minutes after her mother had announced she wanted to move down here. If Jo had just asked, Kate would have gotten onboard. What was here for them but a lot of frustration?

But today?

She just wasn't ready to let go.

Kate sighed then ran her hand through her hair, snagging a few strands between her fingers where she must not have washed away all the stickiness from the work she had done earlier.

Before Jo had left this morning to "run errands," she had set out some light housekeeping for Kate to do, in the thinly veiled guise of giving her out-of-necessity suddenly sedentary sister some much needed exercise. Kate had protested. Pleaded infirmity. Even insanity—saying that staying in the house had driven her batty and begging her sister to let her tag along just to get outside and feel the sun on her face.

"You were outside yesterday," Jo had said flatly.

"I'm like a delicate flower. I need sunshine and fresh air, every day."

"You need to move around in here where it's safe," Jo had argued. "Get your strength back before you venture out too much. There'll be time for going out after you do your chores."

"Thank you very much, wicked thinks-she's-in-charge-because-she-can-take-the-steps sister." Kate had harrumphed, going so far as to lie back on the couch in a picture of overwrought drama to prove the depths of her unhappiness about her circumstances. "Easy for you to say stay put and get better. Your Prince Charming already showed up to offer his admiration and assistance. I'm still waiting for mine."

"Oh, yours showed up all right. Don't blame me that when he did, you fell into a hole, demanded he feed you greasy fish then fell asleep and snored right in his face." She'd grabbed her keys and limped off toward the door, carrying her crutches under her arms in case she needed them for walking any distance.

Leaving "Kate-erella" behind to ponder all that as she labored away helping to get the cottage ready for whatever next step Jo had in mind. Alone. With her thoughts. With her, well, they weren't quite hopes and dreams so much as what-ifs and if-onlys.

Kate hated what-ifs and if-onlys.

Now she was stuck with them. In a place where she could visualize everything from her parents arguing on the front lawn the first time they'd all come here to the way Vince Merchant had looked standing on the front porch yesterday.

If only her father had stayed, how would things be different? Would her parents have found a way to work things out? Or at the very least, would her father not have whisked away the youngest of the sisters? How would that have changed Kate? Would she have stayed with Vince all those years ago?

It all connected in her mind, in her experiences and choices, in the very way she saw herself and everyone she loved. Marriages do not always work out. Children are hurt. Despite God's design, people do bad things. If you care too much for someone, you make yourself vulnerable to loss.

Those kinds of thoughts had driven her from place to place, job to job. They had kept her distant from her mother and sister, and cost her the love and commitment of a good man. And his son.

"Gentry," she murmured and could see that big-eyed already fragile kid looking up at her and saying the words that had made her break her engagement.

"Quasi-engagement?" She crinkled her nose. Made it sound as if she were marrying the Hunchback of Notre Dame. She gazed at her left hand. Vince had never put a ring there. He'd bought one and offered it to her. Gotten down on one knee on a moonlit night on the beach.

Kate sighed and then took in a quick breath, the way her patients did when she hit a sore spot in the course of her exam. He'd asked her to wait to wear the ring until he had told Gentry about it. She had agreed more to buy herself time than out of concern for the child.

She had been fresh out of college, practically a kid herself, and if she married Vince, after just four months together, she would become the child's mother. Responsible for his upbringing, his care, his *safety.* She, who had already failed her sister by not telling anyone when she'd heard her father leaving.

She had never slipped that ring on. Never let Vince tell Gentry about their plans because Kate knew in her heart that people have so very little real control over the way their lives turn out. That was why the wise ones rested their faith in God and surrendered to His will.

That was a wisdom and grace she had not possessed back then.

So, Gentry was the real reason she had run away from Vince, though she could never tell anyone that, least of all Vince himself. Not that she would have the chance to tell Vince anything, nor should she expect it, but…*if only…*

"Enough!" She'd forced the unproductive thinking to the side and fixed her attention on the work before her.

Much to her surprise, it had turned out that she actually enjoyed her time alone in the old cottage. Puttering. Muttering to herself. Going through things. Even throwing things away had a cathartic effect.

In a strange way, doing all that had presented Kate with the opportunity to do something she hadn't done in a very long while.

Nothing.

Not the sitting around staring into space or lying about, waking up just long enough to complain about the abysmal quality of offerings on television. But a wonderful, lose yourself in the moment and the memories of moments gone by kind of nothing that made the hours sail, cleared the cobwebs from her head and lifted up her heart.

And during it all she had never once felt trapped or had to squelch the urge to get away. Instead of that low undercurrent that constantly buzzed in her ear telling her she should be someplace else, she just let herself be.

"That alone had made the trip down here worth the trouble," she murmured, imagining what she might tell people about the whole adventure once she returned to the angst and pressure of her "real" life.

That alone? Oh, brother! Hearing the sappy sentiment out loud made her cringe. Nobody who knew her would ever buy that. Spending the day doing busy work a justification enough for her burst of goodwill today? For her renewed affection for and sense of belonging in a crummy little cottage she had ignored for over sixteen years? For the fact that she had begun to think ahead to when she could return to Santa Sofia for another visit instead of plotting how she could run away and never look back?

"What is wrong with me?" Kate glanced down at the pad and pencil she had just tossed aside.

Grabbing them up and desperate to avoid that couch, she turned toward the dining room. But from there she couldn't see the mystery house.

Not that she cared one whit about the mystery house, but who knew when a prince or handyman in a pickup truck might come riding along and park in its drive?

She glanced around and her gaze fell on the door of the enclosed stairway. They had yet to venture up there because Kate had deemed neither of them ready to do stairs without an able-bodied bystander there to help.

Of course by "neither one of them" she had meant Jo.

Kate herself was always ready, willing and able to take on anything. They didn't call her Capable Kate for nothing.

"Maybe they just call me Capable Kate because Unrealistic, doesn't-know-her-own-limits, so-pigheaded-she-rushes-in-where-wise-men-fear-to-tread Kate takes so long to say they knew I'd have time to take a swing at them before they got it all out." Kate collapsed onto a step halfway up the stairs. She stretched her leg to place her mending foot on the step below where she sat, giving her cast support. She laid her head against the railing.

She had come trying to find just the right spot to sprawl out and make out her list of everything that was wrong with her, and whatever few things she could think of that were right. "First thing on the wrong list…too stubborn for my own good."

She didn't actually write it. Which probably should have been the second thing on that list: too proud to admit even a simple human flaw.

She winced and adjusted her foot to try to get more comfortable. A glance up over her shoulder to the remaining steps, and knowing that the comfort of her old room waited there for her, made her grit her teeth.

She could scoot her way up.

One step at a time.

Once up there she could go through things, look around. Who knew what she might find? If she could do all that before Jo got back and started in with whatever she wanted to do with the place, it would be as though Kate had proprietary claim on the whole of the cottage. Like a mountain climber planting a flag.

Hers.

Kate blinked.

Hers?

Why?

Just to keep Jo from… What? *Winning?*

No, there was more to it than that. Kate wanted the cottage to be more hers than Jo's. Even more hers than her mother's. She had not felt that way until she'd spent the day here, thinking, dreaming. Hoping for…

"Home," she said again.

And besides, if she could make her way to her old room, she could look out over the cul-de-sac at the mystery house and spy on anyone who came over there today.

She looked down at the list.

Had she said she failed to admit *a* human flaw?

Strike that.

Many flaws.

Starting with not being honest, even with herself. She wanted the family to retain ownership of the house because it gave her a reason to see Vince. This place around her did not feel so much like home as it represented what she had lived her whole life trying to avoid—hope.

Hope for a full life. Hope for a healed family. Hope of finding love without the constant fear of loss nagging at her, driving her to move on before she made another mistake.

"Many, many flaws," she murmured, her eyes on the paper. How much sweeter, she thought, was it that no matter how long that list of flaws and things that were wrong with her, they would be balanced out by a single concept? Salvation.

She would not be measured, ultimately, by the sum of her sins but by the magnitude of God's grace. People who did not share her faith might not understand, but to a person like Kate, who'd lived so long in fear and sadness, that promise was the only thing she had ever felt she could fully depend upon.

What had passed was past. She could not change it.

But she could accept her role in it and work with all her heart to do better from now on.

She picked up the pad and held it to her chest as she took a moment for a silent prayer of gratitude.

Then with the word *amen* still humming on her lips, she sniffled and tried to get herself in a position to move. Up or down, she hadn't decided but she didn't want to be stuck sitting here when—

Wham! The back door slammed shut.

"Lousy timing," she grumbled, envisioning yet another fault on the already heavily weighted list. Then, after a deep breath, she used her cane to prod the stairway door fully open so she could call, "Jo, is that you?"

"Where are you, Kate?" The rustle of plastic bags. The thump and bump of objects hitting the kitchen table. The clunk, swoosh, clunk of Jo moving with new confidence using the borrowed crutches preceded her sister peeking around the corner of the door frame and staring at her. "Who were you hoping it would be? Oh, let me guess, Prince Charming?"

Kate winced at the very thought of Vince barging in and finding her not at her best. "Last night, did I just fall asleep or did I drool, too?"

"Vince left before the drooling began."

"Good."

"And only a few minutes *after* the snoring started."

Kate groaned.

"What are you doing in here? I thought we agreed that we'd wait to try the steps when we both felt up to it."

"I felt up to it enough for both of us."

"Obviously you were only half-right." Jo gave a direct deadpan look to where Kate had landed on the stairwell. "Did you get any rest at all while I was gone?"

"Yep."

"Yep? No complaint about being stranded here wanting to get out and about?"

"Nope."

"Whatever meds you are on, your doctor should have prescribed them years ago."

"If only I'd had the foresight to jump in front of Mom's tire sooner." Kate smacked the pad into her sister's palm.

"Oh, good, you did your assignment."

"All of my assignments, including your real dirty work." Kate watched to see if her sister picked up on the double entendre.

"Kitchen and bathroom?" Jo said without giving any evidence that she suspected what Kate was suspecting about her wanting to sell the cottage.

"Not only did I get everything done you asked, I actually enjoyed doing it."

"You enjoyed peeling up dirty old shelf paper from the kitchen cabinets and bathroom linen closet?"

"It gave me a sense of purpose and accomplishment."

"Uh-huh."

"It kept me from dwelling on my problems."

"Oh?" Jo seemed more than a little intrigued by that prospect.

"Okay. First I dwelled, um, dwelt?" Kate scrunched her eyes into narrow slits then bunched up her lips as she rifled back through years of English grammar rules then finally gave up and forged on. "At first I did sulk and brood and worry a little. Then I decided to let it go and just do the work."

"Just like that?"

"Sure." Kate continued with a smirky smile, gesturing to demonstrate what she had done all morning, "And besides, I really liked the sound the paper made when it came up in one great big sheet. *Schlerrrrrrp!*"

Jo shook her head, her soft blond hair catching the afternoon light from the front-room window, as it swept along her neck, barely brushing her shoulders. "Tell me again how that's not the pills talking."

"Do you know how long it's been since I spent the day working with my hands without the responsibility of dealing with other people? Managing staff? Working with patients? Fielding pharmaceutical reps? Juggling accounts payable?"

"Um, change that to contractors, sellers, buyers and mortgage lenders, and you have *my* usual day."

Always a competition with them.

Well, not today. Today, Kate would not try to one-up her sister. Both of their jobs had aggravations, after all. Kate's just happened to be more important, more pressing, more, well, everything. Which was why she had enjoyed the contrast of this day so much. "Then maybe you can understand how doing this today gave me attainable goals, and when it was over I felt something I haven't felt in a long time."

"Stiff? Sore?" Jo stretched her arms up then put her

hand to the small of her back. "So glad you went to med school so you don't have to do that unless you choose to?"

Kate considered the mere mention of med school a sort of mini-coup in her favor, so she smiled even more broadly when she gave her sister the real answer. "Content."

"Content? Working around the cottage made you content?" Jo crossed her arms over her white cotton shirt and clucked her tongue. "Well, if you liked today's to-do list, you are going to love tomorrow's."

"Let me guess. New shelf paper?" Kate rubbed her hands together.

Jo nodded. "And that is just the beginning."

"The beginning of what?" Kate wondered.

But before Jo could elaborate, and Kate had no illusions that her sister would not, indeed, elaborate, Kate's cell phone blasted out her familiar ring tone.

"It's Mom," Jo warned, raising her own phone to indicate she'd just gotten a call from their mother as well.

"Dare I answer?" Kate wondered, knowing that when she didn't get an answer, her mom would try again immediately to give her time to limp to the phone.

"I didn't."

Kate pushed herself up to her feet, clinging to the railing for stability. "You think that's wise to ignore her like that?"

"You'd rather talk to her and try to sidestep her inevitable questions about when she can come down here to stay?"

"Stay?" Kate glanced at the pad in Jo's hand. For one fleeting instant, she thought of grabbing it back and writing in bold letters on the disastrous side of the lists—*MOM*.

She loved her mother but the three of them in a two-bedroom cottage with the two sisters even slightly incapacitated? Those old instincts to run away welled up in Kate again.

"You want to tell her about my ankle? Or your falling through her front porch? How about we regale her with the tale of how we all got thrown out of Billy J's?"

But Kate couldn't run. "Technically we didn't get thrown out so much as we didn't get to stay and eat our food there."

"Mom is not big on technicalities. She hears what we've been through already, what do you suppose she will want to do?"

"Rush down here to the rescue." That meant they couldn't talk to her until they had some really positive things to say. "I don't feel right about just not taking Mom's calls."

The cell phone went silent.

"Oh, but your doctor, the man charged with keeping you from messing your foot up forever? Him you can avoid with not so much as a twinge of conscience?"

"People who live in glass houses…"

Jo scowled at Kate, practically daring her to come up with an applicable finish to that hasty accusation.

"Shouldn't throw cell phones?" Kate gave a one-shouldered shrug.

Her phone rang again, just as she knew it would.

"What about it, Kate? You going to throw your cell phone?"

"Yes. Out a window." She made her way down the stairs. "What are you going to do?"

"I am going to be using my phone to make calls." Jo helped her make the transition from the last wooden step to the carpet, where her cast could get more traction.

"Calls to who?" She moved more quickly now, heading toward the couch.

Jo reached into her pocket and produced a stack of multicolored business cards. She fanned them before Kate like a seasoned poker player glorying in her hand.

"Where did you get those? And what are they?"

"Stopped into a real-estate office, friend of a friend type of deal."

Kate pulled up short.

"Where I went to get references for carpenters and painters and tile layers and plumbers," she read the professions off one by one. "For fixing up the place."

"Toward what end?"

Jo clamped her mouth shut tight.

"You just made it clear you don't want Mom coming down here. So why the big rush to fix the place up, Jo?"

"Be sweet to me, Kate. I'm trying to do a good thing, here."

"I bet you are. But a good thing for who?" If Jo had not pulled out their mom's favorite pouting plea to "be sweet," Kate might have conceded that it was a good idea to fix the place up, no matter what the motivation behind it. But the admonition dragged across her nerves and put her on high alert. For this family, "be sweet" really meant "be careful" because something big was headed right at you. "I thought we wanted to keep things honest between us, Jo. Why don't you start by admitting outright that you want to pretty up this place so you can put it on the market as soon as possible?"

"Do I?" Jo's expression went dark.

Kate sensed genuine conflict in her sister. "Don't you?"

"I don't… I don't know anymore." She leaned one shoulder against the door frame at the bottom of the stairs and looked around. "I thought I did. There. It's out. I wanted to sell this place. I *need* to sell this place. And I justified that by telling myself that my needs were bigger than Mom's whim about living here. But now?"

"Now you've gotten a little bit of a whim yourself, huh?"

Jo looked at the floor. She shifted her weight, using the crutches Travis had given her for renewed support.

"Okay, so we fix the place up some." Kate shut her eyes, hardly believing what she was saying. "How do you propose we would pay for that? How are we going to afford all these fellows on these fancy business cards?"

Jo flicked through them all, humming cheerily as she did.

"Jo?" If there was a bigger red flag in their family than "be sweet," cheeriness was it! Kate braced herself. "You've got an idea, don't you, Jo?"

Chapter Twelve

"He's your ex-boyfriend. Why drag me into this juvenile scheme?" Jo spoke in a whisper so sharp and rushed it reduced her vowels to near silence and made the consonants practically pop and hiss.

"Stop whining." Kate got into position and stretched her hand up toward the doorbell. She could just…almost…reach. "You said you thought you saw him over here. You agreed we need to be good neighbors. This was your idea, after all."

Jo's vivid green eyes all but bugged out of her head. "Coming across the street to see if Vince would consider helping us fix up the cottage was my idea."

Kate strained every muscle in her body, trying to give herself that extra oomph to realize her goal.

"But this?" Knee bent and standing on her good foot, Jo gestured with her crutches, holding them both straight out to indicate pretty much everything taking place on the front porch of the mystery house at the moment.

"Great idea. Hand me your crutch, I need the extension."

Jo obliged, slapping the aluminum into Kate's open palm with a sound that smacked of sarcasm. "*This* is all you, big sister."

Kate scrunched down low to approximate where she planned to be and lifted the ungainly crutch. "If I can just reach the doorbell."

"And then what do *I* do? I can't exactly run for it."

"Hide." Wasn't it obvious what Jo needed to do? Especially given Kate's vantage point, crouched beside a big empty box shoved off to one side of the closed front door.

Jo's expression went positively sour. "What?"

"Hide. Duck out of sight." Kate made a motion as if she were pushing her sister's head down below eye level. Out of sight.

Ahhh. The mere thought of being able to do just that made Kate feel better.

Yes, it was a mean thought, but given the kind of day she'd had and Jo's obstinate and obtuse response to a simple, logical request to make herself scarce so they could carry out Kate's covert master plan? Kate decided she'd leave it off her list of faults for now. She pointed to the enormous elephant-ear plant that stood almost as tall as the porch rail. "Those leaves will provide the perfect camouflage."

"And what will you use for cover?"

"This." Kate stabbed her finger at the oversize cardboard container that, according to its label, had recently held a brand spanking new clothes dryer.

"You wouldn't. You couldn't." Jo sneered then paused. She chewed her lower lip, her worried gaze on the large box. "Would you? How *could* you?"

"Easy. It's slit open all the way up the side and across the bottom. It's practically got its own door. I simply back in, keep low and use your crutch to ring the bell."

"And then what? Single-handedly nab the thieves as they come to the door?"

"We don't know they are thieves." *They* being whoever owned that pickup parked at the back of the house. The one Jo had spotted as she'd driven up, thinking it was Vince's, but which, after they had wobbled and hobbled all the way across the cul-de-sac, they had realized was not Vince's at all.

Or maybe it was.

They weren't sure.

Jo really thought she'd seen Vince standing in the driveway with his back to the street when she'd driven past a few minutes earlier. The old truck certainly looked familiar to them both. Neither could say for sure it wasn't Vince's.

As they'd peered through the branches of a scraggly mess of leaves and limbs by the mailbox at the end of the drive, Kate had tried to recall the truck she'd seen in the drive the day before. But what with dropping through the floor shortly after that, it had blurred a bit in her memory. They'd taken Travis's car to Billy J's and when they'd gotten back, it had been dusk and she hadn't exactly had her eyes on their surroundings.

"The truck could belong to whoever has rented the place out," Jo had suggested.

"Except it has a local tag and a Billy J's Bait Shack Buffet bumper sticker on the back bumper, which is peeling off."

Jo had raised one artistically arched-in-one-of-Atlanta's-best-salons eyebrow. "The back bumper is peeling off?"

Kate had gritted her teeth, unwilling to let Jo get the best of her by playing dumb. "It's an old sticker, then. Must have been on there for ages. Why would anyone who had lived in Santa Sofia for ages suddenly up and rent this old place?"

"You're just rationalizing because you want to snoop around more," Jo had accused. "Admit it. You would use any reason as an excuse to try to get a peek inside this old place."

"All right. You caught me. I'm curious. I'll grant you that." Kate had thrown up her hands, and almost lost her balance. A side effect, she'd concluded, of having overtaxed herself today. "But did you ever stop to think that despite my more self-serving motivations, that this is also the act of a good neighbor?"

"I thought you prayed for us to *have* good neighbors, not to *be* them."

"You can't *have* them unless you *are* them."

Up the eyebrow had gone again. "We're our *own neighbors?*"

"We're *everybody's* neighbors, Jo. You know, like in Sunday school when they taught us about the good Samaritan?"

"Oh, don't you try to turn this into a who-knows-her-Bible-better battle with me, Kate-the-couldn't-sit-still-and-spent-most-of-her-time-in-the-corner Cromwell."

Kate had wanted to argue that she could still hear the lessons from that vantage point but then Jo would bring up the rows of gold stars after her name in every classroom, not to mention her blue ribbons for the annual Bible Bowl. All of which completely missed Kate's point, which was…that Kate wanted to do things her way.

"Hear me out, now. I'm saying that in that 'we are all travelers on life's highway' kind of way, we all have to look out for one another. It's the same principle as those neighborhood watch programs." The moment the words had left her lips, Kate knew she'd found a way to win Jo over to her side.

Jo had confirmed as much with a quick cock of her head and narrowing of her eyes.

"Yeah. That's right. Wouldn't you like to add that to your list of strong points when you put the cottage on the market? Proactive neighborhood watch program in effect."

"That's a bit much to claim even for someone as seasoned at highlighting the bright side of things as me. But I'm more interested in the other part of what you said. If we put the cottage on the market? You're open to that now?"

"No." Kate was less of a highlighting-the-bright-side type of gal and more a never-one-to-gaslight-someone-into-thinking-she-would-take-any-side-but-her-own one. "I don't want to sell the cottage. At least not now. Which is why I want to find out as much about what's going on over here as possible."

"And nothing I do can convince you otherwise?" What Jo had expected to sound disappointed, peevish even, had come out almost hopeful, as if perhaps she didn't really want to sell the house now but needed someone else to take the fall for that decision.

"Have you ever convinced me 'otherwise' in our whole relationship, baby sister?"

A slow smile had overtaken Jo's face.

"Which is why we should not even be wasting time here bickering. Now, let's get up that driveway. Carefully."

On closer inspection, then, Jo had noted that where the truck bed had been empty when she'd arrived home, it was certainly not so now. Though Kate couldn't imagine why anyone would steal the shabby old chest of drawers and swing-arm faux brass floor lamp loaded into the pickup's bed, she had to admit that finding them there did seem quite suspicious.

And so Kate had formulated this plan, which left them on the porch, whispering. "If there are thieves in there, they are unlikely to come to the door. After all, the first rule of a home robbery is not to get caught in the act."

"Then why are we hiding?"

"Just in case these thieves don't know the rules."

"So, if it's not a thief, what do you aim to do? Jump out of the box and yell 'surprise'?"

"If it's Vince Merchant, I just might." Yeah. Right. As if Kate had that kind of nerve where that particular man was concerned. The whole time they'd spent in one another's company yesterday she'd hardly said boo to him. She'd wanted to. Not say boo but say…so many things. Ask so many questions. Talk and talk. Catch up. Make up. Just speak up about all that had gone on between them and in all the years since.

Instead she'd kept her conversation to immediate needs—how they would go about fixing the porch, what they wanted from the grocery store, if Billy J ever, in the decades they had eaten at the Bait Shack, *ever* changed the oil in his deep fat fryers. Kate cringed.

And now she envisioned leaping out of a box on the porch like one of those girls who jumped out of cakes?

"Kate?"

Jo's desperate whisper snapped Kate back to the moment. She scrunched herself down into the box, telling her younger sister as she did, "Hurry and hide yourself in those big leaves. Oh, and Jo?"

"Yeah?"

"After this is over, let's go have some cake."

"Some…what?"

Kate secreted herself in the box then poked the crutch out through the slit.

Braaa-aaa-ppp.

The old doorbell sounded more like a Bronx cheer than a cheerful chime of a quaint beachy hideaway.

Kate held her breath and listened. Nothing. No villainous scramble to get out the back way. No shushing or frantically whispered questions about who it could be or what they should do.

"Ring it again," Jo popped her head up to say.

"You didn't even want me to ring it the first time. Why should I ring it again?"

"Maybe they didn't hear it the first time."

That wasn't Jo's voice! Kate's heartbeat went as faint and flickering as a candle about to be blown out. That was… She turned her head to confirm it with a quick glance. "Vince!"

"Hey!" He grinned and gave a nonchalant little wave the way only a man like Vince Merchant could when finding the woman he had once professed to love tucked inside a dryer box outside the door of a stranger's house. "What's going on?"

Kate looked to the crutch protruding from the box, just inches from the doorbell, then at the man. Then at the doorbell, then at the man, then… Then the momentum of her movement threw her off balance again. She pitched forward and tumbled out of her hiding place.

At that point she could only look up, smile and say feebly, "Surprise!"

"Not really." Vince shook his head and helped her up. "In fact, I made a bet with Moxie as to how long it would take the two of you to come nosing around over here."

Kate got to her feet, brushing off the track pants

with the side of the leg unsnapped to the knee—the only thing she had that she could get on over her cast that didn't need laundering or wasn't a dress.

"Moxie?" Jo batted the leaves aside, looking a bit like Fay Wray or some other beautiful blond, black-and-white movie heroine emerging from the jungle. "Isn't that…?"

"Me."

"Oh." Kate turned to find a young woman standing behind the smudged glass of the old storm door just a few feet away.

She looked familiar. But not familiar.

Kate thought of the time she'd seen a famous television actress buying underwear in a discount store in Atlanta and because the face felt so familiar, she had walked up and asked if they had gone to high school together. Like that. Someone she had never met, but knew by sight. Someone who felt like a critical part of her life, yet was a total stranger.

"Excuse me, but have we met?" Jo asked the question that Kate had been too lost in thought—or was it imagination or emotion or memory?—to pose.

"No." The young woman shifted the baseball cap pulled low on her head, shading her eyes.

Her eyes. They were bright and clear and brown. Kate focused in on them. "Are you sure?"

"Y-yes. I know who y'all are, of course. The Cromwell sisters?"

Jo nodded.

Kate supposed she did as well.

"I was just about to bring this dresser and lamp over to you."

"To us?"

"Why?"

"A dresser was stolen and a lamp broken in your house. Happened on my watch. Feel I owe it to y'all to make it right."

"Oh, no. No." Kate didn't want to insult their longtime caretaker but she didn't want that junk in her home. Not now that she had decided on keeping the place. "You don't have to—"

"Great. Bring it on over," Jo chirped up.

"You two will want the place furnished, right? You're going to stay a while?"

"Yes." The word shot out of Kate's mouth.

"Maybe," Jo amended.

Kate blinked at her sister, slow purposeful blinks she hoped conveyed the message: did you just say *maybe?* You with the car full of supplies from the home-improvement store, the clandestine meetings with a "friend of a friend" Realtor and the scheme to get Vince to fix the place up on the cheap so you can sell it for top dollar?

Jo shrugged at her sister then turned to Moxie. "That is, we haven't decided, yet. We do know the place needs some work." She swung her sweet-faced gaze over to Vince. "For which we could certainly use a pair of expert hands."

Uh-oh, here comes some terrible pun about Vince and me. Kate could feel her face go hot and she imagined she must have looked like a cartoon thermometer with bright red surging up until the whole thing exploded.

"I never said a word," she blurted out.

Everyone looked at her.

Didn't she feel like a big old clown all of a sudden? Except she wasn't a clown. Far from it.

"I'm a doctor." That was probably pride rearing its ugly head, but Kate just felt the need to have something positive about herself, something that spoke to accomplishments, out there. She thrust her hand out to Moxie at last. "Dr. Kate Cromwell. You can call me Kate, of course."

"Oh. I'm, uh, I'm in property management. But I guess you both knew that already?"

"Property management?" Jo came up the stairs as if drawn by a magnetic force. Her green eyes sparked with interest and before she even reached the top of the stairs she had her hand extended. "You work for other people or you own your own?"

"Both." The young woman took Jo's hand and gave it one jerking shake. "Mostly own, but obviously I work for you."

"So you know a lot about property values around town?" Jo took the woman's hand in both of hers, gripping her wrist the way Kate might latch on to a reluctant patient while extracting a splinter. "You know what people are looking for? What moves a property quickly?"

"Are you looking to sell your place quickly, Ms. Cromwell?"

"Call me Jo, please. And yes, we are."

"Not." Kate interjected to finish the sentence more to her liking. "We are not looking to sell quickly or otherwise."

"Hmm?" Jo gave her a sharp look.

"We are not selling."

"We may not be selling." Jo did not release Moxie's wrist or hand. "Probably not. Yet. But maybe. It never hurts to consider our—"

"No." Kate cut Jo off without so much as a sideways glance. Why would she want to do that anyway, to egg her sister on with a look? Naw, she'd matured past that kind of thing. Besides, not looking at Jo gave Kate the upper hand—nyah, nyah, take that you sneaky house-selling sister of mine—and it gave her a chance to keep her eyes on Vince.

"But—"

"No."

"Kate, we should at least—"

"No. We are not selling the house. Not now."

Moxie wrenched her hand free at last. "In that case, I guess I should go over and get the furniture in place."

"I'll be over to help you get that dresser off the truck and up the stairs in a minute," Vince said.

"Great." Moxie eyed Jo's lone crutch. "You want to ride over with me?"

"I would love that," Jo answered the other woman but she made sure she caught Kate's eye as she did.

Kate glared.

Moxie disappeared for a second, then the truck

came backing down the drive, stopping even with the walk that led from the porch to the drive. She popped open the passenger door.

Kate handed her sister the crutch she'd used on the doorbell. "Don't make any deals to sell the house on the way."

"It's just across the street," Vince noted.

"Plenty of time." Jo snapped her fingers.

"You have to have mine and Mom's approval, anyway, and you won't get it," Kate called after her.

Jo glowered but made her way to the truck, climbed in and slammed the door. The whole thing shimmied. The motor growled and off they went the whole distance of the cul-de-sac. Accomplished in seconds.

And still in Rverse.

Suddenly alone with Vince, all Kate could think to say was "She certainly handles that truck well."

"She should. She practically rebuilt the thing herself." His eyes shone with admiration.

I rebuild human feet. It's sort of the same thing. Only harder. And more noble. Not that I'm bragging or desperate to impress you. Kate thought of throwing that, or most of it, into the conversation. But in the few moments it took for her to watch the young woman help Jo hop down to the drive across the way, she matured enough to allow someone else to have some well-deserved credit.

So, she changed the subject. "So, that *wasn't* your truck, after all. Jo and I debated about it before we came over."

"*That?* You thought that was my truck?"

"I know." He probably drove a brand-new, gleaming pickup with all the bells and whistles. Men liked their toys the way they liked their women, she had heard. Showy and without a lot of miles on them. "What was I thinking?"

"I'd love a classic like that."

"Oh." Kate found some comfort in hearing that.

"Naw, mine's got a few years on it. You know, not too flashy, still cleans up good."

"Good to know."

He looked at her.

"You know, in case I see you around town. I can… wave." She lifted her hand to demonstrate.

"Hope you do. See me around, that is."

He doesn't want me to wave? Kate the kid felt slighted, but only slightly. "What color?"

"Stick around a minute and you'll see it. Esperanza should be driving up in the thing any time now."

"Esperanza?" She had heard the name mentioned yesterday, hadn't she? "Should I know—"

"Hey, yeah." He stepped forward, blocking Kate from his line of vision and raised one arm. His whole face lit up. "Here's my girl now."

"Your…girl?"

"C'mon, I'll introduce you to the new love of my life."

New love of his life.

What did she expect? Sixteen years had gone by. He had moved on.

That was healthy.

Good for him.

She made her way down the steps, repeating it again and again. "Good. Good. Good for him. That's healthy."

Vince hurried ahead, pulling open the passenger side of his not too flashy but still pretty new and very red truck and began doing something inside the cab.

"That's healthy. Good and healthy. For him. That's—"

He stepped away from the truck and closed the door to reveal what he had taken from inside it.

"That's a baby!" Kate followed up that brilliant statement of the obvious with a rush of unintelligent babble that she thought went something like "Well. There. Hey, there. It's a baby. Look at the baby. You have a baby. Well. Yes. A baby. How nice. Nice baby."

She might have gone on like that indefinitely if Vince hadn't finally taken his eyes off the child, fixed his delighted gaze on her and said, "Kate, I'd like you to meet Mary Fabiola Merchant."

She didn't know whether to ask him to say that name again or just go with it and shake the baby's hand.

Vince didn't wait for her to do, either. "Fabiola is eighteen months old, my little ray of sunshine."

His words focused Kate in a way neither the strange image of him nor her disappointment at realizing he had a new family, a very new one, could.

The new love of my life. My ray of sunshine. Vince deserved that. "I'm glad for you. And the baby's mother…?"

"Esperanza?"

"That beautiful young girl? She's so…beautiful." And young. *Young,* young. She could be his daughter. She could be Kate's daughter. She could be Kate and Vince's daughter if only…

"Here, I'll take the baby, Vince." The black-haired beauty lifted the bright-eyed child from Vince's strong arms.

"She's lovely, Vince. They both are."

"I may be a little prejudiced. She is my first, after all."

"Your…first?"

Vince watched Esperanza and the child heading up the porch, giving a small, totally goofy wave as they walked away. "My first grandbaby."

"Grandbaby? Oh! Grandbaby!" Kate pivoted to watch them, too. "Of course."

"Of course? Why? What? Who did you think she… Oh, Katie, you didn't."

"I did," she confessed, leaning on her cane. "The odds of finding you here in Santa Sofia after all these years were—"

His eyes glinted with good humor. He laughed as he spoke. "Pretty good, given the track record of vacationers who become locals."

"But that you'd be here when I came back, got dragged back against my better judgment, in fact? And then to think you wouldn't have remarried?"

"I almost did, once."

"Oh?" *Good for him. Healthy. Good.* She forced a smile at him.

"I'm talking about you."

"Oh!" The smile eased into a laugh, the laugh into hushed awe. "Then that means the baby is Gentry's?"

"Yes."

Kate shook her head, slowly. "I always picture him as still a kid himself."

"He is." Vince cast his gaze toward the ground. If he had looked Kate in the eyes, she'd have taken that as defensive, but his refusal to do so told her that he was admitting to her something he had tried to keep hidden, even from himself. "Which is why Esperanza and Fabiola are moving into this place without him. He's just not mature enough to handle a family, that's all."

Kate went to him.

She touched his arm.

You can't stand by and let that happen. No. No, Vince, you cannot enable him in this choice. You of all people, a man who put being a father above everything else in your life, even me. You should rail against this. This is not a game of Wa Hoo, these are lives at stake here, Vince, futures. Do not help your son make the biggest mistake of his life.

Kate wanted to scream all that and so much more at him. But she held back. What good would it do? She was a veritable stranger now. She had no part in this.

Besides, she had argued with this man once about the way he raised his son. All she had wanted was to be a part of telling Gentry about their engagement. To be a part of the when and if of telling him. But Vince had told her to stay out of family business.

That was when she'd known she and Gentry and

Vince might never be a real family. That she would never be allowed to behave toward the boy as if he were anything but Vince's son.

She looked now at baby Fabiola. The light of Vince's life.

If Vince paved the way for his son not to step up and be a man or a husband and father, because Gentry knew his own father would be there to take up the slack, Vince would be left with the task of being a father to his granddaughter. This was family business, and where Kate was concerned, it would always have a big ol' Keep Out! sign posted across it.

She had come all this way, across all these years and borne all this guilt to find herself in the exact same position she had found untenable then.

And suddenly the old Scat-Kat-Katie urges returned. She wanted to run. Run all the way back to Atlanta even though she had nothing waiting for her there. To have nothing by choice was surely better than to have nothing because everything you cared about had been ripped away from you. Right?

Kate didn't know if she was asking herself or wanting an answer from some higher source. She did not wait for an answer, either way.

"I have to go now."

"I'll, uh, get the girls inside then be right over to help with the dresser."

Kate could only nod, her back already to the man, and her gait uneven and awkward in her attempt to get away as fast as she could.

Minutes later, breathless, she wiped away the damp film of sweat on her forehead. She leaned one hand against the fender of Moxie's old truck. She fixed her eyes on Jo's, then Moxie's, then Jo's again and she announced, "I've had second thoughts. I don't think it would be such a bad idea to sell this place. The sooner the better."

Chapter Thirteen

The next day, Moxie stood at the back door clutching a file she had put together concerning the Cromwells' cottage.

The land survey from city hall showing where Moxie's property and the Cromwells' met.

The city zoning ordinances that described how the land could be used, single-family dwellings with potential for commercial zoning and on what sized lot.

Printouts from the Realtor's Multiple Listing Service database to show the prices of similar houses in town.

A list of basic repairs needed just so the house could pass inspection, cost estimates included.

Plus some suggestions from her as to what would appeal to the buyers in the area, paint, landscaping, upgrades.

And an offer.

From her.

To buy the house as is.

She knocked on the back door once, lightly, and waited, knowing it would take either of the sisters a while to get to her.

She took a deep breath. Scanned the chipping paint, then narrowed one eye and tried to imagine the back of the house with a real garden instead of that odd assortment of rocks and tacky souvenirs. "Where did all those things come from, anyway?"

Had renters gotten the idea of bringing a little piece of home with them to sort of say "We were here?" Or had people thought it a good joke to find some awful, ugly piece of statuary and stick it here? She skimmed the collection of birdhouses, signs, concrete mascots and replicas of famous landmarks. It didn't matter, she supposed, unless the strange creation came from the minds, hearts or wacky sense of humor of the Cromwell family themselves. That might tell her if she had made a big mistake with this offer or not.

She thought she heard movement inside the house and her pulse quickened.

One more time she slipped open the file and stared at the preliminary buyer's contract she had drawn up with the proposed numbers and contingencies all in place.

Low end.

Again her eye wandered to the rocks and schlock and then to the most obvious things in need of repair. She studied the offer again. Reasonable given these conditions.

But low. Very low.

A knot tightened high in her chest.

Too low?

Just a starting place, she told herself. A jumping-off point. But jumping off into what?

A family rift? Moxie had no idea whatsoever how to deal with that kind of thing.

When *her* family faced conflict, her father went fishing. He'd gone off fishing today, in fact. Which might have seemed pretty fishy in itself to her, except that fishing was what William J. Weatherby did every Saturday.

He put himself out there, threw a line in and saw what happened. That was all she was doing, wasn't it? Just casting a line and seeing if anyone would take the bait?

If they did, Moxie would pick up a sweet little property that had a special place in her heart—and finally secure her ownership of every lot on Dream Away Bay Court. Her own small empire—with large commercial potential.

Moxie could just see an antique shop in the smaller of the two existing houses. Next to it, a new building that could hold a couple of specialty shops, and then a large, two-story bed-and-breakfast, with a charming café tucked inside. The Cromwell cottage would house her property-management office, a place for her to oversee it all. A community of her own inside a community where she had always been just a little bit of an outsider.

It wasn't the same as having a family, but it was something. A place where she would belong.

If the Cromwells would sell their house to her.

But what if they didn't want to sell? Then Moxie might be perceived as self-serving, opportunistic, out of line. What if they did want to sell but had some starry-eyed nostalgia-fueled view of the nigh-onto-ramshackle cottage's worth? They might see her as…well, the same things. Either way, Moxie would look bad.

She hated looking bad.

She had always worked hard to make sure people thought the best of her because, well, first of all, she thought she was a good person, even if her adoptive mom had never really warmed to her. Then there was the Billy J factor. She loved her dad. Everybody loved her dad. But Moxie strongly suspected that if you hit the Web on one of those universal encyclopedia sites and keyed in the word *curmudgeon,* the last words in the entry would read: *see Billy J. Weatherby.*

That was a lot for a girl to overcome. Moxie did it by working hard to keep people from calling her callous like her mother or crusty like good ol' Billy J.

She put the back of her thumb to her lips as she weighed her options and the consequences of them one more time.

Neither of the sisters seemed to know what they wanted.

It wasn't her place to push them one way or another.

She brushed her fingertips over the offer. It was very low. Making an offer this low now *was* pushy. It also might be seen as callous to their feelings and showing a lot of crust.

She whisked the paper with the offer on it out of the

folder. Hastily she raised her knee so that she could fold the contract in half then into quarters.

"Just a sec," a woman's voice called.

Moxie stuffed the folded page under the nearest flowerpot, thinking she would grab it on the way out.

The door swung open and there stood Jo Cromwell. "Hey! We thought you were the pizza delivery guy."

"Pizza?" Moxie should have thought of that. Brought a pizza or an assortment of sub sandwiches or… She glanced down at what she had brought, then at the contract that left the empty pot slightly off-kilter.

For the first time in her life, Moxie found herself empathizing with a flowerpot.

"Sorry, no pizza. But I did bring by some information for you to chew on." She thrust the file toward the bright-eyed blonde.

It was the kind of thing she'd done dozens of times in her line of work but today it felt different. Risky. Exciting. Bold.

She tugged her hat down low over her eyes, imagining herself engaged in some kind of espionage. Moxie Weatherby, girl spy. "I have an estimate on fixing the porch and a schedule for when work can begin. Also a few things I thought might help you out."

"An estimate? A work schedule? So fast?" Jo flipped open the file, glanced down, then gave Moxie a big smile, stepping back to wordlessly invite her inside. "I love how people with the right connections can make things happen in a small town. How'd you do it?"

"Like you said, the right connections." In other

words, Moxie's behind had connected with the chair in the contractor's office and refused to budge until he'd given her an answer. But seeing how pleased Jo appeared with her, she decided not to divulge that.

"Come on in, I can't wait to show these to Kate." Jo motioned her inside to the kitchen, where people had just begun to take seats.

Jo, her bright blond head bent over the file, didn't seem to notice Moxie's hesitation as she took it all in. Kate sat on the couch, a throw over her legs but with her purple cast peeking out from the soft tangle of fringe. All around her, precarious towers of old games and puzzles, and some large, plain cardboard boxes made her look as if she had secreted herself away in her own pretend fortress.

Vince sat himself down in the bright kitchen and plopped a cooing Fabiola on his knee. Moxie felt a pang of guilt over that.

It was Saturday, and gloomy. No actual rain forecast but Moxie's dad had decided to post this sign on the door of the Bait Shack: The Management of this Fine Establishment Reserves the Right to Chase Through Town any Sorry Soul who Overstays his Welcome or Takes More than his Honest-to-goodness Single-meal Stomach Capacity.

He'd even gone so far as to add to the window under the words All You Can Eat, When I Say You've Had All You Can Eat, That's ALL You Can Eat.

Moxie couldn't help but think the old fellow was courting trouble, so she'd chosen to stay out of his way.

That meant that he had needed Esperanza to come in to work, at least through the lunch shift.

Travis Brandt sat at the table drinking tea from a tall glass. No doubt he had been called into service when Esperanza had had to leave. More guilt.

Moxie paused. The mood seemed amicable. Relaxed. Warm. How she wanted to cross that threshold and soak it all in. But just as she knew she didn't belong in the middle of a family rift, she didn't know if she fit in any better in the middle of a family affair. "Wow, I didn't realize… Did I come at a bad time?"

Please say no, she thought. Fit in or not, this was suddenly where she wanted to be.

When she'd seen Vince's truck at the rental house and Travis's car in the drive behind it, she had expected they'd gone over to do some work on the house. She had planned to go over *there* after she dropped her file off and, well, she didn't know what she would do exactly. She did know she wasn't going to pitch in and help with the unpacking.

That sounded just awful, even in her own head. But it was a matter of principle. She did not agree with Vince sticking his nose into his son's life this way and she was determined not to aid and abet any actions that made it easy for Gentry to avoid growing up and getting on with his life. So finding Vince and Travis and the baby here took that weight from her shoulders.

"Bad time? Naw, I'd say you have perfect timing." Vince grinned up at her from his seat at the kitchen table in a way that hinted that he had her all figured out. "Didn't she, Fabbie?"

The baby in his lap grinned, too, and clapped her hands.

"Yep." Travis took a sip of tea then held the tall glass away from his lips and gazed into it, not trying to hide his own amusement at Moxie's well-scheduled arrival. "Too late to pitch in with the unpacking at Pera's but not too late to pick through things around here before the girls have a yard sale."

"A yard sale, huh?" She eyed Jo, who had gotten as far as the second page in the stack of paper. "Great idea. One of my Realtor connections always has her clients have a big yard sale before she will put their house on the market."

Billy J was not the only one in the family with a knack for fishing, Moxie thought with no small amount of pride. She watched Jo, with her back still pressed to the open back door and her attention fixed on the file.

She hadn't taken the bait right away. Fine. A good angler knew all about casting and waiting. Jo might never stop and think things over or take action, but if she heard the notion, she might take it as her own and that might move the sister more swiftly along toward making a decision about the house. One way or another.

"This friend says," Moxie went on, "that yard sales not only clear away a lot of clutter but they also help people begin to let go of the place and to think in terms of starting fresh."

"Mmm," the younger of the two Cromwell sisters said.

Moxie stole a peek at Kate, making headway through the piles of junk surrounding her. *The smart one and the pretty one.* She wondered how many people had classified Kate and Jo that way? Or did Moxie have it turned around? They were both pretty after all, each in her own way.

Maybe Kate was the pretty one and Jo labeled smart. Either way, people had probably distinguished them from one another in some way like that. She couldn't help but wonder if the sisters resented it.

Moxie was absolutely sure that she would not have. How could anyone resent being pretty or smart? Or having a sister, for that matter? A built-in friend for life who shared your history. Your DNA. Your shoe size.

She glanced down at her own fat feet, then at Jo's. *Whoa.*

They were remarkably similar in shape and size—and not just because one of Jo's was still puffy and swollen.

"You don't happen to be selling any of your shoes, are you?" Moxie had to ask.

"What? Shoes? I hadn't planned to. Why?"

"If she were smart, she'd sell them all," Kate called from the couch without looking up from untangling a ball of yarn still connected to a half-finished knitted… something. "They are killing her feet."

"How dare you accuse my across-the-board-adorable footwear of murder." Jo said it all dramatic-like, making sure every eye in the room would train on her and away from her sister.

Kate—smart, Jo—pretty, she decided.

"And in the future if you want to participate in our conversation, please do us the common courtesy of addressing us from the same room, not merely shouting out random intrusive remarks whenever you feel like it."

Or maybe the other way around on the smart/pretty thing. Of course, both women had both attributes, which made Moxie like them all the more and herself just a teeny bit less.

"Maybe I shouldn't… It really does seem like a bad time." Moxie started to step back out the door when something caught her eye. "Is that a homemade Wa Hoo board I see?"

"It's not for sale." Jo stood back and folded her arms over the closed file at last. She had a sly smile, not mean-sly but more self-assured-sly. "But if you think you can handle it, I'll play you a game."

It was that smile as much as the actual challenge that brought Moxie across the threshold. The "if you think you can run with us, then prove yourself" nature of Jo's expression. It was, at its heart, an invitation to be one of them, if just for a while. How could Moxie refuse that?

"Be warned. I am the undisputed Wa Hoo champion of the greater back booth area of Billy J's Bait Shack Seafood Buffet."

"Well, bring it on, sister." Jo pointed to one of the two empty seats at the kitchen table. "Because you have just entered the domain of the Dream Away Bay Court Big Cottage Wa Hoo master herself."

"I'm greenies!" Moxie said, plunking down at exactly the same time Jo shouted her own version, "I call greensies!"

Vince pointed a finger at his old friend. "Moxie called it first."

Jo slapped the file down in front of the man. "Just for that, you get to go over these estimates and tell me how you can beat them when you take this place on for us."

"Take this place on? Am I still doing that?" He leaned forward, baby and all, and turned his head so that everyone could see him looking at Kate on the couch.

Seemingly oblivious, Kate held up a jigsaw-puzzle box and shook it by her ear.

"You can't tell if there are any missing pieces that way, Kate," Travis called out, his eyes on Jo and not the woman he spoke to.

"I'm not looking for missing pieces," Kate snapped back, also not making eye contact. "I'm listening for my key."

"You sing in the key of jigsaw?" Moxie had no idea where that came from, it just came out.

Jo snorted out a quick laugh, then nudged Moxie in the arm. "Unless you've actually heard her sing, you have no idea how funny—and accurate—that is."

Moxie blushed. "I, um, was just kidding."

Kate did not respond. "The key to my treasure chest."

"Oh, like that makes a lot more sense to these nice

people," Jo called out, then she leaned in and lowered her voice. "She found a metal file box under the stairs—"

"Marked Important Documents or something like that?" Moxie had found that box years ago when she had made a quick inventory of the contents of the whole house for insurance purposes. "I almost sent that to your mother the first year I began looking after this place."

"Thank you for not doing that!" Kate set the puzzle box down, picked up another and shook it.

"Yeah, well, after careful study of the printing—"

"And the misspelling," Jo rushed to point out.

"And the misspelling," Moxie agreed. "After looking that over I decided to leave it. I was a kid once myself."

"You weren't much more than a kid *back then* yourself," Vince chimed in.

"Well, back when I was a kid, I kept all my valuables in there. I think it's mostly postcards and seashells. I was twelve, tops. It couldn't be much. Anyway, I hid the key and now I don't remember where."

Travis leaned in now, too, his hand just inches away from Jo's. "And you don't know, either?"

"I hid it *from* her," Kate interjected.

"And even without having known her long, that's precisely why I can imagine she knew, at least once upon a time, precisely where to find it."

Lowering her eyelids and giving a delicate quirk of her lips, Jo sent Travis the message, "You have me pegged, and then again, there is so much more you have to learn about me," in a look.

Moxie didn't think she'd ever sent out such a flirtatious and yet confident message in one fleeting glance in her entire life. Maybe if she stuck around here, she could pick up a thing or two from this Jo. Not that Moxie's boyfriend's work would ever slow down long enough for him to look at her, even fleetingly.

The puzzle-shaking began anew from the front room.

"I don't have any idea where she last hid the key," Jo confessed. Then she turned to Vince. "Why don't you go help Kate look for it?"

Vince did not move right away.

Jo kicked the leg of his chair under the table.

He scooted back.

A puzzle box hit the floor. "I don't need any help."

"I thought you wanted me to go over these estimates." Vince snagged the file and flipped it open.

Moxie tried to hide her gratitude that she hadn't stuck that offer in there.

"Bring them out here. I can look at estimates while I search for my key." Kate never lifted her head. "The sooner we get through with this place, the sooner we can go ourselves."

Vince sighed and stood. He started to give the baby to Moxie but Travis intervened with open hands.

"I'll take her, if you don't mind."

Fabiola cooed and reached for Travis's face.

The sight tugged at Moxie's heart. That baby needed her daddy so much. Where was he? Why was Vince here instead of Gentry? Moxie looked away.

"You look good with a baby, Travis," Jo said softly.

"Yeah? I like kids," he said. "Always wanted to have a couple of my own."

"Why haven't you ever started a family?" Jo asked.

"Just have to find the right girl, I guess."

Jo scootched to the edge of her seat, clenching the bag of marbles in both hands, probably to prevent her arm from shooting into the air with her fingers wriggling as she begged breathlessly, "Pick me, pick me."

"Keep your eyes open, Trav. She may be closer than you think." Moxie pushed her chair up.

"I'll take that into account, Mox." He put his lips alongside the baby's neck and blew a raspberry.

Fabiola squealed with delight.

Jo emptied the marbles into her cupped palm then picked up a green one and handed it across the table to Moxie. "I think you and I could be friends, don't you?"

"Does that mean you'll let me borrow a pair of shoes sometime?"

Jo hesitated.

She'd asked too much.

To join the game. To tease the older sister. To take a place at the table *and* to borrow cute shoes? Too much.

Moxie wet her lips to buy time and think of a way to kid herself out of overstepping her bounds.

Jo dumped the rest of the marbles then raised her head and offered her hand to Moxie. "If a friend can't walk a mile in your shoes, who can?"

"Nobody could walk a mile in your shoes, little sister." To make it all official, Kate threw her two cents in. "But you are welcome here anytime you want, Moxie."

One firm, resolute shake. Moxie had done it a thousand times over countless deals, but this time felt different. Better. Bigger. As if she had just committed herself to an adventure she could not yet imagine.

Chapter Fourteen

The next morning, Kate awoke in the small bedroom instead of nursing an aching back on the couch. For a moment, no, just a sliver of a hint of a moment, all the years since she had last slept in this bed fell away. She was young. She was on the verge of something new and exciting. She was…

She stretched her arms out. Her joints cracked. Her back ached. Every muscle in her body clenched, leaving her as stiff as the thin, unyielding mattress she had just spent the night upon.

She was fooling herself.

In more ways than one.

She pushed herself upright, careful not to bump her head on the slanted ceiling of the dormer where her small twin bed sat tucked away beneath what had once seemed to her a window that framed her every hope and dream. She did not need to lean forward and put her face near the glass to know what she would see out that window.

Dream Away Bay Court. The mystery house. And beyond that, a good deal of Santa Sofia.

Kate did not want to gaze out upon any of it this morning.

Why bother?

It was not as if she planned to stay here much longer.

With that thought, the image of Vince standing in his drive the other day, holding darling little Fabiola, overtook her. Overwhelmed her, really. The way a swift, deceptively powerful wave rolls in after its gentle predecessors and overwhelms an unsuspecting ocean gazer. Kate dragged air deep into her lungs but that did not chase away the sadness or the stab of pain that thinking of Vince brought on. Not just Vince. Vince and his new family.

No, the baby wasn't his daughter, but unless something changed very soon, he was going to be the child's primary father figure.

"Oh, Gentry. What happened?" she murmured, trying to picture how the boy she had known as a caring if clingy six-year-old had grown into a man who could abandon his own wife and child.

It occurred to her that maybe she had played some part in it. Had her leaving all those years ago caused a sort of disconnect in the boy, or between father and son, that had these kinds of long-term effects? She of all people knew that the smallest of things could have a profound impact on a child.

Why wouldn't they? Children are small. Their worlds are small. Their perception is small. They are so vulnerable and often at the mercy of people, concepts and realities that are much too large for them to comprehend.

Wasn't there a Bible verse about thinking as a child then putting away childish things? She reached out to the nightstand and pulled open the single drawer. There it was, her old paperback Bible with the teal, magenta and orange designs on it, meant to make it look *radical,* the word of the moment back then for *cool.*

She smiled, drew it out and quickly found the verse she had been thinking of, 1 Corinthians, 13:11.

"When I was a child, I used to speak like a child, think like a child, reason like a child; when I became a man, I did away with childish things," she read aloud then set the book back on the nightstand, her curiosity satisfied but her heart far from it.

Kate had done away with childish things when she'd still been a child. That was when she had learned that the people we love do not always love us back. The people we trust are not always worthy of that trust. And things we think we should have for a lifetime can be taken away in the blink of an eye.

She thought of young Gentry.

Then of Fabiola.

Then last and most achingly of her baby sister Christina.

I wasn't born old. I grew old too fast. Kate's own words rang through her mind.

"If only," she whispered.

If only she had called out that night when she'd heard her father creeping out the door and driving off in the brand-new shiny truck that he and Mom had fought so much over. Kate couldn't have known he'd had the youngest of the girls with him, or she would have called out, she had told herself time and again.

But deep down, Kate could still feel that sense of relief that had enveloped her when she knew her father had left their home. The same sweet reprieve she had felt every year at this very cottage when they had escaped from the harsh reality of first a bad marriage and then a broken family. She had been glad he was gone and so she had stayed silent. That was a childish mistake she had determined she would never repeat.

But had she repeated it? Had her silence, her absence, brought about more pain for someone she had loved?

Guilt constricted her chest even all these years later. Heaped on top of that was the new realization that her choice to let fear of that same kind of loss had driven her away from Vince and Gentry when she was an adult and should have known better. What if she had stayed back then?

No one could guarantee that they would have lived happily ever after. They had only been unofficially engaged, after all. She'd loved Vince then, of course. Who was she kidding; she loved Vince still.

But when she had left, had he followed? Had he even once asked her what she was so afraid of? Maybe he hadn't really loved her? Or maybe he'd been scared, too, and young.

Still, if he had learned anything from that time, why would he stand by and allow—no, enable—Gentry to do the same thing to Esperanza? Why didn't he tell his son to go after his wife, to fight for his family? After all, Fabbie and Esperanza were Gentry's family. Unlike Kate.

Then again, Kate had never told Vince how she had felt, so maybe…

If she had it to do over again? Kate shut her eyes. She had made that decision already, hadn't she? She could not stay and risk involvement with Vince and his family. Esperanza was young and pretty. If she and Gentry did not work out their differences, she would surely move on and take Fabiola with her. How could Kate knowingly set herself up for something like that?

A damp draft overtook Kate. She shivered then threw her blanket around her shoulders. Hunched over, she scooted her way to the window to push it shut, only to find it closed and locked. And letting in air from somewhere.

She ran her fingers along the sides and bottom of the sill to try to find the source of the chill. Nothing.

She shuddered again. She'd have to come back and look for the gap later in the day, when it was warm in the upper rooms and she'd welcome the coolness. Of course, by then the breeze would have stopped blowing, she mused, throwing the cover off and sliding out of bed.

The flash of blankets in the confined space caught the Bible by the corner and sent it tumbling downward.

Kate reached out and caught it before it thumped to the ground, but not before something small, metallic and as shiny as a new dime fell out. It somersaulted through the air then pinged against the hardwood floor.

"The key!" She grabbed it up and pressed the icy metal into the warmth of her palm. "Now I remember. I hid it in my Bible because I thought Jo wouldn't have the nerve to snoop for it in there."

Travis had pegged Jo perfectly yesterday when he'd accused her of having a knack for finding Kate's most prized, and secret, possessions.

"Wow." She put the Bible back in the drawer, promising she wouldn't go so long without opening it up again. Then she sent the key sailing in the air like a penny flipped in a coin toss.

Slap. She caught it between her hands and laughed.

Maybe this morning did still have some promise left in it, she thought, edging her way off the bed and onto her feet, using the wall for support. *I'll just make my way downstairs and while the coffee is brewing have a little look-see at what's in that old treasure chest, before Jo starts snooping around trying to find out what secrets are in there.*

She couldn't recall when she had last put anything in the box. So she had no idea what to expect to find. Pictures cut from fan magazines of teen heartthrobs? A piece of driftwood she had thought particularly pretty? Some old photographs taken the year she had gotten an Instamatic camera? Whatever it was, Kate realized she had once thought of it as treasure and she wanted to see it by herself first.

She touched the Bible and said a quick prayer of gratitude. Yes, she had put away childish things too soon, but she couldn't help but feel thankful that in spite of that, she had found this small bit of her childhood again. Maybe seeing those things would help her forgive her younger self, or at least accept the past for what it was—past.

At the very least it would get her mind off Gentry, Esperanza and Fabiola, and her own role in their distressing situation.

From where she stood, she could see the mystery house, if she wanted to see it. She cast her gaze downward as she put the Bible back in the drawer, reminding herself not to allow this treasure to languish there too long. Then she reached out to put the covers back on the bed.

In that instant something caught her eye. A figure. A movement. A flurry of white flouncing and flitting in the street below—and heading directly for her cottage.

"Hello?"

Kate froze at the sound of Esperanza's voice coming from the front porch. *Let Jo deal with it.*

Kate held her breath and listened for Jo's response. Anything, from her already being awake and downstairs to swinging open the door, to her groggily calling out the window of the bedroom across the hall, "Go around back. That porch isn't safe."

Nothing. Not a peep.

"Jo?" Kate called.

No answer.

"Can you get that?"

Still no answer.

"Please. Please. Wake up." The cry came above the pounding on the door.

Kate grabbed the top blanket and wrapped it around herself but she did not make a move for the bedroom door. "Jo? You're faster on your feet than me, take care of that."

Not so much as a fake snore from the direction of Jo's room.

More pounding downstairs, then finally, "It's the baby. I need to see the doctor."

Before she had a chance to think about how stiff she felt or how much her foot would encumber her, Kate was out the door and in the stairwell calling, "I'm coming."

"Please. I don't know what to do. She was—"

Kate flung open the door.

Esperanza's face rivaled her white cotton nightgown for paleness. Her dark eyes appeared enormous and bright with tears and terror. "She was fine last night."

The girl barged in with the baby's pink cheek smooshed against her shoulder.

Fabiola fussed, though quietly, and pushed at her mother's grasp. A good sign, Kate concluded. If the child had gone limp or lethargic or, even worse, stiffened suddenly, that would worry her more.

She put her hand to the baby's forehead. Hardly

scientific but a method that had served mothers and healers for ages. "She is very hot. We need to get that temp down."

Esperanza nodded.

"Have you given her anything?" Kate moved into E.R. mode and began a cursory exam.

Emergency medicine initially had seemed tailor-made for her—fast-paced, little personal involvement and instead of having to move on every so often, an environment that changed constantly. Her rotation in the E.R. had dissuaded her of those notions quickly. Unlike the constant excitement portrayed on TV, the only constant in her experience was boredom, broken up for a few minutes every now and then by sheer chaos.

And in those moments, the chance, however small, that she would have to make one of those big decisions she could not fix or take back. Not for her.

She had learned, however, about dealing with cases just like Fabiola's. Many a panicked parent had passed through the doors with a sick child in the middle of the night. More now that so many people had no health insurance.

She would tell them what she was about to tell Esperanza. "We can do some things to help get the fever down immediately but we need to get her to her doctor as soon as possible so we can rule out any serious underlying causes for the fever."

"But you're a doctor," Esperanza whispered, her face grim.

"But this is not a hospital or doctor's office. I don't

have the equipment or facilities to do anything but basic home care, sweetie." Kate pried the baby from her mother's arms. "Now, I have some liquid acetaminophen in my first-aid kit. I'll give her the right dose and get her into a cool bath. You go back to your house—"

"I don't want to leave my baby." Esperanza reached out to the child.

Kate held firm. "Just long enough to throw on some clothes and shoes and to get her pediatrician's phone number."

The young mother stepped back, hesitated, then said quietly, "She doesn't have a pediatrician. So far her father hasn't stayed at a job long enough to get insurance and I just started working at Billy J's."

"Okay." Again the guilt over how Gentry had turned out and how she might have affected his growth stabbed at her. She did not have time for that now, so she pushed it aside. "Okay. Go home and get dressed. Use the back door, though. We can't risk you falling through the porch and getting hurt right now. When you get back, we'll go."

"Go where?" Esperanza kept at her heels, which meant she had to move in a jerking, quick step-stop movement to keep from overrunning cast-wearing Kate.

"As I recall, Santa Sofia has a small hospital." Struggling to keep her grip on the squirming child, Kate used her shoulder to hit the light switch. The kitchen, where she had left the first-aid kit when she'd wrapped Jo's ankle days ago, flooded with light.

That did not help Esperanza's dim news. "Not anymore."

Kate slowed but did not stop. "What?"

"The hospital closed last year," Esperanza said.

Kate stopped a few feet from the sink, trying to give her brain a shot at processing this info and at assessing what to do next.

"We do have an urgent-care clinic."

"Okay." She took another step. The stopper clinked into place in the drain. A twist of the knob and the rush and splash of water filling the sink underscored Kate's hurried order. "Get dressed. We'll go there."

"I don't have a car."

"My sister will take us." Kate tested the water then moved to the cabinet where she had tucked the first-aid kit away.

Esperanza finally agreed with a nod and headed for the back door.

"Jo!" Kate yelled as loud as she could.

Fabiola cringed then yowled at the rude blast of sound.

A response that Kate took as a good sign. "Jo! Wake up, we have—"

"She's not here." Esperanza stood in the doorway and whipped her head around. "Her car is not in the driveway."

"What? It's early Sunday morning. Where could she be?"

"Church?"

"We don't have a church here." When they were younger they had always just gone to the Traveler's Wayside Chapel for… "Travis."

"What should we do?"

They couldn't exactly call Jo now. If she was in church, she had probably silenced her cell phone. If she hadn't silenced it, then their call would intrude on the service for others. Kate wrestled to get the medicine bottle out of the kit, then measure out the dosage as she mentally ticked off their options.

"I can call Vince," Esperanza said. It was not a question. It was a habit. The same answer the for-all-practical-purposes single mom had learned to give to any problem.

Fabiola fought the dropper at first, but Kate persisted and in a moment had emptied out the medicine. She took a moment to wipe the thick red liquid from the child's chin. "I know, sweetie, sometimes the things that are best for us are the hardest for us to swallow."

The last words slowed and faded on her tongue.

Kate jerked her head up. "Esperanza?"

"What?" The girl's delicate footsteps resounded across the back deck, she stuck her head in the door. "Is she worse?"

"No." Kate gazed down at the child, who had relaxed a bit and was making faces and sticking her tongue out trying to get rid of the medicine's aftertaste. The child wasn't worse, but Kate might just be about to make things between herself and her one-time love worse. She had no business doing it, either. But that wasn't going to stop her.

She had run from the big life decisions, from the looming specter of loss, from her own silence for too long. It ended today. No matter what the costs.

She would put away those childish fears and do the right thing, by giving someone else the chance to do the right thing also. “Don’t call Vince. I am going to call Gentry.”

Chapter Fifteen

"So no service?"

"Are you kidding?" Travis brandished a long silver spatula and in one fluid movement used it to pry an overcooked pancake off a portable griddle on a counter in the chapel's basement kitchenette. "Best service in town, don't you think?"

Jo had arrived early, hoping to, well, planning to make sure the adorable minister knew she had made the effort to come to worship this morning. She'd worn her best non-Realtor business-suit type of dress and a pair of modest—in style but not in price—shoes. And had even managed to tame the shreds of her custom-cut-to-accommodate-her-extensions hair into a fluffy, girlie hairdo. Cute but not out of the question for a minister's wife. Or friend.

A minister's *friend,* she reminded herself.

She had had visions of herself sitting in the front pew, all sweet and blond and attentive. Of listening to the message of grace, singing the Lord's praises from her heart and afterward inviting the resident man of God out for lunch.

But lunch was not exactly on the menu.

"Why breakfast?"

"It's the most important meal of the day?"

Jo put her hand on her hip and looked up at him.

He grinned at her and went back to work pouring batter on the griddle. "The answer is in our name."

"Wayside Chapel?"

He nodded. "Wayside missions have a long-standing tradition of existing for those who are off the path, who have literally fallen by the wayside. We meet those people where they are, not where we are most comfortable."

That made Jo squirm a little. Her life, even life in her daydreams, had stayed pretty much tucked safely inside her comfort zone.

"So we serve meals and run food banks and clothes closets—"

"And loan out crutches."

He grinned. "And loan out crutches, to anyone in need. In Santa Sofia that also includes reaching out to our significant tourist population, of course."

"We used to come here ourselves on Sundays. And sometimes Mom would come for the evening service, also."

"We still do it on Wednesday and Sunday evenings—we call it All Souls Worship and Praise Sing-along."

She smiled at the thought of all those strangers and locals coming together to lift their voices and make a joyful noise. Or as in the case of her own singing, a boisterous noise, emphasis on *noise.*

"Maybe you can come by tonight, then."

"I'd like that."

All around them people had begun to gather, most of them calling out their hellos to Travis first and then to each other. All of them eyed her. They whispered with one another, then stole another peek at her again. And Jo did not think it was because of her darling hairdo.

"Maybe I shouldn't have come by this morning?"

"Don't say that. I'm glad you did."

"Really?"

"Yeah, I could always use an extra hand in the chow line."

She had deserved that gentle but firm reminder. This was neither the time nor the place for trying to get Travis's attention. In this place, and at this time more than any other, he must rightly focus on the people who came to him seeking the love of the Lord.

She made a sweeping glance of the room and noted all the people dressed more for cleaning out a garage than for congregating in a church. At least she thought they had come seeking the Lord. Maybe they just came because McDonald's was too crowded.

She watched a mom kneel in front of a small boy, spit on a tissue then clean a smudge from his cheek. He endured it, but fidgeted the whole time, dancing up and down in his sneakers with the busted seams along the side. And it dawned on Jo. They weren't dressed this way out of lack of respect for the chapel.

As was her habit, she looked at the woman's shoes. They made her son's ragged sneaks look good. Suddenly even Jo's modestly priced shoes seemed a silly extravagance.

"Surely there is something I can do," she whispered.

"You want something to do? Check the ice chest at the end of the table and make sure there is plenty of milk and juice boxes."

Jo took a peek into the chest then at the crowd. "Just barely enough. If you'll tell me where to get more, I'll restock it."

"More? There is no more, Jo. Just tell people as they go through not to take anything they won't use at this meal. That usually works."

"And on the days when it doesn't work?"

"Somebody goes without," he said softly and she could see in his eyes it troubled him.

Not that mother, she wanted to say. Not that child. Instead she licked her lips and thought of how much she had in life. How much she had taken for granted. "Meals, food banks, clothes. What else do you do? Support groups?"

"AA." He kept working away.

"What about a women's group?"

"For…?"

"Women?"

A slow smile crept over his face. He shook his

head. "We don't have a woman on staff to lead that kind of thing."

"I could."

"You?" He looked her over, up and down and up again, his last glance resting on her crazy-expensive shoes.

"Yes, me. I could lead a class. I know the Bible. I have the ribbons from Sunday school to show it." She would have slipped those shoes off on the spot but thought better of it since they were essentially in a makeshift kitchen preparing food. "In fact, we could…we could meet on the beach. No shoes required."

"A regular group of barefoot believers, huh?"

"Why not?" That question burned itself into Jo's head then and there. "Barefoot Believers. Kick off your shoes and walk awhile with the Lord."

His mouth quirked up on one side.

If he said yes, he was saying yes to more than just her help and they both knew it. He was saying they were a team, of sorts. She held her breath and waited for his answer.

"Almost have the first round ready, folks. Why don't you line up and get your plates? I'll stop long enough to say the blessing in just a sec." He motioned with the spatula to the people closest to them, then turned to Jo. "It won't be easy. It sure won't be glamorous."

"I know."

He smiled. A real, warm, genuine smile.

But he didn't say any more. He didn't say yes to her wanting to be a part of his work.

Jo wanted to cry and she didn't know why. Pettiness? Travis cared about all these people as individuals, not just her. Had that realization made her overly emotional? She searched her heart and shook her head slightly. No.

Jo watched an older woman being helped ahead in the line by a young man. They both had plain white plates in their hands and Jo couldn't help wishing she knew their story.

Everybody has a story; it dawned on her then. She certainly did. And Kate. And Travis. He had one that people all over the country had once wanted to learn. These people had their stories as well and those stories mattered. They mattered to the man making them breakfast to make sure they got a meal today and they mattered to God. Each of these people mattered because of God, because His Son had died for all of them.

Jo blinked and to her surprise found tears in her eyes. She never thought like this. She never got all spiritual about, well, anything.

It certainly wasn't the kind of thing that ever came up in the Monday-morning motivational meetings at Powers Realty. The message there was always "Sell. Sell. Sell. Money. Money. Money. There's a boom going on out there. Which would you rather do? Ride the explosion or get caught in the fallout?"

Jo had ridden that explosion *and* gotten caught in the fallout. She had come to Santa Sofia trying to hop on whatever firepower the boom had left, and suddenly she felt ashamed of herself for it. She had a home. She had an apartment in Atlanta, but she also had a home here in Santa Sofia. A home she no longer wanted to sell off for a quick fix.

She had a family who loved her.

And plenty to eat.

And clothes on her back.

And shoes on her feet.

She shifted her heels over the old linoleum floor. Her gaze dropped down to the footwear that had cost her more than Travis had probably paid out to feed the small cluster of folks here this morning.

Why not? Why not the Barefoot Believers? She wasn't doing it to be a part of Travis's team; she would do it to be a part of God's team.

And in that moment, she knew He wanted her.

She waited for Travis to lift a short stack of pancakes onto somebody's plate, to share a kind word, then to wipe off his hands and turn back to the griddle before she asked, "How do you do this?"

He poured some batter then grimaced. "I put the first two aside for the dog."

"What?"

"You wanted to know how I make such perfect pancakes. Right?" He grinned at her.

"This is your idea of perfection?" She pointed to the griddle bubbling with things that looked like paint splatters more than circles, in various shades of barely beyond-batter to burned-beyond-belief.

"I suppose you can do better?"

She took the spatula from his hand without saying

a word and went to work. "My question, by the way, was how do you do this, early mornings, hard work, for people you may never see again?"

"And a few I see every day even though we are supposed to supply temporary help only?"

"Yeah. How do you face that every day?"

"The simple answer is with faith."

"Faith? It sounds like anything but a simple answer to me."

"It's all I've got."

She looked at him over her shoulder, studied his honest, open expression a moment, then finally said exactly what she had wanted to say since the moment he'd walked though her door. "Do you ever regret it? You gave up so much."

"I guess this is where I say look at all I've gained." He spread his arms. The noise of people chatting, scraping forks over plates, of chairs scooting over the dingy floor and of complaints about the coffee being too hot and the syrup too cold rushed at them. Not a single person looked up.

"I have to ask you again, how do you do it?"

He opened his mouth.

"And don't just say faith," she cautioned. "Faith is *why* you do it. I'm talking about how. How do you get up day after day and look at this life over the one you could have had and not become bitter? How do you keep at it when nobody seems to even notice? How do you pay your bills?"

"Some days, I don't."

"Which? Bitter? Ignored? Bills?"

"All of them."

Jo could not understand this man. "So…?"

"You want to talk impossible? Living up to an image that has nothing to do with you, with the real person. With my goals and hopes and even my actual abilities. That was impossible." He handed out another breakfast plate then turned to her, looked her over and began unwinding the big apron from around his neck. When he got it free, he held it up to her.

She ducked to allow him to slip it over her head. "Don't even try to tell me about that. I have lived with that all my life, only the image was a walking, talking, becoming a doctor perfect sister."

He reached around and nabbed the apron strings, brought them around front and tied them together for her. "You have to learn to accept yourself. *Be* yourself. God didn't make any other person more qualified for the job."

"Ugh." She clucked her tongue. "Where'd you get that? From some sign in front of a church?"

"Actually from a book—" he folded his arms as if to say *yeah, I read a book,* then stole a sideways glance toward the crowd before he bent down and whispered "—of sayings that have been used on signs in front of churches."

She laughed.

"So it's corny. That doesn't make it less true."

"For you maybe." She slid the spatula under a fluffy golden pancake and moved it to the pan waiting to be served. "But what if the 'you' that you are stuck being is a person nobody else wants?"

Travis frowned, his arms wound not quite so tightly now. "Could you put that in quaint cliché church signese, please?"

"My mom chose Kate." She poured a pancake. "My father chose my baby sister." Another pancake. "Nobody chose me." No more room for more batter. "Ever."

He shook his head. "I find that hard to believe."

"It's true. When I was five years old, my father left my mother, taking my baby sister with him. We never saw either of them again."

"And you wished he had taken you with him?"

"No. I wish..." Jo paused with the spouted mixing bowl of batter still in one hand. "I wish he'd have at least tried to take me with him."

"Really?"

"Yeah. Really."

"Year after year for all this time you've looked back at what happened in your family and wished that?"

"Yes."

"Jo—"

"Because in the aftermath I became invisible. Like a toy on a shelf the day after Christmas."

"You're breaking my heart." It could have sounded cruel but somehow in the midst of the families just trying to get a meal for their kids, it didn't.

"Mom clung to Kate. For the rest of our lives, she depended on Kate. And Kate never failed her."

"Is that why Kate didn't marry Vince?"

"I don't..." She moved to the second portable griddle and started to pour again, then stopped. "I never thought of that."

"Did you ever think that maybe if Kate could do it all over she would wish she wasn't 'chosen'?"

Jo set the batter down with a clunk. "I just wanted to be somebody."

"Believe me, I've *been* somebody. It's not as great as everyone says it will be."

"I know that, too. I was something of a hotshot with my company until..."

"Until you let your vanity over getting that Powers guy's interest push you into a deal, that not-so-hot deal, huh?"

"It was all false pride and poor self-esteem, wasn't it? And now I have this half-finished house in Atlanta with a payment due in a couple weeks and..." She looked at him. The old Jo would have used this moment to press her case, to ask for help, to close the deal.

Instead she turned to the pancakes. To the simple task before her and found comfort in doing it. She turned them, poured more on the second griddle then checked the serving pan and the crowd to see if she should be slowing down production.

She looked out at all the people. She thought of all *their* stories. Then she looked at Travis.

At this moment, she felt a tug to choose. The life she had once thought of as her only way to "be somebody" or to stop living a lie and start actually being herself.

It was not as difficult a choice as she would have thought a few days ago.

"If I can't raise the cash quickly, I am going to take a huge financial loss on it." She spoke honestly, and without embarrassment. She'd messed up; it wasn't the worst thing in the world. She sighed. "Then I will go broke, have to move out of my pricey apartment and have to start over somewhere else."

Please ask me to start over here, she thought, looking up into his kind, understanding eyes.

"If all that's going on, why are you here?" He asked a question he had posed once before. "Why aren't you back in Atlanta trying to fix things?"

"Because Kate needed me to come here." The answer surprised her. She thought she had come to sell the house, but even more than that, she had come because… "Kate needed me."

"*Perfect Kate?* Needed somebody?"

"Well, maybe she's not exactly always one-hundred-percent perfect." In saying that, something broke free inside Jo. She felt lighter.

"And when she wasn't perfect, you were the one she wanted to help her."

Jo thought of their struggle the first day just trying to get from the car to the apartment building. "*Wanted* might be a bit strong."

"Well, she chose you."

"Yeah, she did, didn't she?"

"Who else could have done what you have for her?"

Not their mother. In fact, their mother had done this

to her. Kate had no real friends, only staff that she had not wanted to get too close to because she knew she might have to let them go. "You are very good at this."

His eyes twinkled. "Maybe I should be a minister."

"Maybe." She looked at the huge mess he had made around them before she'd taken over. "Because you are never going to make it as a short-order cook."

"Well, maybe the Lord will send me somebody who can do a better job at this kind of thing than I can."

"Somebody?"

"Not just anybody. A real somebody," he said softly.

Jo's heart swelled. She flipped a pancake with ease and expertise she hadn't realized she possessed, then smiled at him. "You know, as services go, this might have been one of the best ones I've ever attended."

Chapter Sixteen

The nurse on duty had taken one look at the flush-cheeked child and listened to Kate's brief summary of symptoms before she'd shuttled them straight back to the examining room. Kate wanted to think they could thank her credentials, which she'd all but shouted as they'd rushed in through the automatic glass doors, for the quick response. But after a moment's reflection, she realized the nurse had recognized the small family and had pulled their file, probably when she'd seen them hurrying through the parking lot.

That left Kate and Gentry alone for the first time in sixteen years.

Sixteen!

She didn't feel that much older, really, but he had grown into a tall young man with brown wavy hair, a closely clipped beard and watchful, wary eyes. He stood in the entryway, jangling his keys in a way that suggested he might be using them soon. Very soon.

Kate recognized that restlessness, that urge to bolt when life got too overwhelming, *too real.* She also knew that if the kid ran now, he'd regret it and so would she.

She put her hand on his arm, just barely at first, then when he did not withdraw, more firmly until she had given his forearm an encouraging squeeze. "I am proud of the way you stepped up and took care of Esperanza and the baby, Gentry."

"Stepped up? I can't own that, Kate." He gave her a sly look and in his lopsided smile she could still see something of the kid she had once known and, to her surprise, still cared about. He twirled his key ring around his index finger. "I didn't step up so much as I was given a verbal kick in the pants to get me moving."

"It was more of a nudge to your conscience," she said.

"No, trust me, from my end of the phone conversation, it was not a nudge."

"Fine. Whatever. It got you over to the house."

"Yeah."

Suddenly Kate felt all maternal—and a bit ornery and in need of lightening the mood. "And what do we say when someone gives us a kick in the pants to jump-start us in the right direction?"

He grinned and looked all of six again. "Thank you, Kate."

"I knew you'd do the right thing."

"I haven't so far." He dropped his head and looked at her from the corner of his eye. "But I guess you figured that out."

"I don't think I have anything figured out anymore,

Gentry." Kate patted his arm then moved around to put herself squarely before him. "But I wouldn't have called you at all if I had thought for one minute you didn't have it in you."

He stood quietly.

She had heard it said once that we would be amazed at what would pour out of people's hearts if we weren't all so anxious to fill every silence with words.

So Kate waited.

Finally Gentry lifted his head, gazed off in the direction of the exam room and whispered, "We got married without really knowing each other. Her folks didn't approve. Dad didn't approve."

"But you were in love."

He nodded, glanced down, then nodded again. "Everyone told us that if we were really in love, it would wait. We would still be in love in another year, even two. Give her a chance to get her certification as a dental assistant, let me get my degree."

She felt a swell of pride and relief to know his life had taken that positive course. "You went to college?"

"For three years." He held that many fingers up and peered at her just over the tips of them. "Got the basics down but then couldn't choose a major. I thought changing schools would make me focus but, well, you probably can guess that the schools weren't the problem."

It would have been so easy to lay blame then, but Kate held her tongue.

He shrugged. "I always meant to do better. To try harder but then things got tough and…"

"And your dad rushed to your rescue?"

"He meant well. And let's not pretend I'm not responsible for my part of it. I knew my dad carried a lot of guilt that I didn't have a mom. And because he moved me down here to this place where I had to make new friends every season. He only did what he did to try to make up for all that. And it was easy to let him do it. At least at first."

"Then the cost of always being rescued got pretty steep, didn't it?"

He gazed steadily down the empty hallway, his eyes intense. "I *do* love them, you know."

"I could tell that the second I saw you all together."

"I just… They…" He shuffled his tennis shoes, curled his keys into his fist then clenched his jaw. "The commitment of being a father, them both being dependent on me for so much, doubting myself, not knowing what the future holds, it all scares me. Sometimes I just have to get away."

"I know that feeling."

His expression shifted from anxiety to disbelief. "You do?"

"Yeah, a lot of years ago a little boy scared me like that," she murmured.

"Me? I don't recall any trip to the emergency room with you, Kate. Was I sick?"

"No. But you were hurting. You were vulnerable. You looked to me to help make it all better and it terrified me."

"I didn't think you were ever scared of anything."

"Are you kidding? I was petrified."

"Of what?"

"Of the chance that I might lose you."

"You mean that you might lose my dad?" he corrected, all cynical and so much older than his years suggested.

Kate recognized that feeling. It broke her heart and healed it all at once. She had made something of her life and Gentry could, too.

"No. This wasn't about your dad and me." She paused to gather her thoughts, then pressed on, determined not to hedge or hide anything. "I wasn't afraid of a grown-up relationship failing. I guess I thought that if that happened we'd both have played a part in it, we'd both have options all along the way. But you didn't have any choice and because you weren't mine by birth, that meant I wouldn't have any choice, either."

"You thought that if you admitted you loved me that I wouldn't be the only one left vulnerable." He pegged it.

Kate nodded. "I wasn't able to take that risk. I couldn't love you enough knowing you could be taken from me and I would be helpless to stop it."

"So...you're saying...you didn't love me?"

Promise you will always love me, Kate. Promise you will always be my mom.

The words the young Gentry had said to her that had sent her running so long ago came back so clear in her mind that she could hear the break in his young voice, the rasp of breath he'd taken before he had uttered the thing he longed for most in the world, *mom.*

"I told myself that for so long. That I'd merely been infatuated with your dad and just a little charmed by his son." Kate fought to hold the tears back. She sniffled. "But I can tell you, honestly, that I have thought of you both so often over the years. Wondered what became of you. Even prayed for you."

"Yeah?" The doubt in his face began to fade.

"Yeah." She gathered her composure and found it in herself to say what needed to be said. "I am so sorry, Gentry. I should have been up-front with you even when you were a kid. I should have told you when you asked me if I would stay and be part of the family that that was what I wanted more than anything. And that I was afraid because things don't always work out the way we want them."

"Wow. You know my dad had other girlfriends after you."

"I'm sure he did." Even as she said it, she wondered if she had been sure. In her mind, Vince and Gentry had stayed frozen in time, the two of them living like some TV sitcom duo playing along the beach, learning and growing and trying to make do without her by their side.

"I only say that in case it alleviates some of that guilt, you know, about you leaving me without saying that stuff."

"Oh."

"It would have been cool and all."

"If I *had* said it?"

"No, Kate." His mouth set for a moment, then twitched and his voice barely rose above a raspy whisper as he said, "If you had stayed."

Kate nodded because if she had said anything just then it would have come out choked and ended with a sob.

"But I don't want you to think that Dad couldn't have changed things sooner. Or that I couldn't have changed things these last few years. I mean, not that I had a bad life or have done bad things. But this whole going from school to school, job to job then just getting married, having a baby and now my wife getting sick of my refusing to grow up and moving on without me, I don't want you to think that's your fault, even in a small way."

"I appreciate your saying that."

"And I appreciate your calling me. *And* kicking me into gear." He looked again down the hallway, took a few steps in the direction of the exam rooms, then turned back to talk to Kate. "I would have come if Pera had asked. Any time day or night. But she hasn't asked, so I've been staying away."

"The problem with waiting for someone else to make the first move is that they may think they already have."

"By leaving?"

Kate tipped her head to one side.

"Is that what you did with Dad?"

"Not as a game or a test. I really was scared. I really couldn't see what else to do but if he had come after me and asked me to be a part of his family, not just his wife…"

"Family," he echoed softly. "Scary, huh?"

"The scariest. And the best thing that can happen to a person. That is why I so want you to do the right thing for your child—because I know what it means to live with the regret of having let fear drive you away." She reached out to touch Gentry's cheek when a voice from behind her startled her.

"And just how do you imagine you have any right to say something like that to *my* kid?"

She whirled around. "Vince!"

"Dad? What're you doing here?"

"Dr. Lloyd's nurse just called me to okay billing me for some antibiotics for the baby. That's how I found out the baby was sick, not from my daughter-in-law, not from my son and not from someone who used to be…a friend."

Used to be a friend? What did that mean? She flashed back to that long-ago argument where Vince had made clear that Gentry was his family, not hers. She had tried to amend that today, tried to make up for not standing up for the boy and for her rightful place in his and Vince's lives. But now, seeing Vince here with a chill in his gaze and hearing the disappointment in his voice, she wondered if she had made another miscalculation. Maybe she hadn't matured as much as she needed to where this matter was concerned?

"It's not that big of a deal, Vince." She tried to placate him, beginning with a calming reassurance. "Babies run fevers all the time. Hardly the kind of thing that you call around getting people worked up over without more information. It's probably just a—"

"Haven't you interfered enough? I don't care what you and I were to each other a lifetime ago. We are virtually strangers now. And strangers do not stick their noses into family business."

Apparently it was not her who had failed to mature here. Vince had cowed her with that protective daddy act years ago but she would not slink away from it now. For once, Scat-Kat-Katie would hold her ground. "I'm not a stranger, Vince, I'm a doctor. It made sense for Esperanza to bring the baby to me first."

"And for you to take it upon yourself to call my kid?"

She shifted her weight off her aching foot but did not retreat a single step. "To call the baby's father. Yes."

"To do the 'right thing,' as you put it?"

She planted her cane firmly between them. "Yes."

"Dad!" Gentry stood shoulder to shoulder with Kate, even though his was considerably higher up than hers.

Vince ignored the gesture.

Kate understood it completely. This wasn't about Gentry. This was about Kate coming back to town and acting as if she had a place here, a place in his family.

"So that brings me back to my first question," he said. "Where do *you* get off telling my kid what the right thing to do is?"

"Calling him and expecting him to take responsibility for his wife and child was the right thing to do, Vince." She tried to infuse her words with empathy and encouragement. She needed him to know she had not blasted back into town and immediately jumped to the conclusion that he was a failure as a father. "Any fool could see it."

He jerked his head to one side. "Did you just call me a fool?"

"No. I…" Had she? That was exactly what she wanted to avoid. Why didn't anything between the two of them ever come out the way she hoped? "I…I think I just called myself one."

Vince glowered.

Gentry chuckled.

Kate clutched her cane. If he wanted to, Vince could break the tension by laughing himself. Vince always laughed. It was how he dealt with life. She waited.

He remained silent.

Finally Gentry slapped his father on the back and said, "It's just a loan, though, Dad. I got a job working Mondays through Saturdays with overtime. That's why I wasn't there to help with the move and why I couldn't bring groceries over, Kate. I tried to call Moxie back and tell her, but I couldn't get through."

"Oh." That explained that but did not smooth out the prickling friction between Vince and herself.

"I was going to tell you, Dad, but I thought you'd… Well, it's in construction and I thought if I told you, you'd do that 'let me put a good word in' thing you do."

"You actually know some 'good' words?" Kate had thought it would sound funnier than it did. Lighten the mood.

Kate was wrong.

"Yeah, I know some good words," Vince muttered. "How about *respect?* How about *consideration?* How about—"

"I can pay you back for the medicine when I get my first paycheck, Dad." Another slap on the back. "I put in as much overtime as I could so—"

"You don't have to pay me back for my granddaughter's medicine," Vince snapped, though he never took his gaze from Kate's.

"But I want to."

Vince looked at Gentry, clearly surprised by his sudden assertiveness.

Kate felt protective of the boy. After all, she had been the one to kick-start him. "You should really let him do this, Vince."

"You should really stay out of this." He turned away from Kate, then said to his son, "I am not going to make you pay me back for something Fabbie needs."

"It's not a matter of making him." Kate ignored the message of the man putting his broad back to her, which wasn't easy given the width of his shoulders and the fact that they practically radiated tension, for which she knew she was the source. "It's a matter of *letting* him. Let him be the head of his own household, Vince, let go of him even if it means letting him fail."

"Don't you lecture me on letting go of anything, Kate Cromwell." He turned around, his eyes unable to conceal the old wounds of the loss of his wife, Kate's rejection and now the reality that his son was going to grow up and leave him as well. "Don't even presume you know what you're talking about on that score."

She opened her mouth, about to remind him of the loss of her baby sister. And maybe to tell him how she had grieved over running away from him and Gentry, too.

She didn't get out a single syllable before he narrowed his eyes and said, "You've never allowed yourself to care about anything or anyone enough to know there are some things worth hanging on to."

He yanked out his wallet and handed some cash to his son. "I'm going over to the rental house to do some work. I'll see you there later."

And Vince was gone.

A young doctor came out into the waiting area talking with a relaxed and chatty Esperanza, holding her baby, who was waving around a yellow sucker.

Gentry touched Kate on the arm.

It was all the thank-you he offered and all that she needed as she watched him hurry up to the group, take the baby in his arms and give Esperanza a kiss on the cheek.

Kate rubbed her temple. She had a headache. And a footache. And...if she were totally honest with herself?

She looked at Gentry's relieved expression, then at the door where Vince had just stormed out.

She also had a heartache.

Chapter Seventeen

"I still can't believe they just left you there." Moxie helped Kate around the side of the house. After helping her get out of Moxie's old truck. After helping her get out of a fix when the well-meaning doctor had found herself stranded at the urgent-care clinic.

"They didn't mean to, I'm sure. Dr. Lloyd started asking me questions about my foot and they needed to get the baby those antibiotics."

"Don't you start making excuses for Gentry, Kate. The kid is a—"

"Man. The 'kid' is a man and it's time people around here began treating him that way."

"He left you at the clinic, Kate."

"So did his father and I don't see anyone in this town going around questioning his maturity."

"Present company excepted?" Moxie reached the corner of the house and waited for Kate to catch up.

Kate faltered, grimaced.

Moxie extended her hand for support.

Kate swept the gesture aside with one well-aimed swing of her cane and began forward movement again. "I can make my way into the house from here."

"I was told to get you home and not to leave until I saw you seated, leg up, and checked to make sure you had actually swallowed your meds, not just poked them under your tongue to spit out as soon as no one was looking. Doctor's orders."

Kate shot her a sly glance. "Why do I think you don't really take orders from the cutie-pie doc unless they are orders you already planned to follow through on?"

"He is cute, isn't he?" Moxie picked her way through the junk in the so-called garden, leading the way for a beleaguered Kate. She wondered why Jo hadn't seen to this mess first, as it would be the easiest thing on the list to clear out by herself.

At the thought of the list, Moxie remembered the offer she had jotted down. She took a second to scan the area for the piece of paper that she had stuffed under a potted plant when she'd come over with her recommendations.

"Still there," she muttered.

"Don't I know it?" Kate agreed.

"You...*know?*" Moxie glanced at the paper again, knowing that wasn't really the topic of this snippet of conversation. Opting to retrieve the offer when she left later today, she turned to the woman behind her and confessed, "I'm sorry. My mind wandered and I think I even started talking to myself."

"Oh, you are much too young for that route!" Kate chuckled, wobbled, steadied herself with her cane then began picking her way through the land of tacky trinkets once again. When she reached the deck where Moxie stood, she looked up. "How old are you, anyway? If you don't mind my asking?"

"Thirty-one." Moxie gave a half shrug and waited.

"Thirty-one?" Kate frowned.

Here it comes.

"All these years I pictured the person taking care of this cottage as some sweet dear old thing who took in stray cats and wore aprons and sun hats and high-top sneakers."

"Who knows, maybe one day that will be me! I like the sound of it, anyway." She flexed her fingers to keep herself from just reaching out and snagging Kate to steady her as she took the steps. "Oh, and thanks."

"For what?" Kate took one step then paused to catch her breath.

"Not asking the usual."

"The usual?" Another step. Another pause.

"Thirty-one? And not married yet?"

Kate rolled her eyes, drew in a deep breath then took the last step. "That would be a bit like the pot…"

Clunk. Down came her cane on the deck proper at last.

"…the much older pot and so single she doesn't even have a boyfriend, much less an adorable doctor with his own urgent-care clinic…"

Thump. She swung her cast up and landed it with enough force to make Moxie wince.

"…disparaging the marital status of the kettle."

Moxie clenched her teeth, knowing to the very core of her being that Kate would not welcome help from her at this point. How did she know that? She just did. Because… And even as the thought occurred to her, it also came to her how odd a comparison it was… because that was how Moxie would feel. She would rather do it herself and fail than have somebody take pity on her and offer unasked-for assistance.

"Well, thank you, anyway." Moxie stole one last peek to make sure the offer stayed tucked away, then swung open the back door.

Kate nodded her appreciation for the gesture and kept moving along. "How long have you two been together?"

"His dad, ol' Doc Lloyd, was chief of staff at our little hospital forever, so he grew up here."

"High-school sweethearts?"

"Hardly, I was homeschooled and took my GED when I was sixteen."

"Really?"

"My mom left then. My dad was a mess. It didn't seem like a great time to suddenly learn how to cope with the public school system." Why had she told the woman that? Moxie ducked her head slightly and adjusted the simple straw hat she had worn to church this morning. As soon as she got Kate settled, she'd climb into a pair of overalls and comfy clogs and spend the rest of the day…doing exactly what she wanted. Which probably meant working. "Besides, even at sixteen I already knew what I wanted to do."

"I could tell that about you the first time we met." Kate reached the doorway and took a moment to lean against it before going on. She didn't seem the least bit put off by Moxie practically sharing her life story. "You just seem to know what you want out of life."

"Thanks, but it's not such a big deal. I just want what most people do. To be happy. To have a purpose. To be loved."

"And something tells you that marrying Dr. Lionel Lloyd won't bring you those things?"

"I don't think those things come from other people," she said softly. "Oh, and thanks yet again."

"For?"

"Not assuming *he* was the marriage holdout."

"Him? The man who spent ten minutes chewing me out about not allowing my foot to heal properly then followed it up with an open invitation to move to Santa Sofia and become a partner in his clinic?"

Moxie laughed. "He's also the type who knows what he wants."

"Yeah, he wants some nights and weekends off for a change so he can try to convince you to marry him. That man is anything but commitment phobic."

"Commitment phobic? That your professional diagnosis, Doctor, or more along the lines of it takes one to know one?" Moxie couldn't believe her boldness.

Kate did not appear one bit put off by it, though. She gave a wry laugh and a nod. "Hey, I am what I am. But you? I don't really think you are afraid of commitment. Something else is holding you back."

Moxie nodded. "I keep telling him it's the name."

"Lionel?" Kate crinkled up her nose.

"No. My name. If I married him I'd have to go through life as Moxie Lloyd."

"Not so bad."

Moxie's turn to scrunch up her nose. "It sounds like a chemical ingredient in a fake dietary supplement. 'Now with moxielloyd for fast-acting results.'"

Kate chuckled.

"The only thing worse is how it sounds with my real name."

"Real name?"

"Molly. Molly Lloyd. *That* sounds like a fat nodule you have to have removed from some part of the body you don't want to discuss in public." She rolled her eyes.

Kate shook her head. "And that's the best reason you can give for not wanting to marry that very nice, very cute Dr. Lloyd?"

"Just trying to keep it light. Nobody listens, anyway." Moxie raised her shoulders and looked away. "They don't usually believe I'm the holdout. You know, adorable single doctor with more business than he can handle. Why would he want to tie himself down to one girl, especially one like me?"

Kate turned and latched her green-eyed gaze onto Moxie's eyes. "Maybe because he wants what most people want?"

To be happy. To have a purpose. To be loved.

Moxie's words hung in the air unspoken.

She cocked her head. She'd never thought of that.

While she had dragged her feet fearing that her mother might prove right about the discontent of marriage and life in Santa Sofia, she'd never thought she might be keeping Lionel from realizing his own dreams and desires. She knew he wanted a family. And a home. "But I just haven't been able to make that leap of faith."

"Faith?"

"Oh, not 'faith' faith." Moxie pointed heavenward. "It's not a God issue. It's a human one. Much as I want to be loved, I don't have a lot of faith in it. I don't have a lot of experience with the people I love hanging in there." She thought of her mother's note and of the Weatherby family motto. "How can you believe a person will love you for a lifetime if nobody ever has?"

"People are just flawed, Moxie." Kate touched her shoulder.

"I know. Maybe I expect too much. And I pray a lot about it. Some people think that's corny, I know."

"Not me." Kate took a look at the backyard, her eyes squinted but her face serene.

"Yeah?"

"In fact I've given a lot of thought to my spiritual life since I came to Santa Sofia, seeing how much I've neglected it and feeling a strong tug to change that."

"I'll add you to my prayer list, if you like."

"I would like that."

"Consider it done." Moxie smiled and nodded. "Now, I have doctor's orders to see through. So let's get that foot up."

She held the door open for Kate, who took one step

inside and shouted, "Tell me you did not get up first thing this morning to go shoe shopping!"

"Wow." Moxie crowded in behind the woman to find a small pyramid of shoe boxes stacked neatly on the kitchen table.

Jo's head popped up above the stack. "I'm not shopping. I'm selling."

"Really?" Moxie had to take another look. This time, in a pair of inexpensive flip-flops, she marveled at how much Jo's feet resembled her own. Except Jo clearly indulged in regular pedicures and had allowed herself the small luxury of a simple toe ring, something Moxie would never try. "You brought all these shoes down here and now you're willing to part with them in a yard sale? Do you mind if I…?"

"Help yourself. But keep in mind, the money you give for them is going to the Traveler's Wayside Chapel, so don't try to talk me down too low."

Moxie flipped the lid off the first box.

"I'm going to sit down." Kate lumbered past.

"I'll help you." And by *help,* Moxie meant stay out of her way until she got to the couch, where, if she had to, Moxie could easily grab Kate's cane, give her a push and whisk her cast up onto the table before Kate knew what hit her. "Then I'll come back and try these on."

"Jo, will you get my meds?" Kate called out, not even looking behind her. "And some water."

Jo hurried to comply.

Kate plopped down, covered her eyes with one hand, then propped her leg up and sighed.

"Here's your water and medication." Jo set them on the table by Kate's elbow. "Did you eat any breakfast?"

"No. Esperanza came over with the baby before I was even out of bed this morning."

"Hang on a sec while I make you a peanut-butter sandwich so you'll have some food in your stomach."

Moxie stood and watched the sisters roll with the moment, each interaction a study in effortless ease that only came with blood ties and a very long history. It made Moxie feel like a fifth wheel. A *third* wheel?

Basically, she felt as if she didn't belong.

She hated that feeling.

"If you're all situated, then, I guess I can go," she said.

"Wait!" Kate's hand shot out. "I had a key."

"The extra house key? I brought that over with the paperwork the other day."

"No, this morning. I found the key to my treasure chest and I had it in my hand when I came down to answer the door."

"Where did you put it?"

"I don't remember. Would you mind looking around to see if I laid it someplace in here?"

"I'd be glad to." Moxie looked around in all the obvious places in the room. "Could you have left it in the kitchen?"

"No. I had the baby in my arms by then. But I might have dropped it on the stairs."

"Okay." Moxie threw open the door to the enclosed stairway. The midday sun had not begun to shine through the windows in the front room so she couldn't see well. She glanced up at the lone bulb at the top of the staircase and shook her head. It was on the list. *Put new lightbulb in staircase fixture.*

"Great." She took off her hat, tossed it aside and began searching step by step.

"Save yourself some trouble and check really well in the carpet by the door and in that crack where the carpet meets the steps," Kate cautioned. "I can't help thinking that if it had hit the steps, I'd have heard it and recalled that."

"Okay." Moxie plonked her bottom down on the second step up and began running her fingers along the edge of the carpet.

"Did you hear that?" Jo called from the kitchen. "I thought I heard a car door."

From the stairwell, Moxie couldn't hear anything going on outside.

"It's probably from across the street." Kate's tone gave no doubt that she had no intention of looking and confirming that.

Moxie could hardly blame her. Kate had told her about the scalding Vince had given her for getting involved with Gentry, Esperanza and the baby. Correction, Moxie thought, the *undeserved* scalding. Of all the good people in Santa Sofia who had seen the way Vince had spent his life trying to protect Gentry from, well, pretty much every unpleasant or difficult thing in the world, Moxie alone had been the one to take him to task about it. Moxie and now Kate.

"No. I think I heard something outside." The

clatter of silverware and plates came from the kitchen. Then the rush of water in the sink. "I'm going to go out and see—"

"Bring me that sandwich first. I can't take this medicine until—"

Whomp.

The front door came swinging open and banged against the wall.

Moxie jumped and bumped her head on the doorknob. She put her hand to the throbbing spot and closed her eyes. "Ow!"

"Praise the Lord you girls haven't fallen off the face of the earth!" A woman's voice boomed through the whole of the quiet cottage.

Moxie still had her head bent when she felt a hand cradling the top of her head.

"I know you're always on the move, Scat-Kat-Katie, but you really should be in bed!"

Moxie looked up.

"Oh!" A chubby woman with a bubble of pale hair loomed over her, her green eyes flashing with surprise. "You're not my Katie!"

"No, I'm—"

"Mom! What are you doing here?"

Mom? That was Dodie Cromwell? She looked so… familiar. Moxie stared, and not a subtle stare, either. A big open-mouthed, "what gives here?" kind of stare that, if Mrs. Cromwell were her mother, the woman would have scolded her for and told her to mind her manners. She thought of stepping forward and introducing herself but the woman looked right through her as if Jo and Kate were the only people in the house. In the whole entirety of her universe, even.

"I had to come. My girls didn't answer my phone calls." She went to Kate, pushed her hair back off her face and planted a kiss on her forehead. "I had to come and make sure everything was all right."

The sight made Moxie look away. And in doing so she noticed light bouncing off something metal. She reached down and plucked it up. "I, uh, I found the key."

Kate batted in the air, making her hair fall back into place. She didn't acknowledge Moxie's news, just narrowed her eyes at her mother and demanded, "Where are your friends? How did you get down here?"

The older woman put her hand to her mouth when she said, "Can we discuss this later when we don't have, um, company?"

It couldn't have felt more awkward if the older woman had called her an outsider in Pig Latin. Which would have been super awkward since it would be achingly obvious and imply that she didn't think Moxie still wouldn't be bright enough to piece it together. *Outsider-ay.*

Moxie felt as if she now had the term so firmly imprinted in her brain that it probably looked like a stamp across her forehead. It didn't help that the whole hand-to-mouth thing actually had the effect of amplifying Dodie Cromwell's brush-off instead of hiding it, as she must have thought it would. Moxie stared at the woman some more.

Something about her made Moxie want to smile. Maybe it was the soft, motherly figure or the hairdo that must have taken a couple hours and at least one can of hairspray to construct. Or the funny little shoes that almost went with her outfit, but not quite, that almost fit her feet, but…no.

Moxie winced at the way the woman's foot looked crammed into the shoe and at how the heel seemed to thrust her forward at an odd angle. Dodie Cromwell looked, well, a bit dotty.

And still, Moxie wished with all her heart that the older woman would like her.

For a moment she thought if she introduced herself it might ease the tension in the room. But a glance at Kate, and then at just the back of Jo working in the kitchen, made her realize that the woman had generated her own tension by just showing up today.

She thrust the key out toward Kate. "I'll leave y'all to talk."

"Don't run off." Jo touched her shoulder as she came into the room with Kate's sandwich. "Go. Try on shoes. I know you want to. It's not like we don't see our mom every few days."

"In fact, I'm a little embarrassed we didn't realize she would do something drastic if we didn't answer our phones." Kate took the plate with the sandwich on it then swung her gaze from her sister to her mother. "Or if she just *felt* like it."

"You did not drive all this way alone, did you, Mom?" Jo demanded.

Dodie did not answer. She just clucked her tongue at the plate in Kate's hand. "Is that what you're having for lunch? Surely we can do better than that."

"Mom?" Jo folded her arms.

"Just give me ten minutes in the kitchen. I think I remember where it is!" She went breezing by.

Moxie could not take her eyes off the woman.

"Mom, you haven't answered my—"

Kate held up her hand to cut her sister off. "If she's cooking, she's not stirring up trouble."

Jo shut her mouth.

Moxie looked around and wondered how unsafe it might be to go out the front door. She could probably make it.

"Here, before she gets back in here, hand me my treasure chest. That way I can see what's in it without her sticking her nose in and..." She made a face at Jo.

Moxie supposed that was some kind of sisterly code for *and you know what.* Moxie did not know what the woman would do, however, and it piqued her curiosity. Enough so that this time when she tried to excuse herself she did it without any real enthusiasm. "Okay, then, I guess I should get going."

"Here's the treasure chest." Jo plunked it down in Kate's lap.

Kate inserted the key and wriggled it.

Neither of them said goodbye to Moxie, which she took as a casual invitation to stay.

Kate stuck her tongue out and concentrated, trying to get the old lock to budge.

"Maybe it's not the right key," Jo suggested.

"No, I can feel it. I just need to use a little—"

Clank.

The metal lid flipped back and smashed into the body of the file box.

"Ta-da!" Kate exclaimed.

"What's in there?" Jo whispered, crowding in close.

"Which would you girls prefer—tuna salad or grilled cheese?" Dodie called from the kitchen.

"My retainer!" Kate's voice rang out.

"What?" Dodie asked.

Kate put her hand over her mouth.

"Anything you make will be great, Mom," Jo replied, then pinched the pink-and-wire contraption between her fingers and held it up. "You got in so much trouble for losing this."

"That's not the only thing." Kate put her hand deep into the box.

"What? What have you found?"

Kate did not say a word but her eyes rimmed with tears. She held her sister's gaze and slowly, her hand trembling, withdrew an old photograph.

"Oh," Jo whispered, her own eyes wide and her hand on her cheek as they all stared at a photo of two young girls in a driveway in Anytown, America, standing in front of a truck not unlike Moxie's with a brown-eyed man and a nearly colorless sky.

Moxie's heart stopped.

Her mind stopped.

Her ability to speak stopped.

But her feet did not. They carried her out the front door and to her truck as fast as they could.

Chapter Eighteen

"What was that about?" Jo looked at the door Moxie had just slammed, then at the photo that had seemed to set her off, then at Kate.

"What on earth?" Their mother looked out the kitchen window then ran to the back door. "Give me a minute and I'll move my car!"

"Mom?" Jo hurried to the kitchen only to practically collide head-on with her mom coming back inside.

"Have you ever seen the likes of that? She just whipped that old truck over alongside my car and backed out without using the drive!" Dodie shook her head, then looked at a piece of quarter-folded paper in her hand. "And what is this?"

"What's what?" Jo touched the picture of herself and Kate standing beside their father in front of his new truck. The truck he had driven away in so many years ago. The truck that looks so much like...

She glanced up and the paper in her mother's hands

grabbed her attention. She instantly recognized Moxie's handwriting from having pored over the list she'd made regarding improvements to the cottage. "Where did you find that?"

"Outside on the porch under a plant." Dodie strained to read the page, holding it as far away as she could, then bringing it almost to her nose, then out again. "It looks like… Is this yours, Jo? It looks like your handiwork."

Jo took the paper from her mother's hand and without reading the details recognized it immediately as a tentative offer to buy a property. She made a closer inspection. *This property.*

It *did* look like her handiwork.

"Of course." If the situation had been reversed and Jo had been in Moxie's place, she'd have done the exact same thing. Jo squinted to go over the bottom line a second time. "It's an offer to buy this house as is. A low offer, but fair."

Dodie shook her head and went back to making sandwiches. "Why would anyone think we wanted to sell our house?"

"Because we do." Kate came into the kitchen, her face drawn with pain and weariness. "Or, at least *I* do."

"Scat-Kat-Katie wants to sell the house and move," Dodie muttered. "Now there's a surprise."

Kate scowled. "Jo had the idea first."

"It's a sisterhood, not a competition," Dodie advised for about the umpteen-millionth time in their lives. "It doesn't matter who wanted to do what first."

"She wanted to fix this place up for a fast sale," Kate

went on. "Had the idea we needed to do that to keep you from the wild notion of trying to live down here. She might have had another agenda, though. And after a few days down here, she might have changed her mind, I can't say. Jo?"

Jo gazed at the paper again. A low offer but one that left her with a share big enough to make the first month's mortgage payment on the house in Atlanta and finish off the upgrades so it would sell for enough to keep her from further debt. Then she looked at the picture, the two innocent faces and her father, proud of only his truck. Then she stared at the shoes that after a morning at the chapel in the company of a man whose priorities she greatly admired now represented the frivolity of her life.

It was as if her whole life were now laid before her and she had to choose. Could she ever go back to the way she had been just a few short days ago?

"No," she murmured.

"No?" Dodie frowned. "No to me living down here? No to another agenda? No to changing your mind?"

"No." Jo took a deep breath then went from not looking at anything in particular to focusing on her mother's expectant gaze. "No, I do not want to sell the house. No, I do not want to go back."

"Not go back? I didn't know that was on the table." Dodie sliced through a freshly made tuna sandwich from corner to corner then set it, on a plate, in front of Kate. The whole while she never took her worried gaze from Jo. "But you have a full, exciting life in Atlanta. You have your work and your…all those business deals you've told me about. And, uh, didn't your boss—"

"Listen to yourself, Mom." Jo paced the length of the kitchen then pivoted. "My work. My deals. My boss. That's hardly a *whole* life, is it? Coming here made me realize that."

Kate reached out to touch the photograph with two fingers then looked up at Jo. "Meeting Travis Brandt had nothing to do with that?"

"Travis?" Mom's eyes lit up. "A *man?* You met a man?"

"A *minister,* Mom," Jo emphasized.

"*Travis Brandt,* Mom." Kate waited a moment to allow that to sink in.

Dodie looked at her daughters, the photo, the offer, then at Kate again. She shook her head.

"He's a sports guy? On TV? Really cute. All-American type. Dated supermodels. I know you saw his picture in magazines."

"Not the magazines in your office, Scat-Kat, those things had to be at least five years old."

"Don't be so quick to look down your nose at my outdated magazines, that's probably about the time this guy's picture was everywhere."

"What happened to him? Not some sort of scandal, I hope."

"No. I get the feeling a scandal you would have remembered." Kate lifted her leg to rest her foot on the chair across from her. "He just walked away from it all. The girls, the money, the fame."

Dodie shook her head.

"That doesn't matter, anyway. That's not who he is anymore." Jo held up her hand.

She got it now. In this instant, almost two grand worth of shoes lined up before her and the meaninglessness of her life spelled out by her mother moments earlier, she got it.

Standing here, hearing people talk about who Travis had been as though he had no more dimension than the photographs they had seen him in, she got it.

Looking at the picture of her father and herself and her sister and seeing in his eyes that he had not chosen their baby sister and rejected her but that he had chosen himself, he had chosen an unfilled life and to cause pain to those he should have protected, she got it.

Thinking of all the possibilities still open to her, knowing the man Travis had become, Jo got it. Got how he could walk away from the emptiness of money, fame and, yes, even adoring supermodels just to end up flipping flapjacks in the fellowship hall. "What matters is that he is a good guy."

"And you like him, this good guy?" Mom asked.

"Yes. But that's not the reason I don't want to go back to that life in Atlanta."

Kate scoffed.

"Okay, it's not the whole reason."

"But if you don't go back, won't that nice Mike Powers be angry with you?" Dodie wrung her hands.

"In the first place *Paul* Powers is not nice. And furthermore I no longer feel the need to impress him at all costs."

"But you were doing so well," Mom said softly.

"Don't you see? My work is not enough anymore." She thought of the chapel, of the needs she could help meet there. She thought of bringing together women throughout the community to form a worship-and-action team that would meet on the beach. With their bare feet in the sand and their hands ready to serve the Lord. "Mom, I am feeling a pull to do God's work."

"What does that mean?" Kate sat up straighter than before. Her intense features echoed the expression of their father in the photograph before them. "How could you possibly know for sure what to do? People spend their whole lives trying to do good, to do the right thing when faced with life's monumental questions, Jo. How can you be here in Santa Sofia a matter of days and presume you know what you should do with the rest of your life like that?"

Kate the perfect didn't understand? A wave of forgiveness washed through Jo. Forgiveness for her sister, her father and even her mother. All of them had been seeking, she realized. Trying to find the right path. They had no idea what *they* wanted or how to find it.

They had not intended to make her feel unwanted, but how could they not? They, like far too many people in the world, felt unwanted themselves.

Jo marveled that somehow it had come to her. Through Travis. Through her own anxiety. Through service.

"It means that I feel that I can't serve two masters. I can't serve my own need to be the biggest and brightest and best in pursuit of money and recognition to assuage my own hurts and make me feel loved *and* serve the Lord and love others with all my heart." Jo held up her hand to keep them from jumping in. "Some people can. But not me. It meant too much for me to try to bring the focus onto myself. I didn't put my clients first, I put my numbers first, my deals, my place in the company."

Dodie set a second sandwich down. Through it all she had kept right on doing the mom thing, putting her kids' needs first. Even the ones she did not understand. "I want to support you, sweetie. But…you're giving up being a Realtor?"

"No. Yes. Maybe. I don't know. It's not the job that's the issue, Mom. I can do or be anything but whatever I do, I have to get my priorities straight or none of it matters. I do not want to go back to my life the way it was in Atlanta."

"Jo, I can't believe I'm hearing this." Dodie looked to Kate as if Kate were the final determining factor in whether or not this news would be true or not.

"Why? Mom!" Jo made her mother look at her and when she did, she reached out and put her hand on her mother's soft upper arm to anchor her attention. "You're the one who wanted to start life over here in Santa Sofia herself. You're the one always saying 'If you're heading in the right direction, you have no reason to look back,' aren't you?"

"Yes."

"Well, for the first time I am heading in the right direction, Mom. I thought you'd be happy." For an instant the old insecurities arose. She wanted her mother to be pleased with her. To approve. But did she want it badly enough to waver on her new commitment? She thought of the chapel and the shoes and then of Travis and the talk they had had this morning. She took up Moxie's offer and held it out. "But even if you don't understand my decision, I'm sticking with it. If we're taking a vote, mine is not to sell the cottage."

Dodie slid the paper from Jo's hand. "Kate?"

"If Jo stays here, I guess she can take care of you. I'm not going to do it." The words had hardly left her lips when Kate gasped, put her hand over her mouth and sat there, blinking in complete shock at her own bluntness.

"I never expected you would, my little Scat-Kat-Katie." Mom laughed.

Sure. Jo announced a turnaround in her life plans and Mom gives her grief. Kate does it and Mom…

Jo narrowed her eyes at her sister, the way she had when they were kids and Kate had gotten all the attention. What she saw made her breath catch in the back of her throat. Where there had been pain in her sister's face before, Jo now saw hurt there instead.

There was a difference, Jo understood, and her heart went out to her sister for it.

Mom gave Jo grief, sure, but Mom also gave Kate grief. It just came in another form.

Jo looked at her mother, who had stuck out her lip in a half-teasing pout but whose eyes shone with concern and maybe a little fear as she looked from

Kate to Jo and back again. Yeah, their mom gave them grief but they gave it right back to her again.

Jo spread out her arms, her hands making a slashing motion. "This stops now."

"What?"

"This... This... This whole cycle." Jo took the paper and snatched up the old photo. "This whole way we have of jabbing at one another, then retreating and pretending it never happened, or we didn't mean it, or somehow the other person is to blame for taking it wrong."

"We never—"

"Mom, we *always,*" Kate corrected.

"And now that we know this, or rather, that we have acknowledged it, we cannot go back." Jo took a deep breath and exhaled. It felt good.

"I don't—" Dodie wrung her hands.

"Sit down, Mom." Jo pulled out a chair.

"And take off those shoes," Kate demanded.

Dodie obeyed.

The chunky shoes banged against the old floor as she kicked them off.

Jo followed suit, even though tossing off her flip-flops did not have the same impact. What did she care? She wasn't going to rely on shoes to make her statements anymore, anyway. "Mom. We cannot go back. We are finally headed in the right direction. We've been honest."

"O-okay," Mom agreed. She didn't look as if she wanted to agree but there it was.

"I don't want to sell the house," Jo went on. "Kate

does. Kate doesn't want to take care of you and… neither do I."

"Jo!" Kate and Dodie spoke in unison.

"But I will. As much as you need me to," Jo went on. "And the best place to do that is right here in Santa Sofia. In this cottage on Dream Away Bay Court."

"I never asked you girls to take care of me," Mom protested.

"Yes, you did, Mom." Kate said it first, carrying on what Jo had started with them dealing honestly with one another at last. "When you sold your condo, making yourself literally homeless. Then when you showed up at my office—an appointment *you* made—to announce your wild idea about coming down here. What do you call that?"

"A plan. I called that a plan."

"As I recall, that plan involved friends?" Kate prodded.

"They made *other* plans," Dodie confessed.

"Oh, Mom." Jo came over and put her arms around her mother.

Kate put her hand on Dodie's.

"Guess it wasn't a very good plan, huh?" Dodie sighed, laughed a little, then picked up the old photo and looked at it, really looked at it, at last. "I can't believe you found this after all these years. I thought it was lost for good."

"I put it in my treasure chest," Kate said.

"Hiding it or saving it?" Jo asked.

Kate opened her mouth then shut it again, not giving an answer.

Dodie turned a hopeful gaze to her oldest daughter. "And the other one?"

Kate shook her head.

"What other one?" Jo asked.

"Mom took this one and didn't get all of the new truck in it, so Dad took a second photo with Mom and Christina in it." Kate put her hand on her mother's arm. "It wasn't in the box, though, Mom. I don't know what happened to it."

"I do." Moxie Weatherby stood in the back doorway, her eyes red and wide, and a picture frame clutched high against her chest. "It's been hanging in Billy J's Bait Shack Buffet for more than twenty years. Not that you could find it in the junk."

"Billy J had a picture of our mom and sister?" Jo tried to make sense of it.

"No." Moxie turned the frame around to show them all as she choked back a sob and managed to say, "The picture he had was of *me* and...and *my mom.*"

Chapter Nineteen

"My birth father told my adoptive parents that you were an aunt and had no interest in finding me. He didn't give a name or where this supposed aunt lived. We had no idea." Moxie spoke to Dodie, despite the fact that Dodie could not seem to hear her words.

The older woman sat in the kitchen, stunned, staring at the photos and shaking her head. "It can't be. It just can't be."

"Wait." Jo put her hand to her forehead. "You were here in Santa Sofia all this time?"

"My birth father left me with the Weatherbys when I was five. He gave them the right to adopt me and I assume that's what happened. I have always used their name, I never knew my whole name before that. I think my birth father may have used aliases."

The other women all exchanged anxious and then knowing glances that all but confirmed they believed Moxie's suspicion.

Moxie pulled her shoulders up protectively but it did not shield her from her doubts and anxieties. What if she'd gotten it all wrong? What if she had it right but the Cromwells didn't care? "I just know that this is the only remnant I've ever had of my life before the Weatherbys. It fits. It's the companion to your photograph."

All of them stared at the two pictures now.

"Isn't it?" Moxie barely managed to whisper.

Kate touched the faded old photo in the frame.

Jo gaped at her in what could have been awe or maybe she was appalled at Moxie's nerve at making this assumption. Moxie couldn't tell.

Dodie looked up at last.

"Isn't it?" Moxie asked again, pleaded really, for some answer. "Isn't it me in that picture? Doesn't that mean—"

"Christina?" Dodie raised her trembling hand. "Is that really you?"

"Molly Christina," she murmured in what sounded as though her voice had had to travel from a long ways away. "They used to call me Molly Christina."

Tears streamed down Dodie's round yet wrinkled cheeks, blurring the brilliance of the green of her eyes.

"Yes. I can see where that would have come from." Dodie dragged in a deep breath. "Molly was your grandmother Cromwell's name."

"It's true then?" Jo asked.

"It's true," Kate confirmed.

Then the room fell silent.

Moxie had no idea what she had expected but it wasn't this. Silence. Awkward, aching silence.

The tightness in her chest pressed inward, closing, clamping. She couldn't breathe. She couldn't speak. The greatest mystery of her life had been revealed and she had no idea what to do about it.

Kate got up from her chair, her eyes searching, her whole body rigid as if she were restraining herself from actually bolting out of the room.

Jo leaned forward, one hand on her mother's arm, the other on one of the shoe boxes.

Moxie took a step backward. "This is all so much to process, for all of us. Maybe I should—"

"Christina. My Christina. My baby." In the time it took for Dodie to say the words, she had Moxie wrapped in her arms. She said the name again and again as she kissed Moxie's hair, her cheeks, even her fingers. At last she stepped back, took Moxie's face in her hands, put her gaze in direct line with her newfound daughter's and said, "I have been looking for you for your entire life."

"You have?"

"There hasn't been a day gone by that I haven't cried for you, prayed for you, hoped for you. I always loved you, Christina. Always."

She'd always loved her. Always. All those years when Moxie had felt unsure and unlovable, someone had been out there praying for her, loving her. Moxie gasped and tears flowed freely from her eyes. "Really?"

"Yes. Really." Dodie hugged her close again. "Why

do you think I kept this cottage? Why do you think we came down here every summer and sent our distant cousins the McGreggors here every winter?"

"The McGreggors were your relation?" That was probably where Billy J had gotten the idea that the lady in the photograph was a relative but not her mother. "I… I don't see what that has to do with looking for me."

"Because I knew at some point your father would bring you here. Between jobs, between relationships, he'd have to have a place to stay at *some* point and since he knew we only came down here once a year…" Dodie let Moxie fill in the blank.

"But didn't you look for me? Really look for me?" Moxie had been right here for most of her life. Though with homeschooling, and her fierce independent streak, not to mention that the Cromwells hadn't come here in person for sixteen years, it might not have been as simple as it seemed.

"I looked every year, though I have to admit, honey, I might have looked straight at you a time or two and never realized it. I was looking for a child who looked like Jo or Kate, and you look…"

"Like you, Mom," Jo observed. "Right down to your feet."

Every one of them looked down.

Jo wriggled her chubby toes.

Dodie did the same.

Moxie felt compelled to wiggle hers, though no one could see through her shoes.

Dodie looked up first and began smoothing back Moxie's hair as she went on, "When I didn't have any luck finding you in Santa Sofia, I used the revenue from the cottage to fund going places to search for you during the summer."

"That's what you did on all those vacations by yourself?" Kate appeared absolutely incredulous.

"Going places?" Moxie tried to imagine what she meant. "Like?"

"Like places I knew your father had contacts or where he had talked of going. Mobile. Savannah. St. Louis. Nashville. You want evidence of all the places I went, it's all in the rock garden."

Moxie lifted her head as though she could see through the walls to the odd assortment of ornaments. "You sent those souvenirs?"

"I knew I'd find you one day and I wanted there to be a record to show you that I never gave up, Christina, um, Molly?"

"Moxie. I like Moxie."

Dodie stroked her cheek. "I like it, too."

"What? She is our sister all of two minutes and you approve of her picking out her own nickname. Kate has like a thousand nicknames but no one ever gave me—"

They all looked at Jo. She pressed her lips shut.

That only lasted a few seconds before she broke into laughter.

Jo opened her arms and threw them around Moxie. "I can't believe this. I really can't."

Moxie hugged her sister back.

Her sister. It felt so weird and so wonderful to say it, even just in her head.

When they pulled apart, Dodie slapped her hands together. "Sit, baby, we have so much to talk about. You want me to make you a sandwich?"

"A...sandwich?" In context of the monumental discovery they'd just made, it seemed far too small a response. And just exactly the *right* response. They were family. This was her family. These were her sisters and this, her mom. Why wouldn't they want to sit down and eat together? "I think a sandwich would be great."

Chapter Twenty

They talked until long past all of their bedtimes and Moxie ended up spending the night. The next morning, wanting to both reciprocate for the tuna sandwich and snacks and because she said she needed to find a way for her new mom and old cantankerous dad to come to terms with what had happened, Moxie offered to open up the Bait Shack Buffet and cook breakfast for them all.

Kate begged off, saying she'd done too much the last few days and needed to rest her foot. It was the truth. Though when she looked out the window of her upstairs bedroom and saw a certain red pickup truck pull in across the street, she figured her foot had rested enough and up she got.

She made the trip around the house and across the way with practiced ease but the last little bit, coming up the drive, she slowed. Vince had gone inside. Probably already engulfed in a project to make the place more comfortable for Esperanza and Fabbie.

And by doing so, making Gentry all the more comfortable *not* being here.

Suddenly not being there sounded like a great idea.

She paused, her cane firmly planted, then began to turn away to go home again.

"Well, there she is." Vince came down from the porch with a leather tool belt slung over one shoulder, a can of paint in one hand and a power drill in the other. "Kate the wise."

Clang. He set the paint can in the back of his truck.

"Kate the righteous."

Thud. Next came the power tool.

"Crowing Kate."

Ka-chunk. He unburdened himself of the tool belt then made the two long strides to stand before her with his hands on his hips.

Kate took a moment just to look at him. Vince Merchant. Hardworking handyman. Loving father and grandfather. Good neighbor.

The man she had never completely stopped loving.

The very thing he had recently accused Kate of never allowing in her life—something worth hanging onto. But in order to do that, she would first have to let go.

Of fear.

Of her defenses.

Of the past.

And mostly, of the man himself. Of all she had built him up to be. Of all the things he never would be.

She had to let go in order to hang on.

If she could do that, then maybe…

"Actually, it's Humble Kate." She leaned on her cane with her left hand and extended her right as if introducing herself for the first time to the man she had loved for half her life. "I'm here to apologize."

He opened his mouth, probably to zing her with a quick comeback, then froze, cocked his head and shut his mouth again.

Kate smiled. She'd left Vince Merchant speechless. That was a start.

Emboldened, she asked, "Aren't you going to invite me in so we can talk about this?"

"I would but this isn't my home." He jerked his thumb over his shoulder toward the quaint little "mystery house." "Gentry and Esperanza are moving his things in later today. He's in. I'm out. They want to do the work here themselves."

Which was as it should be, she almost said, but caught herself. The man knew that. She could see it in his eyes. He did not need Kate the Great to point it out to him. "I'm glad to hear that."

He nodded. "No sense in pretending you had no hand in it. If it were left up to me…"

I'd have botched it big time. The man knew, even if he couldn't bring himself to say it out loud.

Kate put both hands on her cane, which she imagined made her appear quite humble. "Oh, I just made one little phone call."

He narrowed his eyes and studied her. "Don't kid yourself."

"Well…" She wondered if she was blushing.

"Nothing is that simple."

"Oh. Um, yes, you're right of course." Now she knew for sure she was blushing because the heat reached from her neck to her temples.

"But your being there, your calling him, your finally telling him why you left all those years ago, gave Gentry a message that I hadn't gotten across to him in a lifetime." He shuffled his feet, dropped his gaze. "No matter what passes between people, love hangs tough. It gives the best and expects the best, even when 'the best' hurts or is inconvenient or comes at a personal sacrifice."

"I think I've read that somewhere before." She smiled to hear this rugged handyman sum up the "love" chapter from Corinthians so simply, and from his heart.

"And obviously the kids wanted their marriage to work."

"Of course."

"When Esperanza moved here with the baby, she had given Gentry an ultimatum. Get a job and grow up."

"And he did get a job."

"Yeah, but he never had any real reason to grow up. I mean, I raised him to believe he'd always get a second chance. And a third." Some people might have at least chuckled as they said something like that, to soften the harshness of such a painful confession. This time, Vince did not try to make light of it. "And if those didn't work out, I'd swoop in to the rescue."

"You always let him win."

"Hmm?"

"At Wa Hoo. You always let him win at Wa Hoo, Vince. Even as a kid he knew that wasn't right."

"Wa Hoo." His smile quirked up on one side, showing a hint of the old Vince again. "Thanks, Kate."

She nodded. *Let him go.* "So I guess this means I won't be seeing you around this place anymore?"

"Not around *this* place." He put one hand on the tailgate of his truck and raised his head so that his line of vision fixed on the only other house on Dream Away Bay Court.

"Is that your not-so-subtle way of angling for an invite over to my place?" she asked, not even pretending to play it coy.

"I don't know. The two of us? What would the neighbors say?"

"It's about time," she muttered a guess through a sly smile.

"Why, Kate!" He feigned shock badly.

"Let me finish." She held up her hand. "It's about time the two of them stopped acting like lovestruck kids and did a little growing up themselves."

"Lovestruck? Kate, to be lovestruck you'd first have to be in—"

"I love you, Vince Merchant. On some level, I always have and the biggest regret of my life was not sticking around and fighting for that love, and for our family."

"Our family," he whispered, then slowly, wistfully nodded his head in acceptance of that. "It's a little late in coming together, Kate. Do you think we can get past that?"

"I do."

"Remember those words, you may need to say them in front of a preacher later," he said softly just before he took her in his arms and kissed her. When he lifted his lips from hers, it was only to whisper "I love you, Kate. With all my heart."

"Vince… I…" Kate's cell phone blared out and cut her off. She glanced down to see Jo's number. "I have to take this."

"Go ahead. I'm not going anywhere," he said.

"You're not?"

He smiled at her and shook his head.

When she flipped open her phone, she practically sang her greeting, "Hey there!"

"Kate, we need you to meet us at the urgent-care clinic."

Kate's pulse quickened at the breathless rush of Jo's words. "What's wrong? Is it the baby?"

"Is it Fabbie?" Vince stepped up. "Is she sick again?"

"No. It's Moxie," Jo said, still struggling to get her breath.

"Moxie?"

Another gulp of air and then laughter as her sister spilled out the explanation. "Billy J tried to sneak out of the restaurant to go fishing. Mom decided that sounded like fun and took off to tag along. Moxie grabbed the fishing poles, snagged a giant plastic swordfish, which fell from the ceiling, and she tripped over it and there's blood everywhere and—"

"A swordfish? Fell from the ceiling?" Kate rolled

her eyes. She had given up a second kiss from Vince for *this?* "What?"

"Please don't make me say that again. The upshot is that she has a gash that is probably nothing but may need stitches."

"Oh, I get it. She's our sister for less than one whole day and already she's gotten the competition bug and is trying to get a better bad-foot story than the two of us."

"It's not her foot."

"Moxie? Your sister?" Vince squinted and shook his head.

"What?" Kate held up a finger to ask him to hold that thought a moment.

"Knees and shins," Jo explained.

"Aww, upping the ante. I see where this is going," Kate teased.

"Shall I call Travis and ask him to swing by and bring you to the clinic?" Jo asked.

"No. I think I can get a ride."

Vince nodded his head. "Why not? I don't have any more work to do here. And you can tell me about Moxie on the way."

Later that day, when the sun had begun to set, the sisters put their feet up on a footstool on the back deck overlooking the most wondrous tacky garden in all of Santa Sofia.

Mom and Billy J had not yet returned from their fishing trip. Gentry, Esperanza and Fabiola were probably sitting down to their first evening together as a family in their new home. And the men in their lives had gone out to pick up something for their supper.

"So, beach wedding at sunrise or chapel wedding with all the trimmings?" Jo looked up from taking off the last bits of her once-fancy toenail polish.

"We're not even officially engaged." *Yet.* Kate shook her head. She wondered if Vince still had the ring he had once bought for her and if he did, how would it feel to have him slide it on her finger? She held her hand out and admired the place where it would rest, as if the diamond were already winking at her.

"After all these years," Moxie marveled, shifting about her bandaged leg.

Kate wasn't quite sure if she was talking about the belated romance or their finding each other again. Did it matter? She decided it didn't. They were both awesome examples of God putting things right in His time.

"Anyway, given our history, you may be married before I am," Kate reflected wisely.

"Who? Me?" Both Moxie and Jo looked up at her.

"Yes. Either one of you. *Both* of you." Kate looked first at one sister then the other, then laughed. "Don't tell me it never occurred to you. No dreams of white gowns, frothy veils and gorgeous jewel-encrusted wedding slippers?"

"Only if those shoes are my something borrowed." Moxie aimed a keen eye at Jo. "I can't imagine ever *owning* something like those."

"Sorry. My days of buying shoes that cost an arm

and a leg are over. How do you feel about rhinestone-encrusted flip-flops?"

"Works for me." Moxie clinked her iced tea glass to Jo's.

"I can't believe what I'm hearing." Kate blinked and pretended to clean out her ears. "Jo is giving up expensive shoes?"

"Maybe all shoes."

"You plan on going barefoot?"

"I just might. I'm thinking of starting a group down at the beach to meet, study the Bible, take on service projects, whatever needs to be done."

"Sign me up," Moxie volunteered. "What do you plan to call this group?"

"Well, in honor of how me and Kate got down here again and as a way of making anyone who joins feel equal as sisters in Christ—"

"Which really *should* be a sisterhood, not a competition," Kate just had to throw in.

"I'm thinking, the Barefoot Believers."

"I like it." Moxie wriggled her toes. "Imagine the chance to show how much you love God without having to put on shoes that pinch!"

The iced-tea glasses clinked again.

Then all went silent for a moment.

Kate looked out over the yard, then lifted her head and found that if she tried, if she really concentrated, she could still hear the ocean. In that instant, she was connected to the past, her childhood, her memories, to the poet inside the podiatrist, to her mother—and in a small way, her father—to her sisters, to Vince and Gentry and most of all to God. She had run for so long and gone so far only to find Him waiting for her at every turn.

Even in Santa Sofia.

"This isn't really a bad place to settle down, is it?" Kate observed, wriggling her bare toes in her now grubby but still vibrant purple cast.

"Good place to lose yourself," Jo murmured, her eyes shut and a peaceful smile on her face for the first time in a long time.

"When my adoptive mother ran away," Moxie said quietly, "she left a note that asked a question—'Isn't there something better than this?' I think I finally have an answer."

Kate and Jo waited.

"To be loved. To feel productive. To be happy." Moxie took a sip of tea and sighed. "It's a blessing. Is there anything better?"

"Maybe," Kate conceded, sipping her tea as well. "But if there is, I'm in no hurry to run off to try to find it."

* * * * *

QUESTIONS FOR DISCUSSION

1. Kate and Jo decide on their own that it's time to take charge of their mother's affairs. What do you think motivated their decision?

2. Many members of the "sandwich" generation, people who are caring for their own children and their aging parents, find themselves taxed on all levels. How do you think the longstanding family dynamic of the Cromwell sisters affects their decisions about home and family?

3. Jo struggles with perfectionism. Is this an issue you have dealt with either in yourself or in others? Do you see it as a real problem or is Jo blowing the issue out of proportion?

4. Knowing we are all flawed, even those of us who seem perfect (as Jo does to the world and Kate does to Jo), how do you think Christians can better minister to people who seem to have everything together but are actually hurting and lost inside?

5. The sisters' memories of their childhood, both good and bad, have affected the choices they make regarding career and family. Is there a specific time, place, and/or event that you can pinpoint as having had a life-altering impact on your choices in life?

6. Kate has the chance to meet her first love and to try to explain some of her choices and to make new ones regarding the relationship. Many people often think back on old relationships and wish for the same opportunity—why? Given the chance, would you reunite with someone from your past?

7. Kate was named for Katharine Hepburn, Jo for a character in *Little Women* and Moxie changed her name from Molly Christina because she wanted a name with more gumption. How big a role do you think names play in people's lives, including your own name in your life?

8. Is there a character in this book you would have renamed? Have you ever chosen not to read a book because of a character's name?

9. In her daydreams Moxie creates her own little kingdom on Dream Away Bay Court. In books, where setting plays a big role, authors often create whole towns that suit their vision. How important do you think the setting, the cottage, the town, the chapel, Billy J's Bait Shack Seafood Buffet are to creating a believable fictional world? What would you have changed about the town to better serve the book or your own preferences?

10. Jo has to put aside material things when she realizes they come to mean more to her than

doing the right thing. Given her perfectionism, financial problems, sibling rivalry and wanting to impress the chapel's minister, how do you think she will handle her conviction to give up her love of shoes and fine things? Have you ever vowed to renounce something? How did that turn out for you?

11. Moxie seems to be very much in transition in various areas: her love life, her wish to expand her business, her role as caretaker to Billy J. After she learns the truth about her past, she feels some closure and hope for the future. Given her situation, do you see her moving into this new life with ease, or do you see trouble ahead.

12. Do you approve or disapprove of the way Kate steps in and meddles in Vince's and Gentry's lives? If you felt a friend was going awry in their parenting, would you ever say anything?

13. Did you see the twist in the sisters' relationship coming? If you were another character in the book outside the Cromwell family, what advice would you give them about going forward from this point?

14. The Cromwell clan pretty much decide to uproot themselves and begin again in Santa Sofia. Many people do this kind of thing at midlife or later.

Do you aspire to relocate and if so why? Does it seem a realistic choice for these characters?

15. What did you think was the overall message of *The Barefoot Believers?* What made you decide to read this book?